Broken dreams...

Part of Joy had always hoped that if Gabe had known she was pregnant he would have stayed with her. Part of her had always hoped that he had loved her.

"I was too young, too ambitious," said Gabe bleakly. "It was nothing against you. It was simply too soon for me."

"I understand," Joy said. Even as she spoke she withdrew from him.

"Then why are you turning away from me?" he asked, his voice husky, urgent.

"Because you don't understand. It was too soon for you to love six years ago—and now it's too late for me."

Dear Reader,

When two people fall in love, the world is suddenly new and exciting, and it's that same excitement we bring to you in Silhouette Intimate Moments. These are stories with scope, with grandeur. These characters lead the lives we all dream of, and everything they do reflects the wonder of being in love.

Longer and more sensuous than most romances, Silhouette Intimate Moments novels take you away from everyday life and let you share the magic of love. Adventure, glamour, drama, even suspense—these are the passwords that let you into a world where love has a power beyond the ordinary, where the best authors in the field today create stories of love and commitment that will stay with you always.

In coming months look for novels by your favorite authors: Maura Seger, Parris Afton Bonds, Elizabeth Lowell and Erin St. Claire, to name just a few. And whenever you buy books, look for all the Silhouette Intimate Moments, love stories *for* today's women *by* today's women.

Leslie J. Wainger
Senior Editor
Silhouette Books

IMRL-7/85

Sequel

Elizabeth Lowell

Silhouette Intimate Moments

Published by Silhouette Books New York

America's Publisher of Contemporary Romance

SILHOUETTE BOOKS
300 E. 42nd St., New York, N.Y. 10017

Copyright © 1986 by Ann Maxwell

Distributed by Pocket Books

ISBN: 0-373-07128-0

First Silhouette Books printing January 1986

10 9 8 7 6 5 4 3 2 1

America's Publisher of Contemporary Romance

Printed in the U.S.A.

Silhouette Books by Elizabeth Lowell

ELIZABETH LOWELL

writes in several fields. When friends ask her why she decided to write "*romances*, of all things," she just smiles. She has been married for eighteen years to the only man she has ever loved. How can she help but write novels that celebrate love and life?

for Evan
again
because he deserves it
always

Chapter 1

I couldn't have heard right.

Joy Anderson closed her gray eyes, then opened them quickly, as though she hoped that what she had just heard was part of a nightmare from which she could awaken. But it wasn't that easy. She was already awake, sitting in a patch of hot gold sunlight pouring through the cottage's four-paned kitchen window. The phone was hot to her touch, all but burning her ear. Though she couldn't see her caller, the memory of Harry Larkin's broad, professionally amiable face was imprinted in her mind.

"Yeah, it's quite a shock, isn't it?" asked Harry, chuckling, wholly misunderstanding Joy's silence. "The great Gabriel Venture is coming to your very own boondocks to do a major article. Although someone said he was there some time ago, back when nobody but your parents knew much about Lost River Cave."

Five years, eleven months and twenty-nine days ago, give or take a few hours.

But the words went no farther than Joy's mind. She was too shocked to speak and too careful of her privacy to reveal that she knew the time of Gabe's departure to the day and hour. The date was hard to forget. Kati had been born nine months to the day after Gabe had driven out of New Mexico's pale, searing deserts in pursuit of the Orinoco River's steaming mysteries.

" . . . Be only too happy to help him," continued Harry, unaware that he had lost his distant audience, "because it's about the only way the Lost River grant might be renewed. I don't have to tell you what that means. Not only your own job, but those of the people who work for you. Not to mention the university's prestige. Lost River Cave has been quite a feather in our cap, publicity-wise. I'm sure you agree, Dr. Anderson." He paused. "Dr. Anderson?"

Joy pulled her shattered thoughts together with an effort. From her subconscious she called up the last few moments of Harry's speech. *Only too happy to help him.* Joy shuddered lightly. *Oh God. All I want to do with the Great Gabriel Venture is never to have to see him or hear his name again. Ever. Barring that piece of good fortune, I'd like to drop him down Lost River Cave's deepest, blackest hole and throw the rope in after him!*

The intensity of Joy's emotions shocked her. She thought she had forgotten Gabe's sweet smile and sweeter touch, and the bitterness of his betrayal.

Wrong. He didn't betray you. He never promised you one damn thing. He just took what you offered, thanked you kindly and left you holding the bag. Literally.

It was the opening refrain of an argument that was as old as the day that Gabe had left her. Joy had argued his side and her own, trying to understand what had happened, until she was emotionally exhausted. Then she had found out she was pregnant.

"Dr. Anderson?"

Harry's words came as though from across a deep canyon, distant, echoing. It had nothing to do with the radiophone's reception and everything to do with Joy's state of mind.

"I'm thinking," she said, her voice thin.

Harry chuckled and continued soothingly, "Don't you worry about a thing, Dr. Anderson. We know how busy you are wrapping up the Lost River explorations before the grant runs out. The magazine editor who made the arrangements assures us that Mr. Venture can handle himself in any kind of country and won't get in your way." Harry didn't wait for Joy to make polite noises. He simply marched ahead like a man with two days of work and only a day to do it in. "Now, I've sent all the information about Mr. Venture's schedule that you'll need. It should be at the Carlsbad post office, along with a package of his most recent articles and a summary of his needs while at Lost River."

Dazed, her normally quick mind floundering, Joy let Harry's words pour over her in a numbing cataract. His enthusiasm should have been contagious. As the man in charge of gathering funds, grants and gifts for the university, Harry had been her angel on more than one occasion. Without him she might never have gotten the original federal grant that had made exploration of Lost River Cave possible. Now he was talking about the kind of publicity that could ensure eventual funding for further explorations, and all she could do was stare through the window across a rumpled desert hazed with sunlight and heat. She wasn't really looking at the desert anymore than she was comprehending anything Harry said beyond one fact.

Gabe here, in Lost River Cave, again.

The thought was like rope whipping out of control through her hands, burning her until she bled.

"Dr. Anderson," said Harry a bit impatiently. "Are you there?"

"Yes," she said, her voice barely above a whisper. She cleared her throat and gathered her thoughts with a resurgence of the determination that had brought her through the shattering year after Gabe had left her. "We've been working very hard," she began firmly. Which was true, as far as it went. A thought came to her. She grabbed it and hung onto it like a lifeline. "There's so much for me to do. Someone else can show Gabe—Mr. Venture around. Jim Fisher. He's the best amateur caver west of the Mississippi. He's been working with us on the weekends and—"

"No, not Fisher," interrupted Harry, his voice both calm and certain. "This was bucked all the way up to the university president. It came back down with your name on it."

"Why?"

Harry chuckled again. "Got a mirror handy?" he asked wryly.

Joy grimaced. She didn't need a mirror to know that she was small, slender and feminine. With her sun-streaked blond hair and unusual eyes, she would make great photo material, as Harry had pointed out more than once in the past. Add to that her youth and expertise in an unusual area of academia and you had a publicist's dream.

"The president and I agreed that you're our best hope of keeping the Lost River grant alive," summarized Harry.

"The article won't be finished and printed in time to do us any good," said Joy flatly.

"Not this year," agreed Harry, "or maybe even the next. But the cave has been there a long time. It'll be there a lot longer. Sooner or later the money will come in again."

Joy said nothing. She already had her résumé out to the few other employers in the world who might need someone with a thorough knowledge of how water shapes caves and the expertise to explore even the most treacherous underground passages in search of new knowledge. Unfortunately, the demand for hydrospeleologists wasn't great. Add to that the fact that she was a woman and the answer was simple. No.

She had been offered other kinds of jobs, but the prospect of teaching geology or hydrology to bored freshmen in well-scrubbed classrooms made her extremely restless. She would do it in order to support Kati, but she would rather not. If she couldn't have the velvet darkness and unearthly beauty of Lost River Cave, then she hoped for work in some other remote and unusual place. There were so many incredible landscapes on earth, so many of the planet's secrets that had barely been rumored, much less researched. She wanted more than a classroom, more than the security and the closed horizons of tenure.

If helping the Great Gabriel Venture would make it possible for her to get out of the classroom sooner and return to unraveling the mysteries of Lost River Cave or some other equally unique place, then she would be the most helpful cave guide ever born.

"You're right," she said, her voice normal again, crisp. Her wide storm-colored eyes focused on the sunny vastness of New Mexico's southern desert. "I'll do whatever I can to help Lost River Cave get the recognition and funding that it deserves."

She could hear the satisfaction in Harry's voice as he said, "You be sure and let me know if Mr. Venture needs anything."

Joy replaced the radiophone on its hook and looked past the black shortwave set to the hot serenity of the late-afternoon desert. Finally, she stood with the lithe grace of a dancer or a gymnast, someone who was accustomed to testing the limits of her body on a regular basis. With her short hair, casual clothes and barely five foot two inches of height, she appeared more like an undergraduate than a Ph.D. The impression faded when she was close enough for her eyes to be seen clearly. There was a maturity in her glance that came only with hard experience.

It was a long dusty drive from Cottonwood Wells to the nearest post office. The closest city of any size at all was Carlsbad. Undoubtedly Gabe would be flying in there. Hopefully he would be able to rent a four-wheel drive vehicle and find his own way to Lost River Cave.

Even as the thought came, Joy shook her head. The dirt tracks leading to Lost River headquarters were carefully unmarked. No one wanted hordes of visitors demanding to be shown around or amateur cavers determined to leave their mark on the virgin cave. She had been coming out to Lost River Cave since she was sixteen. Even now, at twenty-six, she sometimes had difficulty finding the way home after one of the season's torrential cloudbursts washed out the tracks of previous vehicles.

Someone would have to pick up the Great Gabriel Venture and lead him by the hand to Cottonwood Wells.

For a moment Joy toyed with the idea of letting Davy Graham fetch Gabe. That would save her the trouble of thinking of polite things to say during the long drive in from Carlsbad. It was a tempting thought, but she rejected it. No one alive knew that she had fallen in love with Gabe when she was nineteen, had his daughter when she was twenty and had been unable to trust herself with a man since Gabe's betrayal. Few people even knew that she had worked with him once before in Lost River Cave's seamless darkness. She couldn't hope to keep the latter a secret, but the former was no one's business except hers and, eventually, Kati's.

As for Gabe, he hadn't cared enough even to write and ask if the baby had been born.

Yes, she would have to be the one to pick up Gabe if she hoped to keep the extent of their former relationship a secret. And if the thought of dealing with Gabe again made her tight, brittle, angry, then she would just have to put a lid on her emotions and screw it down tight. The Great Gabriel Venture couldn't affect her unless she let him. She had had nearly six years to think about many things. She wasn't worried about succumbing to him again. She knew now what she hadn't known at nineteen: Gabriel Venture was a man who put his career first and everything else last. He was a man who valued sex, not love. He was a man who could casually father a child and leave behind enough money for his lover to have an abortion. He was a man who had taken a young girl's physical and mental innocence, left her pregnant and never looked back.

No, she wasn't worried about loving Gabe again. She was only worried that he might find out how deeply she hated him.

The echo of her own thoughts shocked Joy. For years she had turned aside all thoughts of Kati's father, deflecting them, ignoring them, refusing to acknowledge them. She didn't want to feel anything for Gabe at all, love *or* hate. He was in her past, frozen, like the dry upper reaches of Lost River Cave where water no longer came to dissolve and reform the very stone itself. What Gabriel had once meant to her was fixed in her past, unchanging. Dead. She couldn't let her emotions eat into her until she was raw and wanted to scream with pain. She owed Kati more than that. She owed herself more than that. She hadn't hated Gabe in years. Why should she hate him now, when he no longer had the power to make love run hotly through her with a single touch, a single smile?

Joy let out the breath she had been holding in a long sigh. There was a lot to be done—she didn't have time to explore the dangerous, brutal landscape of her past. What she had felt for Gabe was buried now, like Lost River itself, consumed by darkness. Let it stay that way.

With a quick glance at her watch Joy assured herself that she had time to pick up Kati at the Childer ranch, which served as a school bus stop. Then she remembered that Kati was spending the week with Laura Childer. A feeling of hollowness settled in Joy. For a moment she wished that she had refused permission for Kati to stay with her friend.

Joy quickly chided herself for the thought. It would be cruel to keep Kati from sharing a large family's warmth just because her mother missed her. Susan Childer was a wise, laughing ranch wife who had eight children and would have loved to have had eight more. At times it seemed that half the kids along New Mexico's southern border lived at the Broken Bar X, what with the comings and goings of all the Childers and their friends. Joy had lived and worked at the ranch until she received her master's degree, and with it an invitation to complete a Ph.D. while living at Cottonwood Wells and exploring Lost River Cave. It had been wrenching for Kati to leave the Childer family. Even now she spent as much time there as she did in the cottage at Cottonwood Wells, because Joy didn't have the heart to deny her daughter the warmth and companionship of a large family.

Joy sighed unconsciously, remembering her own childish dreams. She had been her parents' sole child, a "lonely only" as she labeled herself. She had promised that she wouldn't do that to a child. She would have a house full of kids, and they would all grow up laughing and fighting and sharing and exploring caves and everything else the world had to offer. It hadn't turned out that way, though. The older Joy got, the more she realized that life offered everything and promised nothing.

Deliberately Joy turned her thoughts elsewhere. Kati would have no sisters or brothers, for Joy had written men out of her life after Gabe. She had tried dating a few years before. It hadn't worked. Gabe's betrayal had killed in her the passion that sent a woman willy-nilly into a man's arms. It wasn't that she didn't hunger for sensual satisfaction. She did. But she had learned that such satisfaction came only in her memories and dreams. Gabe's betrayal had cut too deeply, too completely for her to risk passion again. Being touched by other men made Joy very uneasy—and at the same time, being touched brought a longing for Gabe so vivid that it terrified her.

"Dr. Anderson?"

The deep-voiced call came from the front porch of the converted resort cottage where Joy lived, although "resort" was a rather glorified name for the weathered, sand-smoothed cottages scattered beneath cottonwood trees. The trees were silent testimony to a rarity in the desert: year-round water just beneath the dry surface of the earth. But not enough water for cattle or crops, or even a decent resort. The man who had once owned Cottonwood Wells had gone broke. When he died he had willed the remains of his dream to the university.

"Come in, Davy."

The screen door snapped shut behind Davy. He seemed to fill the doorway with equal parts of muscle and eagerness. Both were very helpful to Joy in her job as leader of Lost River Cave expeditions. Davy's broad shoulders, however, had become a joke around camp. He had to strip down to his shorts, put one arm over his head and the other along his side and wiggle on his stomach in order to get through Gotcha Passage, one of the main thoroughfares on the way to the cave's lower levels. There had been talk of renaming Gotcha everything from Bloody Shoulders to Naked

Squeeze in Davy's honor, but Joy had stood firm. Gotcha it was and Gotcha it would remain.

"Did you get the message to call Harry?" asked Davy, curiosity in his blue eyes.

"Yes. It wasn't a reprieve," she added softly. "The grant still runs out in six weeks."

Davy looked away for a moment. At twenty-three he hadn't had enough harsh experiences to teach him how to hide his feelings. His disappointment was as clear as his smile had been. Joy touched Davy gently, her hand looking fragile on his broad arm.

"I'm sorry," she said. "I know how much you want to finish mapping what we've discovered. I wish you could, too. Your maps are extraordinary. Some day they'll save cavers months of time, and the techniques you've worked out will revolutionize underground mapping. No matter what happens, you should be very proud of what you've accomplished."

Joy's words were not only comforting, they were true. Despite his size, Davy was one of the best cave mappers she had ever seen. His large, blunt hands had miraculous patience with muddy clinometers and Brunton compasses, as well as drafting tools of incredible precision.

"As for your three-dimensional model—" Just before Joy removed her hand, she squeezed Davy's arm, trying to reassure him that there would be a way for him to complete the work that his doctoral thesis depended upon. "We'll find a way for you to finish it. In fact, I've been talking with Dr. Weatherby in cartography. I asked him to consider funding your research. He seemed interested, so I sent copies of your maps. If that doesn't work out, there are other things we can try. USGS, for one. It will get done, Davy."

He smiled down at her. "Thanks, Dr. Anderson. Your support has meant a lot to me. Most faculty I've worked with only want to take credit, not give it."

Joy didn't argue. She knew better than Davy how fiercely competitive the supposed ivory tower was. Her lips curved into a small fleeting smile. "How could I possibly take credit? Everyone knows that I couldn't have hauled all that stuff through the cave without you."

Davy made a comic, pained face. "That's all you see in me—a strong back and a weak mind."

"And a fine hand with maps. Don't forget that," said Joy, teasing him as she always had, gently keeping him at a distance while reassuring him that she valued him as an assistant and a person, though not as a potential lover. There would be no other lovers for her. Ever.

Davy grinned. "Yeah. I'm dynamite with maps." He looked at his watch. Like Joy's, it was a hardy stainless-steel model that could take water, mud and banging on rocks. "The afternoon group out yet?"

Automatically Joy checked her own watch. Five o'clock. "They haven't checked in. Give them ten more minutes, and then we'll start for the cave."

He nodded and turned away. "Meet you at the Jeep."

The screen door snapped shut loudly behind Davy. The wind blew with a dry sound, then ceased, leaving only silence beneath the sun. Joy listened for a long moment before turning and going to the back porch where her caving clothes waited.

An oversized industrial washing machine looked out of place on the small cottage porch. The clothes looked even more unexpected in the desert setting—long underwear of wool mesh, full-length wool pants and shirt, a wetsuit of the type worn by scuba divers, a pair of long-sleeved coveralls, multiple pairs of wool socks and canvas-leather boots that had been developed for use in the jungles of Vietnam. There was also a crash helmet to which had been attached a bracket for holding the battery-powered light that would allow Joy to find her way through Lost River Cave's timeless night.

Coiled to one side were the freshly washed ropes that she would use in the cave. Washing the ropes wasn't done for aesthetic reasons, but for safety. Unless the ropes were kept clean, muddy grit that worked between the strands frayed and ultimately cut through them, weakening the ropes dangerously. Specially shaped pieces of metal designed for use with the ropes lay nearby on a shelf. Each curve of steel had the subdued polish that came from use and meticulous care. Joy never begrudged the time she spent on her equipment, for her life quite often depended on it.

Besides, there was for Joy a sense of being part of history when she worked over the ropes and lamps, steel carabiners and ascenders. Each of the smooth metal shapes and ropes represented the culmination of years of human exploration, risk and achievement. Cave explorers had spent their lives experimenting with and refining the equipment that they carried down into the darkness with them. Her father and mother had been among them, as had her grandfather. She herself had entered her first cave when she was four and had learned to handle the equipment at an age when other children were playing with dolls and toy trucks. When she was older, other cavers had teased her about being her parents' ''secret weapon''—the reason for their success in discovering new passages hidden within well-known caves. It was partly true; being small was a distinct advantage when it came to exploring caves.

Joy went through her rucksack quickly, checking off each item against a mental list. With automatic movements, she packed everything into the small, heavy canvas sack that she could sling over her shoulder or around her hips. She could have used a backpack, but had found the rucksack approach easier, especially when she was climbing on a standing rope. A pack slung from her hips kept her center of gravity where she wanted it—low, close to the rope.

Just looking at the wool clothing made Joy hot. With a grimace she stripped to her bra and panties and pulled on a cotton gauze shift that had no sleeves and just enough fabric to be legal. As she gathered everything, the wool pants felt unpleasant against the sensitive skin of her palm. She was grateful she wouldn't have to wear any of the heavy clothes until she was ready to enter the cave.

She ignored the wetsuit, which she used only on the third, deepest level of the cave where water went from ankle to chest and deeper, and mud was everywhere. Today she would be helping Davy survey the Voices, a chamber on the second level of the cave that was alive with water sounds. Running water itself, however, was largely absent. Somewhere within the huge echoing room was one or more passages that would lead to unexplored portions of Lost River Cave. She was certain of it, for nowhere within the explored parts of the cave was there a waterfall, yet the sound of the Voices could come only from one or more waterfalls. Despite repeated attempts, she had never been able to find one of the passages. Only the sounds were present—tantalizing, promising.

Maybe today she would get lucky. Maybe today she would discover the possibilities that had haunted her since the day after her parents died, when she had pushed her way through an obscure passage on Lost River Cave's second level and discovered the Voices. Nearly six years had passed since the discovery. Now she had only six weeks left.

She pushed aside the impending closure of Lost River Cave as she had pushed aside thoughts of Gabe. Mourning what would happen in six weeks wouldn't help her today. She had work to do, years of effort and memories and dreams to wrap up, and she couldn't do it with tears in her eyes.

Quickly Joy assembled the rest of her equipment and carried it to the worn, tattered Jeep that cooked quietly beneath the sun. The Jeep had been her parents' only legacy to her, except for her caving skills and a shoebox full of family photos going back more than one hundred years. And love. Her parents had taught her to laugh and trust and love.

Then Gabe had taught her to hate.

Joy dumped her equipment in the backseat, stacking a canvas sack of ropes on top. Davy came from his cottage and joined her, putting his own equipment in the back. Like Joy, he was stripped down to normal underwear—navy briefs that looked rather like a swimsuit. Unlike Joy, he hadn't bothered to put on anything else. They had worked together for two years, so neither one noticed the other's clothes or lack thereof. After pushing and pulling, laughing and cursing each other through some of Lost River Cave's tighter squeezes—from which a caver often emerged wearing nothing more than a liberal coating of mud—there was nothing of false modesty left in her or him. It was the same for the other students and professional cavers Joy worked with.

The Jeep's seats were hot enough to cook eggs. The lean-to that once protected the vehicle had rotted beyond repair and blown down in March winds. There was no money for a new structure. Silently Davy handed Joy one of the two-gallon jugs of water he had brought with him. Together they wet down the front seats and steering wheel. Everything dried almost immediately, but the evaporating water cooled the surfaces to the point where they wouldn't burn skin.

Joy climbed in and started the Jeep, waiting for Davy to get settled before she headed across the desert between clumps of mesquite, ocotillo and prickly pear cactus. Patches of yucca bristled with brutal spear points, making it impossible to believe that in the right season the plants would send forth cascades of creamy flowers. It was the same for the rest of the desert. Given rain, even the bizarre, whiplike ocotillo brought forth a froth of scarlet flowers.

The drive to Lost River Cave's entrance took only fifteen minutes. The road was nothing more than ruts winding over the rocky, rumpled desert terrain. In the distance rose the Guadalupe Mountains. South and east, Carlsbad Caverns National Park was just over fifty miles away. Lost River Cave was formed from the same thick limestone beds as the other much more famous cavern. Joy believed that somehow, somewhere, someday, Lost River Cave would be found to be as extensive and as enthralling as Carlsbad itself. Perhaps the two were even connected, as was the Mammoth-Flint Ridge Cave system which comprised more than two hundred miles of interconnected passages snaking beneath the Appalachians.

Once, in the geologically recent past, the southeastern corner of New Mexico had enjoyed abundant rainfall. There had been more than enough water to sink into limestone and dissolve out an extensive system of caves that might even rival that of Mammoth-Flint Ridge. But it would take years, perhaps generations, of effort to prove that Lost River Cave and Carlsbad were connected. Joy had only weeks.

A battered Toyota Land Cruiser was parked just beyond the entrance of the cave. Joy pulled in next to the other vehicle, looked at her watch and frowned. Five-thirty. They should have been out of the cave by now. If they still hadn't emerged in fifteen minutes, she would have to assume that they were in trouble and begin search and rescue operations.

"They're probably just using every minute of their margin," said Davy, glancing up from his own watch. He sighed. "I don't blame them, either."

Joy didn't say anything. She knew what Davy meant. The six-week cutoff was like a goad driving all of them. They spent every possible minute in the cave, urgently trying to finish projects that had been in the works for months and years. It was the pressure of time that was sending Joy and Davy into the cave with no one else to back them up. Two was the absolute minimum number of people required to enter a cave safely. Three was better. Five left a decent margin for error or accident.

If they had been mapping the treacherous lowest level, Joy would have insisted on having at least one more person present. That way if someone were injured, one person could stay and give aid while the third person climbed out to bring help. But the second level of Lost River Cave, especially the Voices, was very safe—open and relatively dry. It could be reached by a route that had no vertical descents, no deep water, no truly dangerous passages across slippery walls or breakdown—the piled debris that remained to mark the collapse of a ceiling. The need to complete as much mapping as possible had convinced Joy that the benefits of entering the cave in twos more than offset the increased risk.

As Joy and Davy climbed out of the Jeep, the sound of voices floated from a jumble of rocks that marked the mouth of the cave. The entrance was barely six feet by four and all but lost in the piled boulders. Although she hadn't really been worried about the other cavers, Joy felt herself relax slightly as they emerged. Being responsible for a group of students varying in age from eighteen to twenty-four was rather like being a parent. It aged her in subtle ways.

The first one out into the hot evening sun was Maggie Donovan, a tall undergraduate who had the body of a showgirl and a mind like a steel trap. Above ground, Joy envied the girl her height and stunning curves. Below ground, Maggie frequently and loudly envied Joy's svelte, petite grace. Maggie should have been a freshman, but she had skipped grades when she was younger. The result was that at nineteen years and three days, she was the youngest junior in the university. She turned off her light, took off her helmet and shook out chin-length auburn hair that curled wildly from the humid cave air. Her smile flashed from her muddy face.

"Hey, Davy, looking *good*!" she called, giving him a laughing, once-over glance.

Davy glanced up from the task of pulling mesh underwear over his thick, powerful legs and leered comically at Maggie's muddy, clothes-wrapped body. "Better than you, babe."

"Stick around," she said, reaching for the mud-plastered zipper. "It'll get better."

The three other cavers behind her called out encouragements that no one took seriously. By the time Maggie stripped to muddy underwear, no one was watching. They were all too tired and dirty and chilled to be eager for anything but a hot shower, hotter coffee and dry clothes. Davy gave the redhead a brotherly swat on her rear as she went past him. She swatted him right back, yawned and turned to Joy.

"I wish you'd been down there. For once I was the smallest one in the group, so I had to try that new passage we found on the second level."

"Did it go?" asked Joy.

As she waited for an answer, excitement suddenly animated her delicate features. She didn't notice Davy's quick look at her or the admiration in his eyes. Maggie did. It had bothered her when she had first joined the cavers a month ago, until she realized that a lot of men admired Joy and she treated them all the same—like first cousins or brothers or friends. Even Davy, who was to Maggie a most impressive chunk of man, brains and brawn both. If it weren't for Kati, Maggie would have sworn that the beautiful Dr. Anderson didn't know why God had put men on earth.

"The passage was awful," said Maggie bluntly. "I got stuck and Fish had to jerk me out. I tried it again in the buff." She shrugged. "No luck. I don't think even you would fit."

Joy looked at the compact, muddy man who had followed Maggie out of the cave. Jim Fisher, or Fish as his friends called him, was an amateur caver and full-time mechanic who arranged his work schedule so that he could spend every spare moment in Lost River Cave.

"It was a real pig," drawled Fish. "Thought Maggie was going to be chewed right small by the time I pulled her out. That passage don't go worth a damn."

Joy nodded and sighed. "Thanks anyway, Maggie. I'll take the next squeeze."

Maggie grinned and slapped the lush line of her hip. "No problem. Keeps me trim. I've never been in better shape than a month of cave crawling has made me."

That brought a chorus of remarks from the remaining two cavers, both of whom were male grad students with excellent vision and quick tongues. Maggie paid no attention. She had five older brothers and was utterly unflapped by male ribbing of any kind. She added her coveralls and long underwear to the growing pile in the Toyota. When everyone was down to shirts and mesh underwear, or underwear alone, they packed themselves and their mud-encrusted gear in the Land Cruiser and took off for Cottonwood Wells.

"Your poor washing machine is going to have a real workout," commented Davy, buttoning his wool flannel shirt.

"That's what it was built for. Just hope Maggie remembers to rinse off everything before she puts it in the machine this time. I'm out of filters until Fish goes into town again."

Davy grinned. "Yeah, that was a mess, wasn't it? First time I've ever seen Maggie blush."

Joy gave him a sideways glance and silently hoped that he was finally noticing Maggie in the way she so obviously noticed him. Not that she was embarrassing about her preference; she simply made no secret of the fact that she thought Davy Graham was a very attractive man.

Just as Joy had once let Gabriel Venture know that she found him exciting. Nineteen was such a vulnerable age.

Joy's fingers tightened around her bootlaces until her knuckles showed. She had to stop thinking about Gabe. She knew all there was to know about love and the Great Gabriel Venture.

Lost River Cave, however, remained to be explored.

"Ready?" she asked, settling her helmet in place, checking the light, picking up rucksack and rope.

"Ready," said Davy.

As they approached the cave, Joy tried very hard not to remember the many times it had been Gabe by her side, Gabe who had explored beauty with her, Gabe who had tapped the heat and sensuality deep within her, Gabe who had taught her about love.

And betrayal.

Chapter 2

Gabriel Venture shifted against the weight of his carryon baggage. His left leg and hip ached, the muscles protesting old injury and recent confinement. He walked a bit stiffly down the plane's narrow aisle. He wasn't due in Cottonwood Wells for another week, but he had worked overtime wrapping up his Asian story. He had saved another day by swapping his first-class ticket and catching a plane out of the Philippines that stopped in Los Angeles only long enough to clear customs and take on a few passengers. Despite the fact that it meant a long, nearly unbroken flight in tourist class, he had leaped at the ticket with an eagerness that had made him almost uneasy.

You're riding for a fall, fool. Nothing is as good as time and distance make it seem. Especially a woman. Besides, she'll be long gone from Lost River Cave. With her brains and looks she probably married a French count or a Greek shipper. She sure as hell didn't hang around a small town like Carlsbad waiting for her first lover to come back.

"Have a nice trip, Gabe," said the stewardess, smiling with unusual warmth. Her eyes roamed over Gabe's curly dark hair and wide shoulders as she murmured, "If y'all get to Dallas, remember to call, hear?"

Automatically he responded with a smile. "Sure thing—" *What the hell was her name? Cindy? Sandy? Mandy? They all ran together after a while. Except one. She was in his blood like malaria.* "—dear," he finished hastily. "You'll be at the top of my list."

Gabe heard his own words and winced. The stew didn't seem to mind being one of a list, however. She simply smiled more warmly and touched Gabe's arm with searching fingertips, tracing the hard line of muscle beneath. It was all he could do not to draw away. He squelched his own reaction and wondered if he were going crazy as he approached his thirtieth birthday. The stew was pretty, bright, experienced and probably came with a USDA stamp of approval. There was no reason for him to act like a kid getting his first proposition on a grubby street corner.

"Jet lag," he muttered to himself as he stepped out of the plane into Carlsbad's hot, slanting sunlight. "It's still yesterday where I came from."

Though it was late afternoon, the intense heat of the day radiated back from the tarmac in waves. Gabe broke into a sweat immediately, for his body had been conditioned for the last nineteen hours to a temperature that was at least twenty degrees cooler than the Carlsbad afternoon. His heartbeat increased as the dry hot air wrapped around him. Even as he blamed his accelerating pulse on the heat, part of his mind jeered silently. It was heat all right, but its source wasn't the sun. It was memories brought on by the unique feel of summer in New Mexico, the first vague scent of the desert seeping through the machine odors of the airport.

Dryness. Pungence of creosote. The taste of Joy sweep-
ing through him as he kissed her beneath a noon sun that
wasn't nearly as hot as the first touch of her tongue against
his.

A passenger jostled Gabe none too gently. He realized
that he was standing at the bottom of the plane's metal
stairway, lost in memory, blocking other people from
whatever awaited them inside the artificially cool terminal.
He muttered an apology, cursed himself silently and went
into the building with long strides. No one was waiting for
him. He hadn't expected anyone. He went to a car rental
desk, smiled at the bored young woman behind the counter
and talked her out of the only four-wheel drive she had left.
It had been promised to someone on an incoming flight, but
Gabe was here, now, displaying an easy male charm that had
melted much colder, harder material than the car rental girl.
He paid the extra insurance, picked up his luggage and
loaded everything into the car.

Although it had been almost six years since Gabe had left
Carlsbad, he found the post office on the second try. It
didn't surprise him. He remembered everything about his
time in New Mexico with unnatural clarity, a vividness that
alternately tantalized, infuriated and confused him. He
could see everything in his mind as though it had just happened—the long drives into Carlsbad to pick up the mail,
and Joy sitting close, watching him with eyes as clear and
inviting as spring water welling up from the desert.

Gabe forcefully turned his mind away from Joy and
walked into the post office. As Dan had promised, there was
a package of mail and two trunks waiting for him. Mentally Gabe thanked the younger brother who was also his
mail drop, business manager and fiscal consultant. Without Dan to forward clothes and equipment to Gabe around
the world and keep track of the day-to-day details of the life

that he had left behind, Gabe would have found it much more difficult to vanish into the unlikely places of earth and return to find his apartment intact, bills paid and mail neatly weeded out to the essential business communications. It was Dan who had stepped into the fiscal chaos when their father had died of a heart attack, Dan who had shown a shrewdness about money and people that had baffled Gabe even as he admired it. After years of living on the brink of financial ruin, Dan had finally managed to salvage the family fortune.

The only thing the two brothers had ever argued about was Gabe's penchant for getting into trouble with women. But that had been when he was young and believed that women—and men—told the truth to each other. They didn't. When a woman said "I love you," it could mean anything from "You turn me on," to "Rich man, I'm going to take you to the cleaners with a paternity suit." The latter had been a joke, if the girls had only known it. The fabulous Venture wealth had existed only in the minds of the press, for his dead father's interlocking corporations hadn't been worth the paper they were incorporated on. Gabe had worked for every penny he spent—and he had spent as little as possible.

Few people knew that, for Gabe was always referred to as the "scion of the wealthy Venture family." It was the lure of easy money that had put him in the center of two paternity suits the year before he came to Cottonwood Wells the first time. The fact that he hadn't even slept with one woman and positively hadn't impregnated the other was proved only after long, very public wrangles that had taught a much younger Gabe more about yellow journalism, women and avarice than he had ever wanted to know. Since then he had become very adept at spotting women who wanted more from him than a mutually pleasurable romp.

It had been different with Joy. He had trusted her not to be after his supposed wealth. He had been wrong again. When she discovered that he wouldn't be paying lavish child support, she had had an abortion. So much for her protestations of love.

Then why in hell had memories of Joy become an obsession?

"Mr. Venture?" asked the postal employee patiently, watching the weary man in front of her with sympathetic eyes. He looked dead on his feet, pale beneath his tan, his green eyes the only thing alive in a face lined with something deeper and more painful than physical exhaustion.

Savagely Gabe yanked his mind back from the questions that had been haunting him more and more since the accident in the Andes. He had come here to find answers, not to repeat the same old middle-of-the-night questions until he wanted to scream or curse or cry like a child.

"Yes?" said Gabe, his normally controlled voice ragged.

"I noticed that we were supposed to forward that package and the trunks to Cottonwood Wells if you didn't pick them up in ten days. Are you going out there right away?"

Gabe nodded and picked up his package, in no mood for casual conversation.

"There's other mail for the Wells," continued the employee hurriedly. "Fish has been out at the cave for three days, so no one has picked it up, and he won't be back for three more. Would you mind taking the mail with you? One of the packages is express. Must be important."

"Sure," said Gabe, vaguely ashamed. He should have thought of that himself. In many ways, Cottonwood Wells was as isolated as any place he had visited anywhere on earth. No electricity except by a portable generator which rarely worked, water pumped by windmill into a tall tank and delivered by gravity to the cottages, communications dependent on rare visitors or shortwave radio. As for Lost River Cave itself, it was like another universe. There had been nothing to equal it in all his years as a roamer.

Or was it simply that nothing had equaled Joy?

"Thanks," said the employee, handing Gabe a pile of mail for Cottonwood Wells.

"You're welcome," responded Gabe. *For almost taking my mind off an obsession,* he added bitterly, silently.

He carried the small trunks one at a time to the car. The pavement sent transparent, shimmering waves of heat up to meet him. It was hard to believe that in a few hours the air would be frankly chilly, the sun's searing embrace just a memory. It was one of the stark contrasts of the desert that always surprised and fascinated Gabe. Australia's Outback, Africa's Sahara, the Atacama of Chile, the Great Sonoran Desert of America—it didn't matter. The underlying principles were the same everywhere in the world. Drought. Heat. Unveiled sun. A clarity of life and death that knew no equal in any other landscape on earth.

Except one. The unlit mysteries and startling beauties of a cave carved by water deep within the very bones that supported the desert itself. Water glistening on impossible stone sculptures, air saturated with moisture, coolness that varied only two degrees from season to season. In all ways the opposite of the arid, light-drenched land above. Except one. Life and death were intensely focused in caves too. The margin was very fine—a frayed rope, a body too tired and chilled to revive, rocks kicked loose to strike a caver far below. The rewards, too, were very fine. Virgin landscapes of a beauty seen only in dreams. A sense of being in the presence of something far greater and more enduring than a single human life. The feeling of having touched eternity.

That's why you came back. That will still be here long after the woman and the I-love-you lies are gone. The fan-

tastic stones and the silence and the darkness pierced by a single cone of light. That's still here, waiting for you. It will answer some of your questions and make you forget the others. It will give you peace. It will be enough.

And the other half of his mind retorted quickly: *It better be. The cave is all there is. The woman is gone as surely as the baby she got rid of. Yeah, fool. She really loved you a lot, right?*

Gabe had no answer for the sardonic voice within him. When he had left Cottonwood Wells and Joy, he had planned to be in South America only for a few months, four or five at most. It had stretched into a year. When he had come out of the Orinoco Basin five years ago and read Dan's old, brief message that the New Mexican cutie had been satisfied with $5,000 and an abortion and in the future would he kindly stay the hell zipped while in the States, Gabe had felt a fury that still surprised him to remember. His rational mind had said that of course a young girl wouldn't have wanted to be tied down with a kid and no husband and no money to help her out. The intractable, furious part of his mind said that a lot of girls got pregnant and kept the baby and worked their asses off, especially the girls who truly loved the man they had slept with. Besides, Joy had been very close to her parents. They had been a long way from rich, but they would have helped her until Gabe was back in civilization and able to help her himself.

Five years ago it had been all Gabe could do not to track Joy down and tell her what he thought of her. Two things had prevented him—an urgent assignment in the Indian Ocean and the certain knowledge that if he confronted Joy he'd want to beat her within an inch of her selfish, careless, lying young life. Although he had gotten over the sting of being taken in by sexual experts, he had never gotten over the rage of being taken in by innocence.

Gabe realized that he was sitting in the rental car, staring out of the windshield as though the answers to all his questions were written on the car parked in front of him. They weren't. There was nothing but dusty paint and blinding brightness where the sun ran hotly over chrome strips.

Exhaustion hit Gabe like a wave of blackness welling up from the hot earth. He knew he should get a motel room, catch up on his mail, find out what arrangements his editor had made for Lost River Cave and memorize the names and accomplishments of the people he would be working with. He should do each of those things and then he should sleep around the clock before he went to Cottonwood Wells.

But he could not wait. An irrational sense of urgency drove him. As he had so often in wild places, he held his own fatigue at bay by sheer will. He started the rental car and began driving toward the desert waiting beyond Carlsbad's irrigated emerald fringes.

He left the town behind quickly, driving too fast, not really caring. There was no traffic after he left the main highway and turned off onto a gravel road. He began to wish that he had stopped for coffee to keep him awake, but knew that a mild dose of caffeine wouldn't have done much good. Making a dent in his exhaustion would have taken enough coffee to fill Lost River Cave. He had worked without stopping for fifty-eight days, had been awake for thirty-seven hours and had crossed so many time zones that he had lost track of them.

The muscles of his left thigh and hip ached, then burned, then sent lancing pain messages up his back and down to his foot. Time to stop, stretch, walk around, baby the muscles that hadn't fully recovered from the climbing accident that had come within a quarter inch of taking his life—the thickness of unfrayed rope that had remained after he had finally dragged himself back up the face of the cliff. He had spent a long time dangling head down over an endless drop, banging against granite with each pendulous swing, his weight entirely suspended from his left leg. He had been luckier than his native guides, though. The landslide had swept them over and down and down until their screams were lost in distance and grinding stone. His article on "Aerial Surveys and Mountain Trails" had nearly been his epitaph.

Gabe pulled over to the side of the narrow gravel road and turned off the ignition. The sun's thick, slanting light poured like honey over the hushed land. He got out of the car and walked a short way into the desert, moving slowly. It had been months since he had been this stiff. The doctor had warned him that long plane flights and tension would be harder on the tender muscles than anything but going head down over a cliff again. The long plane flight Gabe could accept. But tension? He had no reason to be so tight. He had wanted to come home to the States, to explore once again the velvet night of Lost River Cave, to—to what? What had driven him from a hospital bed in Peru to the Great Barrier Reef, to Tierra del Fuego, to the steamy Philippines and then finally back to a stretch of New Mexican desert that few people knew existed and even fewer cared?

Memories, whispered part of his mind.

Dreams, scoffed the rest of him.

There was no answer but the tension aching in him, a tension that had begun when he crawled off that deadly Peruvian mountain asking himself every inch of the way why he had lived and other men had died. What was there in his life worth saving? Was he so fine and good and pure and kind that he should live and others should die?

He had spent his twenty-ninth birthday in a hospital bed, his only present life itself. He had looked very carefully at that gift, reviewing the years and himself with the cool, sometimes almost cruel intelligence that made his articles crackle with insights. But his life wasn't a mountain or a sea or a mysterious, impossible cave growing beneath the land. Emotions blurred his personal insights, reshaped memories into doubts, turned dreams into treachery. He had come out of that hospital as tight as a rope in the instant before breaking. He had accepted one assignment after another, his only requirement that each place be different from the New Mexican desert and the wild, incredible cavern that haunted his dreams.

Nothing had worked. He had finished the last assignment in a rush that bordered on frenzy and booked the first flight that would connect to Carlsbad, New Mexico, United States of America. He wasn't even sure why he had returned. He only knew that he had to. In some way that he didn't understand, the cave had become an enigmatic symbol to him. He had lost or found something there that he could not name and had learned or forgotten something that haunted his waking and sleeping dreams.

The desert wind moved gently over Gabe, ruffling his thick chestnut hair and tugging at the open collar of the blue cotton shirt he wore. He stretched unconsciously, turning his face into the wind and the fiery, descending sun, giving himself to the moment with the intense sensual appreciation that was as much a part of him as his bones. The smell of the desert swept over him, heat and dust and pungent plants, an ascetic, almost astringent fragrance that pleased him more than the thickly layered perfumes of jungle flowers.

Memories welled up in him, laughter and smooth skin and the taste of Joy on his lips. At first he fought the memories viciously, reflexively, as he had fought them for nearly six years. The tension in his body increased until the muscles of his left leg knotted. He walked on stiffly, cursing the pain and the memories, haunted by desert scents condensing around him as delicately as time itself.

And then he gave in, understanding at last that this was one reason he had come back. To remember...

...heat and a fragrant wind caressing the land, whispering promises of the cool night to come. He and Joy were on the way to Carlsbad. Her father had given Gabe the keys to the Jeep, a warning about the difficult shift into third gear and a grocery list. Joy had jumped in at the last minute, saying that if she didn't get out of Cottonwood Wells she would get cabin fever. Sam had ruffled her hair affectionately and told her to have a good time. Gabe had offered dinner and a show in the interests of mental health. Sam hadn't objected. Joy had dated since her sixteenth birthday, and many of her dates had been university students years older than she was.

Gabe hadn't realized how hungry he was for Joy's smile, her laughter, her company, until he felt elation spread through him as he drove toward town with her at his side. During the weeks that he had been in Cottonwood Wells, Joy had first amused, then fascinated and finally compelled him. Now, two weeks before he had to leave, he knew that he had never wanted a woman half so much as he wanted her. From the way that she responded when he had held her beneath the brilliant desert moon and learned just a few of the secrets of her body, Gabe believed that Joy wanted him, too.

As soon as they were beyond Cottonwood Wells he turned and slowly ran his fingertips over her cheek.

"I'm glad you came," he said simply.

Color rose beneath her skin. She turned her head quickly, brushing her lips over his palm. "So am I."

The rest of the day was a kaleidoscope of vivid, sensual images. The sun-colored flash of Joy's hair beneath the grocery store's cold lights. Her small hand brushing against his fingers as they both reached for salt at the same time during lunch. Her tongue catching up a drop of peppermint ice cream that had run onto her knuckle from the cone. Her laughter and sudden breathless silence when he had neatly licked the minty mustache from her upper lip. The swift, hot weakness that had come to him when she had returned the favor, removing every trace of ice cream from his lips, sending all the blood in his body rushing toward the hungry flesh that strained suddenly against his jeans.

The movie was an exquisite torture. He put his arm around her and pulled her close, drowning in her fragrance, her warmth burning hotter than any desert sun against his arm. She had watched him, not the movie, and at some point during the matinee she discovered that she wanted him. He could see it in her eyes, feel it in the infinitely yielding flesh so close to his. He had kissed her then, a kiss that had narrowed the world to the heat and sweetness of their joined mouths. The honesty of her response, the small sound she made when his tongue stroked hers, was as exciting to him as the far greater intimacies he had known with other women.

As they left the movie Gabe considered taking Joy to the motel at the edge of town, but even the thought left a sour taste in his mouth. She wasn't like the other women he had known. It was more than just her relative youth. There was a transparency to her that simply didn't admit to the possibility of hurried encounters in grimy motels. Perhaps it was simply that although she was more sensual than anyone he had ever touched, she wasn't as experienced as the women he had bedded in the past. He knew as certainly as if Joy had told him that whoever her previous boyfriends had been, whether there had been only one lover for her or several, no man had ever truly set her afire and then burned deep inside her.

He wanted to be the man who did.

Gabe took Joy's hand, threading his fingers through hers, feeling her smoothness and warmth even as he let her feel his restraint and strength. He didn't want to take her to a restaurant for dinner, to stare across a table at her with a hunger that no food could appease. He wanted to be alone with her, away from everyone else. It was as though the mere presence of the town could somehow smudge Joy's rare honesty. He wanted to feel as though she and he were the only two people on earth, utterly removed from all reality, each knowing only the other.

"How about a picnic dinner in the desert on the way home?" Joy asked, watching Gabe with eyes as clear and deep as a rain-washed sky. "Senora Lopez packs great fried chicken to go. Unless you really want to eat at the House of Sirloin . . .?"

"How did you know that I didn't want to be in a restaurant and share you with everyone in town?" he asked, squeezing her hand.

Her breath caught visibly. Her sudden smile and her husky words made him feel as though he had fallen into the sun. "Because that's the way I feel, too," she said.

They drove out into the desert, following the faded road, lured by the thickly slanting rays of the late afternoon sun. Joy gave him directions to a tiny, mossy seep visited only by the wind and fleeting desert creatures. There was no sign of other people, not even a faint trail as they parked the Jeep and walked the last hundred yards. The land was pristine, shivering with light, a creation as new and hot as the first time Gabe had kissed her.

Joy made a tablecloth out of a bedroll from the collection of camping gear that her parents always left in the back of the Jeep. Gabe set down the bag containing dinner. He watched her small hands smooth the bulky fabric of the bedroll and wanted nothing more than to feel her touch on his body, easing the hunger that made him ache. He knelt in front of her. She looked up questioningly. He wanted to reassure her that he would be gentle, that he wouldn't hurt her, but he couldn't think of the words. He could think only of touching her.

"A kiss," he said, his voice almost hoarse, his hands trembling slightly as they curved around her face. "Just a kiss, sweetheart."

He kissed her lips and found them soft, firm, unbearably sweet, and he could not stop. He teased their inner softness until she gasped and then he drove his tongue deeply into her mouth, groaning as he felt her fingers dig suddenly into the muscles of his upper arm. Her tongue moved against his caressingly. Without knowing, without thinking, he pulled her down and covered her body with his while hunger raged through him, shaking him, and still the kiss had not ended. He could not end it. He wanted to pour himself into her, filling her until she overflowed and turned to him with her own need, her own demand that he be part of her until they were one and that one burned with a fire that knew no end.

The snaps on Joy's western blouse gave way with a slow inevitability that made her whimper deep in her throat, the only sound she could make for she was learning the hidden warmth and textures of Gabe's mouth. The curious, searching touches of her tongue excited him, telling him that she enjoyed the taste and intimacy of the deep kiss as much as he did. Her surprisingly strong hands kneaded down his back and up again before spearing into his hair as a passionate tremor shivered through her body. His hands released the catch on her bra as he slowly surrounded the sensitive flesh of her breasts. He rubbed over their softness until he felt as though his palms were afire and her nipples were hard, and he tugged at them with hungry fingertips. He felt her response in the sudden, wild arching of her body and cry that he drank wholly from her mouth, wanting to share her with nothing, not even the desert silence.

Finally he pulled his lips from hers, lured by the soft promise of her breasts, wondering if she wanted to know the feel of his tongue on her nipples half so much as he did. His teeth raked lightly over her neck, down the firm swell of a breast and he nuzzled the peak with a teasing sweetness that brought a murmur of pleasure from her. The murmur became a gasp and then a ragged sound as he bent his head over her breast and drank from her as deeply as he had drunk from her mouth. He heard his name moaned into the silence, and her response was a fire bursting inside him. His tongue rubbed against her, cherishing the flesh that changed from smooth softness to textured hardness. With each shifting pressure of his mouth he heard his name break and re-form on her sweet lips.

His hand traced her body from shoulder to waist to knee in hungry, urgent sweeps that echoed the rhythmic pressures of his mouth. His hand slid underneath her denim skirt and rubbed gently between her thighs, moving slowly upward until he felt the steamy heat of her against his palm and groaned. He took her mouth again, thrusting deeply into her as his fingers moved between her silky pants and her even smoother skin. Blindly he searched her resilient flesh until he felt the rough warmth of her hair and touched the hot, incredible softness that waited between her thighs.

She cried his name aloud as he unerringly found her most sensitive flesh and caressed it as thoroughly as he had caressed the tight peak of her breast. After a few moments she responded with a twisting sensual movement of her hips that inflamed him. He swept off her pants with a single motion of his arm.

"Gabe?" she asked raggedly.

"It's all right," he said, pushing up her skirt, kissing the skin around her navel. "I won't hurt you, sweetheart."

"I—I've never—you're the first—I—" The words were swallowed up in a moan as his mouth caressed her.

And then her fragmented words penetrated Gabe's sensual haze. He looked up and saw her swollen lips, her eyes dilated with passion until there was only a tiny rim of clear gray surrounding the black pupil, her nipples hard and glistening from his mouth.

"You're a virgin?" he asked softly, knowing the answer before it came, knowing that he should stop, put her clothes back on, control the desire that had claimed him as fiercely as the summer sun claimed the sky. Yet even as he waited for her answer, he tasted her on his lips, felt her passionate heat moving against his fingers and knew that no matter what she said he could not let her go. Unbidden, his fingertips traced her layered softness with maddening delicacy.

"Yes," she moaned, twisting against his knowing touch. "Oh God, Gabe, don't stop!"

Smiling, he watched Joy in the pouring golden sunlight, savoring her uninhibited movements as she responded to his touch. Within the shattering intensity of his desire grew a unique calmness, a certainty that was like nothing he had ever experienced. He knew then that he would touch Joy in ways that he had touched no other woman, that he would match her sensuality with a perfection that no other man could ever equal. He would melt her to her bones, and when she re-formed in the aftermath of passion she would never be touched again without remembering him.

"Gabe?" she whispered, eyes closed, body tight with the intensity of her response.

"I won't stop," he promised in a husky voice, peeling away her remaining clothes until she was wearing only the shimmering gold light of late afternoon. He hesitated as he bent over her, wondering if his caresses would shock her; and then knew that it would be all right, that despite her innocence she would understand, accept, glory in her own sensuality as he did. She was a lover to match his dreams. "I have to show you how perfect you are," he whispered, kissing her lips, the frantic pulse in her throat, the nipples thrusting against his tongue, the shadowed navel, the triangle of molten gold hair. "God," he groaned as his tongue flicked over her, tasting her, "so sweet."

The words ended in a wild sound as he succumbed to his own sensuality, caressing her with an intimacy that he had neither offered nor desired with other women. When he finally moved back up her body she was crying and twisting against him, offering him everything that he had ever dreamed of in a lover. She was hot, tight, deep, and if there was pain when he took her neither of them ever knew, for fire knows nothing but its own sweet flames. . . .

Gabe stood without moving as the hot dream-memory faded, leaving him aching in ways that had nothing to do with the fall he had taken nearly a year ago in the Andes.

You bloody fool, he raged silently. *Did you come halfway around the world for a piece of ass?*

You bloody fool, he answered sardonically. *Do you really think what's bothering you is that easy?*

Lust was easy. It demanded nothing but its own satiation. The last few years had taught him the limitations of lust, the depression that came when he realized that sex was over but the hungry emptiness went on and on. When he had understood that, he finally had understood why Joy had haunted him through the years. Of all the women he had known, she was the only woman who had enriched his silences as well as his sensuality. She was the only woman who had left him feeling complete rather than hollow. She was the only woman whose mental and physical response to him had made him reach down to the deepest parts of himself, satisfying needs that were both less tangible and more enduring than lust.

But it had taken him six years to explore that reality.

Fool. You lost something before you knew what it was worth. By now she's probably married and has a batch of kids.

The thought made Gabe's mouth flatten, remembering the child that had never been born. He hoped that every time Joy's husband reached for her, she remembered the man who had made love to her perfectly.

And left her, pointed out part of his mind.

I didn't know she was pregnant. And even if I had known, what the hell was I supposed to do? Dump a career I loved and needed in order to eat, marry a teenager and spend the rest of my life resenting it—and her!

There was no answer. There hadn't been since the first time he had asked himself that question in a hospital bed in Peru. He had searched, but he hadn't found the answer in the South American mountains, beneath the Australian seas, in the jungles of Asia. The answer wouldn't be in New Mexican deserts, either. There was no reason for him to have driven himself to exhaustion just to come back here. Time went in only one direction. Forward. He had borne the pain of remembering Joy for nothing, nothing at all.

Weariness settled in Gabe, a chill that wasn't related to the increasing coolness of the evening air. He walked to the car and started it, forcing his mind to deal with the necessities of the moment. He'd better hurry. There was one more turnoff before he reached Cottonwood Wells. If it got much darker, he would miss the subtle natural signposts that marked the route.

The way you've missed other things?

Shut up, he told himself savagely. *Just. Shut up.*

The car leaped forward, tires spinning, sending dust and gravel boiling upward in a confused cloud.

Chapter 3

Joy scrambled up the last steep pitch of the collapsed ceiling that was the entrance to Lost River Cave. With muddy fingers she unclipped herself from the rope. All around her was the luminous shade of darkness that was desert night. The Milky Way swept overhead like a river of diamonds. Other stars sparked in subtle colors and shades of silver. She switched off her light, removed her helmet and shook her head. The air was cool, dry, crisp, like a fine white wine. She heard a noise behind her and saw a patch of light bobbing and glowing out of the cave's mouth. There was a clear metallic sound as Davy unclipped himself from the rope, then the softer, slurred sounds of the rope being retrieved and wound carefully. The thought of that heavy rope dragging on her bruised arm made Joy glad that Davy was along.

"Ready, Dr. Anderson?" he asked, coming up behind her. He lifted his wrist into the cone of light from his helmet. "We'll have to hurry to make it back on time."

"Ready," she said, stifling a groan as she pulled off her muddy cotton gloves.

"Want me to drive? You banged your arm pretty good on that slope."

"If you don't mind..."

"No problem," he said, switching off his helmet light and resettling the heavy rope with a casual motion.

"Thanks."

Joy sighed, wishing she had Davy's strength. Then she frowned, realizing that it wasn't her body that was worn out and dragging. It was her mind. It had been pushing frantically against the knowledge of Gabe's return, as though that fact were a tight passage which could be put behind her if she just struggled long and hard enough. Wearily she rubbed the back of her hand across her forehead, leaving behind a dark streak. Cave mud worked its way through everything, even gloves and layers of clothing. The thought of the hot bath that was waiting for her made her groan again, this time in pleasure.

"Dr. Anderson?" asked Davy, anxiety clear in his voice.

"Just thinking of a hot bath," she said reassuringly.

"Oh." He laughed. "Yeah, I know what you mean. C'mon."

They piled everything in back, adding another coating of dirt to the Jeep's already liberal supply. After the absolute blackness of Lost River Cave, night was alive with subtle expressions of light—stars of every intensity, the brilliance of the rising moon, the warm yellow glow of the headlights. Cottonwood Wells looked equally alive with golden light as mantles burned incandescently inside Coleman lanterns, sending rich yellow illumination spilling out from the cabins.

"Generator's down again," said Davy, pulling up in back of Joy's cottage and turning off the Jeep.

"Poor Fish. He swears that machine was old when his great granddaddy drove a mule team into New Mexico."

"That's not all he swears," Davy muttered.

Joy almost smiled. The mechanic's inventiveness with profanity was a matter of envy among the other cavers.

"If cussing will make it go," began Joy, "then Fish—"

Her words faded beneath the ripping snarl of the generator. White light flickered, faded, then caught and held, flooding Cottonwood Wells with an electrical sunrise. The sound of the generator jumped raggedly before settling into a steady noise that was somewhere between a purr and a growl. The sound diminished even more as Fish shut the door to the generator's shed.

"He must have cussed it something special," said Davy, his deep laughter rippling through the night. "Hasn't sounded that good since I got here two years ago."

"At least I'll be able to recharge the headlight batteries," said Joy. She had a carbide helmet lamp for emergencies, but she preferred the flameless electrical headlamp she had used that night. "Not to mention having a mechanical slave to wash the clothes for us."

"Amen," said Davy feelingly. He had drawn the short straw on the washboard often enough to dread it.

Together Joy and Davy carried all of the equipment to Joy's screened-in back porch. She flipped on the light and began fighting with the muddy zipper of her coveralls. She had tried using buttoned coveralls, but Gotcha Passage had a way of twisting off even the most carefully concealed buttons.

The zipper didn't budge. Joy swore under her breath.

"Stuck?" asked Davy sympathetically.

"Stuck," she admitted.

"Hang on," came his muffled reply as he quickly shucked out of everything but his normal underwear.

Joy didn't really notice the brawny, mud-streaked, nearly naked perfection of Davy's body. The only thing she felt when she looked at him was the hope that his strong, blunt fingers would have better success than hers had with the stubborn zipper.

"Let's have a look," said Davy, turning her into the light. He frowned as he bent over the zipper. "Mud," he said succinctly.

Joy's answer was a cross between a snarl and a laugh. "Davy, you have a gift for—"

"Restating the obvious," he said, finishing the sentence before she could. "Yeah, I know. Comes with being a cartographer, I guess."

With one huge hand he held the collar of her coveralls. With the other he grasped the elusive zipper tongue and tugged. His muddy fingers slipped. He tried again. They slipped again. He started talking to the zipper the way Fish usually talked to the generator.

Gabe walked up silently to the back porch just as Davy turned Joy again, trying for better light. All Gabe could see was the silhouette of a huge, nearly naked man—Dr. Anderson, he presumed—and the outline of a much smaller person still encased in caving gear. From what the laconic yet fluently profane mechanic had told Gabe, Dr. Anderson was just coming back from Lost River Cave. That and "Pleasedtameetcha" had been the mechanic's only comment when Gabe had driven up and spoken to the first person he spotted. The name Anderson had given Gabe a shock until the rational part of his mind coolly reminded him that Anderson was hardly an uncommon name.

The bare porch bulb cast a harsh glare over the man, emphasizing his powerful build. Gabe decided that the heavily muscled Dr. Anderson would be an asset to any shot-putting or weightlifting competition. Young and handsome, too.

With a rather cynical smile, Gabe pictured the response of Dr. Anderson's female students to their muscular professor.

The smile faded as illumination washed over the smaller figure on the back porch, revealing short, sun-streaked blond hair and delicate features. Gabe stiffened as though he had received a hard body blow. Even as he told himself that it was impossible, that he was hallucinating, he was reaching for the screen door. It banged shut behind him as he stared at the nearly naked young giant who was tugging without success at Joy's zipper.

"I'll take care of her," said Gabe from the doorway.

Though his voice was even, it was a command more than an offer. Davy backed away instantly as he saw the intensity of Gabe's look.

Joy's head snapped up as she heard the voice from her memories. She felt every bit of blood drain from her face as the father of her daughter walked toward her, his expression dark, unreadable. All she could think of was that she was supposed to have had a week more to prepare herself before she had to confront Gabriel Venture, that it wasn't fair that he should find her muddy, tired, off-balance...vulnerable.

Even as the frantic thought came, Joy all but laughed at herself. Life never turned out the way you expected it to, and certainly life made no promises about being fair along the way. Surely she should have learned that lesson after Gabe's seduction, her pregnancy and the helicopter crash that had killed her parents and left her floundering alone in a situation she had never imagined in her worst nightmares. She had survived a lot in the past. She could survive one more unpleasant surprise. She had to. There was no other choice.

Reflexively Joy used the lessons she had learned at such great cost in the past. She simply put away the tumult of conflicting thoughts/emotions/memories and concentrated on the single instant in which she was living. Later she would sort through the tangled mess that passed for her mind. For now it was enough that she controlled herself, revealing nothing, protecting her vulnerable core—the ability to love that had barely survived her nineteenth year.

She turned away from the hands reaching for her, hands she had once kissed in passion and still remembered in her dreams.

"That's not necessary, Mr. Venture," said Joy, reaching for a bottle of liquid soap she kept over the washing machine, biting her lip against the ache from her bruised arm. "I can take care of myself."

Gabe froze. Listening. Staring. The voice was the same one that spoke softly in his memories and whispered among many illusive dreams. The same, yet different. Where emotion once had shimmered and enriched to the point of music, there was only neutrality and precision now. The eyes were the same, a luminous gray, haunting in their clarity. Yet her eyes were also different. She had learned to draw veils over their marvelous transparency, shutting out the world. Shutting out him. Or were they shadows rather than veils, a legacy of disappointment and loss?

"Joy," he said softly, urgently.

She stiffened as though he had slapped her. No one but Gabe had ever called her Joy. It had started the first time she had met him. She had been laughing at something a caver had said. She was still laughing when she turned at her father's call and went to meet Gabe. He had looked at her for a long moment before saying, *With that smile, I can't call you Joyce. Hello, Joy. I'm Gabe.*

"My name," she said distinctly to Gabe, "is Dr. Joyce Anderson."

She turned into the shadows to conceal the betraying tremor of her hand as she squeezed liquid soap onto the zipper. "Go ahead and take the first shower, Davy, before you get chilled," she said, holding her voice as though it were made of extremely fragile crystal. She tugged experimentally at the zipper's metal tongue. "Just be sure there's enough hot water left for me," she added, "or the next time you're stuck in Gotcha I'll leave you there."

Davy hesitated, sensing the odd tension in Joy's voice.

The zipper came halfway down before the tab slipped from Joy's soapy fingers. With the lightning quickness she had almost forgotten, Gabe picked up where she had left off. The zipper opened obediently beneath his hand.

"Thank you," Joy said stiffly, stepping away from Gabe without looking at him. He was too close and she was too tired, too frayed to control her conflicting impulses for long. Hate him. Hug him. Scream at him. Soothe the lines of exhaustion from his face. Take a piece of muddy rope and strangle him. Kiss him as though the world were ending around her.

The tug-of-war was endless. The result was an emotional limbo of neutrality, a volatile calm at the focus of a storm.

With luck, Gabe would be out of her life again before the storm exploded. At the very least she would be alone, nothing but the walls and unspeaking night to witness the raging emotions beneath Dr. Anderson's smooth exterior.

Belatedly Joy realized that Davy was hovering at the edge of the porch. She stifled a flash of irritation at his unwanted protectiveness by reminding herself that Davy had no way of knowing who Gabe was, what intimate strangers she and he had become. "Davy, this is Mr. Venture," Joy said, shrugging out of her mud-encrusted coveralls, revealing almost equally muddy wool pants and shirt beneath.

"He'll be with us for a few days while he updates an old magazine piece on Lost River Cave."

"Gabe, not Mr. Venture," he corrected as he held out his hand to the younger man. "And I'll be here several weeks, not a few days. The piece I'm doing is more in the nature of a sequel than an update."

Davy looked at his muddy hand, hesitating before offering to shake Gabe's hand.

"I've done my share of miles on hands and knees," said Gabe, smiling. "A little dirt won't offend me."

Davy shook hands. "Mr. Venture—Gabe, pleased to—" The reflexive flow of polite words stopped abruptly. "Gabe? Are you Gabriel Venture, the writer?"

"Guilty," acknowledged Gabe with a smile.

"Sonofa—" Davy's expression became a pleased grin as he shook Gabe's hand. "I'm a real fan. You're the only natural history writer I've ever found who was as accurate as he was exciting to read. The story you did on the discrepancies between aerial and foot surveys of that peak in the Andes was nothing short of brilliant."

"Thanks. It nearly killed me."

"Yeah? What happened?"

"Landslide," said Gabe succinctly.

Davy winced in sympathy. Joy closed her eyes and fought not to remember the instant of spinning nausea she had felt when she had heard over the radio that the famous adventurer and writer, Gabriel Venture, had barely escaped death in the Andes and might be crippled for life. Irrational pain had wracked her, an inadvertent sharing of how it must have felt to lie in an alien hospital bed, wondering if you would ever walk again. She had forgotten the incident until now, having swept it into the invincibly irrational part of her mind called *Gabriel Venture, hated lover*. He was like her parents' sudden death—an experience she had finally, painfully, learned to accept without understanding it at all.

"You okay, Dr. Anderson?" asked Davy, concern clear in his voice. "Maybe you better let me see your arm before I go."

Gabe turned swiftly, looking at Joy with searching green eyes. She was very pale beneath the rich earth streaking her face. "What's wrong?"

"Nothing a good night's sleep won't cure," said Joy, bending over, sending blood back into her face as she unlaced her boots and stacked them to one side. She stepped out of her coveralls and stuffed them into the sink to be rinsed off with Davy's discarded caving clothes.

Davy hesitated by the door, obviously wanting to help Joy but not knowing how.

"Shower," she reminded him. "Solar heating doesn't work worth a damn by moonlight."

"Right you are, professor," he said, relieved to return to their normal conversational mode, a combination of pragmatism and teasing that was astringent without being acid. "I'll go get my towel and be right back."

"Your towel is behind you in the cupboard," said Joy, unzipping her damp wool pants. "You left it here last night."

Davy found his towel and trotted off into the house. Within seconds the sound of the shower filtered out into the small back porch. Gabe stood very still, literally immobilized by the conflicting emotions sleeting through him. The rational part of his mind knew that he had forfeited any rights to Joy nearly six years ago, when he had walked off not even knowing if she were pregnant. The irrational part of his mind—the primitive, deepest part of him—raged that she had no right to stand around on her porch at night with a brawny, nearly naked, potently masculine student.

"Does he live with you?" asked Gabe finally, his voice as cooly neutral as the moonlight pouring down on the empty land.

"No more than the rest of my graduate assistants," said Joy, ruthlessly clamping down on her first impulse, which was to tell Gabe to go directly to hell. That, however, would only lead to an argument. Her emotions were too wild, too reckless, for her to risk an argument right now.

"The professors and students that play together stay together?" asked Gabe sardonically.

"Davy's shower is plugged solid. Why don't you go play with some caustic drain cleaner?" she suggested, glancing up at Gabe. Her eyes were like Lost River Cave's deepest pool, transparent and cold.

"Joy—"

"Dr. Anderson or Joyce," she said. "Take your pick." Then, despite her effort not to speak, more words tumbled out. "No one calls me Joy anymore."

"I can see why," he retorted, stung by the comtempt buried just beneath the calm surface of her voice, and too tired even to try controlling his response. "You've turned into a sharp-tongued, flat-lipped old maid who has about as much joy in her as a squeezed lemon."

Gabe's words cut like razors, a pain more intense than any Joy had known since he had left her. "Thank you," she said huskily, hating him, wanting to hurt him as badly as he had once hurt her, as badly as he still was hurting her.

"Don't thank me—" he began harshly.

"Oh, but I must," she said, cutting him off, her voice vibrating with emotion. "You helped to make me everything I am today."

Joy's eyes were no longer veiled. Gabe looked into their transparent depths and for the second time that night felt as though he had been kicked in the stomach. He had imagined many times how it would be to see Joy again. He had imagined anger, laughter, shock, sensuality, tears, elation. He had imagined every emotion but the one he saw staring out of her eyes right now.

Hatred.

Rage swept through him, burning through civilized restraints. He grabbed Joy by the upper arms, making no allowance for his greater size and strength.

"Listen, you little—" he began harshly.

An anguished cry ripped from Joy's throat as Gabe's fingers ground into her bruised arm. The room spun around her in a dark haze of pain as she sagged against him.

"Joy—sweetheart? Oh God, I'm sorry!" he whispered against her hair, cradling her in his arms, rocking her against his chest. "I didn't mean to hurt you."

She leaned dizzily against his chest for a moment, letting the room settle into its normal place. When she breathed in deeply his scent went through her like a shock wave, dragging widening rings of memories in its wake. He had made love to her so gently, so wildly, so perfectly; then he had walked away without a backward look, never calling, never writing, leaving her to bleed in silence.

Weakly Joy pushed away from Gabe. His hands hesitated for a moment before they relaxed, letting her go. She reached for her familiar routine, pulling it around her like darkness around a cave, concealing everything within. Her fingers plucked at the waistband of her slacks. She had the wool partway down over her hips before she realized what she was doing. She was accustomed to stripping down to her muddy underwear with anywhere from one to twelve other people crowding around, jostling and cracking jokes about the state of their clothes and their aching muscles, making bets on whether the washer would quit on the first or third cycle. When Gabe had gone caving with her, it had been the same—no hesitation, no useless modesty, nothing but the camaraderie that was unique to cavers.

It was different now. But to show that would be like announcing to Gabe that his presence disturbed her in ways that had nothing to do with hatred. Like his voice calling *Joy—sweetheart. Oh God, I'm sorry! I didn't mean to hurt you.* Once she would have sold her soul to hear those words from his lips. But that had been years ago, centuries ago, when she was young and believed in life and love. Now she believed in only those things which she could touch—Lost River Cave's unearthly beauty and Kati's small arms wrapped around her in a hug.

With numb fingers Joy peeled off the muddy wool pants and went to work unbuttoning the equally damp, gritty wool shirt. As she began to pull the shirt down her arms, she winced in pain. Gabe reached for her instantly, trying to help.

"No," she said, pushing away his hands with cold fingers, her voice as exhausted as her eyes.

"Let me help you," he said. Then, softly, "I won't hurt you again."

The words echoed in Joy's mind, returning to her slightly changed, a voice from six years in the past reassuring a shivering, passionate virgin. *It's all right. I won't hurt you, sweetheart.* She looked into Gabe's pale green eyes, saw them darken, heard his sudden intake of breath and knew that he was remembering the same words and the same wild afternoon when he and she had burned together as hotly as any sun.

"No," she repeated, meeting his eyes without flinching.

"Joy—"

"No!" she said again, her voice shaking. "I don't want you to—"

The sound of Davy bumping into a piece of furniture in the living room and swearing roundly reminded Joy and Gabe that they weren't alone. Davy walked out to the back porch wrapped in a blue bath towel that was as oversized as he was.

"Arm stiffen up?" asked Davy, seeing that Joy wasn't out of her wet clothes yet. "Need some help?"

"Please," said Joy, turning toward Davy with obvious relief. "If you could just peel off the top layers, I can handle the rest."

With a feeling halfway between helplessness and rage, Gabe watched Davy's big, gentle hands reach for Joy.

"No point in you getting all muddy again," Gabe said curtly, stepping between Joy and Davy. "Which arm hurts, Dr. Anderson?"

Joy looked into Gabe's hard green eyes and knew that she could allow him to undress her or she could precipitate an argument that would tell Davy exactly why she didn't want the Great Gabriel Venture's hands anywhere near her.

"My left," she said, her voice as expressionless as her face.

"Will you be able to handle dinner?" asked Davy, looking anxiously at Joy's pale skin.

"I'll give her whatever she needs," said Gabe in a voice that was too calm, too clipped. "Don't worry," he added. "I'll take good care of her. Joy—Dr. Anderson—and I go back a long way. She was closer than my right hand when I did the first *Geographic* article on Lost River Cave. Couldn't have done it without her."

Davy's surprise told Gabe all he needed to know. Joy had never mentioned him to her students, despite the fact that he was sure the article on Lost River Cave was required reading for everyone with any interest in the cave.

"Oh," said Davy, pausing at the back door. "She never said anything to us."

"Modest," suggested Gabe dryly, deftly removing Joy's damp wool shirt.

"I'd shout," agreed Davy, letting the door slam behind him. "Thanks for the help tonight, Dr. Anderson."

"Anytime, Davy."

"Tomorrow?" he suggested hopefully, his voice floating back from the darkness.

"We'll both go with you," said Gabe, his hands quick as he undressed Joy.

"Great!" responded Davy.

Joy realized that the wool shirt was sliding down over her fingertips.

"There, that wasn't too bad, was it?" asked Gabe, his voice subtly challenging.

In truth, it hadn't hurt at all. "Thank you," said Joy through stiff lips.

"You're welcome," he said grimly. "Hold up your arms," he ordered, eyeing the wool mesh underwear which was every bit as damp and almost as muddy as the shirt had been. "This, I'm afraid, will smart. Unless you want me to cut it off?"

"What?" asked Joy, the tone of her voice telling him that she thought he was crazy. "For a broken arm, maybe. For a bruise, never! Do you know how much these things cost?"

Gabe's answer was lost in Joy's gasp as he peeled off the undershirt in a single smooth motion, leaving her standing in the cool air wearing nothing more than the black cotton underwear she had found to be most practical for caving.

In the instant before she turned away, Gabe saw the firm curves and soft promises of the woman who had haunted his dreams for thousands of nights. Like her eyes and her voice, her body was the same and yet different from his memories. The breasts were still firm, graceful, and like the line between waist and hip, still begged to be caressed by a man's hand. Yet there was a difference, too. Joy was no longer a girl. Nothing of her body was unfinished, nothing was in transition. All past promises had been fulfilled. She was every inch a woman, complete.

And she couldn't turn her back on him fast enough, couldn't pull on the cotton shift quickly enough, covering herself as though he were no more than a rude stranger who had wandered in off the desert.

"For the love of God," he said harshly, "don't give me that blushing maiden crap. I've already seen what's underneath the muddy bra and pants!"

Joy's only answer was a stiffening of her body that made Gabe regret that he hadn't waited until morning to meet "Dr. Anderson." Jet lag and exhaustion had reduced his normal self-control to little more than impulse and apology. Jet lag and something else, something much deeper, far more painful: after six years all that remained of his haunting love affair with Joy was hatred.

What did you expect, fool? She's the one who flushed your child. Remember?

Joy turned around and saw the harsh contempt on Gabe's face. It confirmed the fear that had burned in her for six years. He had never cared for her at all, not really. She had been just a passing amusement for him, an unsophisticated native of New Mexico's desert boondocks. And easy, so easy, falling into his arms like sunlight. But was that any reason for him to hate her? The only crime she had committed was being gullible enough to fall in love with a man who was completely out of her league. "The Great Gabriel Venture."

Joy didn't realize that she had spoken his name aloud until she heard the echoes of her own outrage quivering in the small porch.

"What did you expect?" she asked. Before Gabe could answer she smiled with a cynicism that surprised him. "No, don't bother to tell me. You expected the green little native to fall all over herself again on the way to your bed. April Fool, hotshot. The little girl grew up."

"I didn't even know you were still at Lost River Cave," snarled Gabe, "so how the hell could I expect anything from you? As for being in my bed, don't flatter yourself. When I want a female viper I'll go out in the desert and get a fresh one."

"Be sure to get her young, before she grows teeth," said Joy curtly, stung by the knowledge that Gabe had come back to the cave, not to her. "Otherwise you'll wake up with fangs in your throat."

"You'd like that, wouldn't you?"

"Actually, I'd prefer that you not wake up at all!"

Even as the words left her mouth, Joy knew that they weren't true. She remembered her pain when she found out that Gabe had been badly injured, hovering at the edge of death. Whatever else he was or wasn't, whatever his accomplishments and failings, this man was the father of her child.

Unconsciously Joy moved her hand over her bruised arm, trying to ease an ache that went to the marrow of her bones. "I'm sorry," she said, her voice empty, drained of all emotion. "I didn't really mean that."

"You could have fooled me," said Gabe sarcastically.

"Not as easily as you once fooled me," she retorted. When she saw a flush of anger burn across his cheekbone, she said almost desperately, "Gabe, this has to stop. We both have a job to do, and to get it done we'll have to go down into Lost River Cave together. If we're slashing away at each other, it won't work. You can't go down into darkness with someone you don't trust!''

''Oh, I trust you all right,'' said Gabe coolly, thinking about the abortion she had purchased simply because it would have been inconvenient to have his baby while she was working her way up the academic ladder. ''You won't let personal feelings get in the way of something important like your career. Without me you don't have a snowflake's chance in hell of getting more money for Lost River Cave, *Dr.* Anderson. I know you'll take very good care of me when I'm on a rope down there.''

''How odd,'' she said huskily, hearing Gabe's condemnation of her in each cold syllable, ''that you see me only in terms of yourself.''

''What does that mean?'' he demanded.

''It means that you are exactly what you accused me of being—someone who puts career first and everything else last.''

Joy's words slid through his angry defenses like light slicing through darkness; but unlike darkness, Gabe felt pain. It angered him that she of all people had the ability to hurt him. She was the woman who had casually aborted his child. She knew nothing about love. Who was she to lecture him on selfishness and lack of sensitivity?

''But that doesn't matter,'' Joy continued, her voice unnaturally calm. ''We're adults. We should be able to control ourselves long enough to get this job done.''

''Does that mean you trust me?'' he asked, his voice cold, controlled.

''As long as it's directly related to *your* career, yes,'' she said, turning away wearily.

Gabe saw the blue-black bruise spreading from Joy's elbow to her shoulder and forgot the cruel words he had been about to speak, remembering only the moment when his fingers had clamped over her arms and she had cried out in pain.

"Joy," he said, his voice hoarse with exhaustion and something else that he could not name, something very close to shame. "Your arm."

She looked down at it with an expression of surprise, as though whatever she was feeling had blocked the more tangible signals from her bruised flesh.

"Is there any ice here?" asked Gabe. "I'll get a towel and wrap—"

"That's not necessary," Joy said, walking away from him, back to the peace and loneliness of her empty cottage. "I was bruised long before you grabbed me."

The door to the house swung softly shut, leaving Gabe alone on the porch while exhaustion and futility closed around him more darkly than any night.

Chapter 4

Gabe crossed through the blinding morning to the shadowed heat of Joy's back porch. Four people were already there, sorting through caving gear. One of them was Joy. The honey-and-sunlight flash of her short hair was like a beacon in darkness to Gabe's eyes. He quickly controlled the rush of conflicting emotions that seeing her caused. Fourteen hours of sleep had restored his usual self-discipline, despite the fact that the hours had been as riddled with dreams as Lost River Cave was with hidden passages. But unlike the cave there had been no beauty in Gabe's dreams, simply shapes looming out of the darkness, voices calling his name in anguish and passion and regret. And hatred. That had been a new voice added to old dreams, a cold thread of darkness stitching through remembered light.

Deliberately Gabe turned his attention away from his thoughts and toward the other people on the porch. Davy looked as big in daylight as he had at night. Though only a few inches taller than Gabe, Davy was nearly half again as thick. His broad blunt hands made the climbing ropes look almost frail. The girl standing next to him came up to his jawbone and was as lavishly proportioned for a woman as Davy was for a man. Like the black bikini she wore, the word "statuesque" was barely adequate to cover the tall redhead's reality. Gabe found himself hoping that she was keeping Davy's mind—and hands—off Joy. The redhead looked like all the woman any one man could handle, and then some.

The third person looked vaguely familiar. Medium height, wiry build, a face that was both shrewd and calm. The mechanic from last night, the man who had directed Gabe to Joy's cottage. For a moment Gabe searched his memory for the man's name. It was something odd—Fish. Yes, that was it. Fish was tinkering with a battery pack. Sweat gleamed on his naked back as he bent over a toolbox. He looked up as Gabe opened the porch door.

"Mornin', stranger." Fish stood and held out his hand. "Sorry I wasn't real sociable last night. That old generator can be right trying at times."

Gabe smiled and shook Fish's hand. "I wasn't feeling very chatty myself last night. One way or another, I'd been on the road for seventy-three hours by then."

"Burma or Cambodia?" asked Fish.

Gabe gave the man a searching look. "How did you know?"

"Came in from there once or twice myself when I was in the service," said Fish, the skin around his brown eyes crinkling in an almost invisible smile. "Took damn near eighty hours the last time. That's when I decided that being a world traveler was a mighty big pain in the bucket. I mustered out, bought a service station in Carlsbad and commenced to swear at machines other than airplanes."

"He's real good at it, too," said the tall woman. "You ever want something talked to, you just holler for Fish."

"Now you know I never spoke poorly to nothing that didn't have it comin'," drawled Fish. "You met Gabe yet? No? Maggie, Gabe. If you go to fallin' down in that cave," said Fish, winking at Gabe, "you just be sure that this here gal is underneath when you land. She come factory equipped with some right nice cushions."

"Whisper, Fish. Davy might hear," said Maggie, looking over her shoulder to where Davy was carefully coiling ropes. "If that mountain of muscle fell on me, I'd flatten like a drop of water."

Davy smiled slightly but otherwise ignored the raillery. Gabe held out his hand to Maggie.

"Are you really Gabriel Venture, the writer?" asked Maggie, taking his hand. Her eyes were wide and a tinge of disbelief lurked in her voice.

"Disappointed?" he asked.

"No way! I expected you to be old and ugly," she said frankly, looking at him with open approval.

"You're half right," said Gabe.

"Which half?" she asked smartly.

"Both. I'm half-old and half-ugly. Looks like you got my shares of young and beautiful."

"Oh, I'm falling in love," gasped Maggie theatrically, staggering and clutching the general area of her heart.

"Don't fall on me," said Joy in a crisp voice, stepping out of the way. "I don't have any cushioning to speak of."

"Now that," said Davy, glancing up suddenly, "isn't true." He gave Joy a brief, intense look before he went back to folding a rope. "Some cushions just aren't as, er, *stuffed* as others."

"Are you calling me overstuffed?" asked Maggie, turning quickly, her fists on her firm hips as she confronted Davy.

He glanced up again, smiling. "Do I look like a man with a death wish?"

Maggie feinted with her fist. Davy blocked it with his broad upper arm. Her fist smacked lightly against his biceps. It was a teasing blow, hard enough to be felt but not hard enough to hurt.

"Someday, shrimp," she taunted, "I'll take you home to meet some really big men. Roy would make two of you, and he's my smallest brother!"

Davy cocked a blond eyebrow at Maggie, handed her a tangle of rope and said, "Since you aren't decorative, be useful."

Joy thought that she was the only one who sensed Maggie's tiny flash of hurt at Davy's words. Then Joy turned and caught Gabe looking thoughtfully from Maggie to Davy. Gabe's sensitivity surprised her. She didn't remember Gabe as being aware of other people's emotional nuances—unless sex was involved. Then he had an instinct as hypersensitive as a seismograph. Maybe that was why he was tuned in to Maggie. Maybe he wanted her. What was it he had said last night? Something to the effect that if he wanted a woman, he'd find a fresh one. Well, Maggie was that and then some.

The thought slashed through Joy, catching her unaware with its pain. Echoes of last night broke around her, cutting her with razor edges. *Sharp-tongued, thin-lipped old maid. As much joy in you as a squeezed lemon. Female viper.*

"Don't listen to him, Maggie," said Gabe in a casual, teasing voice. "You're a knockout and Davy is just too tongue-tied to admit it."

Maggie looked up from the rope she was winding. "That's okay, Gabe," she said, her voice almost casual. Almost, but not quite. "I've spent my whole life with five older brothers telling me what I look like. I know I'm 'over-built and under-pretty.' But—" she hesitated, then smiled up at him almost shyly "—thanks anyway. It was nice to hear."

Davy's intense blue eyes narrowed and he looked at Maggie as though seeing her for the first time, hearing the wistfulness and sensitivity beneath the constant clowning that was Maggie's usual exterior.

"You tell your brothers," said Gabe seriously, hearing the vulnerability in Maggie's voice, "that they wouldn't know pretty if it tripped them and laid them out flat. You're more than pretty, Maggie. As for being over-built—" Gabe grinned "—I don't know a woman who wouldn't kill to be put together like you."

"Amen," muttered Fish.

"Such wonderful lies," sighed Maggie deeply, clowning again, but this time there was pleasure rather than wistfulness beneath her voice. "Or maybe you've just been out in the wilds too long?" she teased, slanting a blue-green glance at Gabe.

"Don't slander Gabe," Joy said dryly. "Didn't you know he's a world-class expert on women? And his specialty is nineteen-year-olds. A real connoisseur," she added, her voice resonant with barely stifled emotions.

She heard her own words and all but winced at what they revealed. She'd have to guard her tongue, stop the bitterness from seeping out with every word. It wasn't Maggie's fault that Gabe was gentle with her and harsh with his former lover. It wasn't Maggie's fault that she was young, stunning, innocent, and that Joy was not.

But that simple fact also filled Joy with an irrational rage. So she smiled brilliantly and turned to face Gabe's glittering green eyes, discovering just how angry he was. Joy's eyes stared back, as transparent as spring water—and as cold. "I know you're very experienced in many areas, Gabe," she said, speaking in a casual low voice that belied the transparent ice of her eyes, "but it's been a long time since you were in a cave, so I—"

"Five years, eleven months and thirty days," interrupted Gabe, giving her a smile that lowered the temperature on the hot porch by about half. He saw the look of surprise on Joy's face echoed on Maggie's and Davy's. "Oh yes, Dr. Anderson, I remember to the exact day how long it's been. You see," murmured Gabe, including everyone in his words without releasing Joy from his icy smile, "Lost River Cave was a unique experience for me. I've climbed some of the world's tallest mountains until I ached for lack of oxygen. I've nearly drowned in the warm rhythms of some very exotic seas. I've come close to succumbing to the hot seductions of a few deadly jungle flowers. But I have never been as fooled by anything as I was by the transparency of Lost River Cave's waters. So pure, so perfect, so innocent, seeming no deeper than my hand. But if you believe that innocent, sweet, deceptive surface, you'll stumble in and drown—if you don't freeze to death first."

Fish gave Gabe a swift, shrewd glance and went back to tinkering with the battery box. Joy saw the look and felt color stain her cheeks; Fish knew that Gabe was talking about exploring women as well as landscapes. So did she. She supposed she deserved it for her crack about connoisseurs and nineteen-year-olds. The fact that her words were true didn't make the comment any less cutting.

But he had no right to call her deceitful and cold. She had never lied to him, and Kati was the living proof of a warmth that still haunted Joy's dreams.

"Since you're aware that what little you know about Lost River Cave isn't trustworthy," Joy said grimly, "you won't object to being treated as a total novice."

"Would objecting do any good?" asked Gabe with deceptive mildness.

"No."

Gabe smiled mockingly. "Then by all means, *Dr.* Anderson, teach me whatever you think you can."

Davy looked up sharply, disliking the sardonic emphasis of Gabe's tone. "Why don't I show Gabe the ropes," offered Davy. "We can catch up with you later in the cave. In fact, maybe you should stay here this morning. Your arm must be giving you fits."

Gabe remembered the instant when he had grabbed Joy, punishing her far more sharply than he had intended. He turned on her with a swift, almost violent movement. "Is it still bothering you? Didn't you put any ice on it?" he demanded harshly.

"There wasn't any," she said.

"Let me see your arm."

"It's fine."

"The hell it is. I'll have a look at it, Dr. Anderson, or I'll know the reason why. If you think I'm trusting my life on a rope with a belayer whose arm is half dead, you're—"

"I'm not a fool, Mr. Venture," Joy said curtly, cutting him off and pushing up the sleeve of her loose gauze shirt at the same time. "I wouldn't go caving at the risk of someone else's life. *Even yours.*"

Gabe swallowed his response to her last crack and looked carefully at her arm. The bruise that had seemed so huge last night looked much better this morning. Without the added dark streaks of mud and livid chaffing that came from cold, it was clear that the bruise wasn't a serious one. She would be able to go caving safely. The blue-black area was barely half the size of his palm. What made seeing it like a blow to Gabe was the fact that there were two blurred yet unmistakable bars where his fingers had closed over the bruise, further damaging the tender flesh.

Very delicately Gabe stroked his fingertips over the discolored skin, seeking any hard knots that would indicate the presence of true injury. There were none. He cupped the bruise gently against his palm, restraining Joy with a hand on her wrist when she would have flinched away.

"I won't hurt you," he murmured, watching her gray eyes, seeing the pupils expand, sensing the sudden intake of her breath. "I just want to see if it's hot." He ran first his palm, then the back of his hand, then his fingertips down her arm from shoulder to wrist. "Feels fine," he said, his voice husky. Then, too softly for anyone but Joy to hear, "Very fine."

Joy felt her pulse accelerate and knew that in another instant Gabe would feel it too. She wanted to snatch her wrist from his intimate grip but knew that such an act would be as revealing as anything she could do except slap him or return the caressing motion of his fingers with her own.

"Are you taking notes, Davy?" she asked, her voice light, her eyes icy. "This is how a connoisseur acts. Of course I'm not nineteen, I don't have a shape other women would kill for, and I'm, shall we say, *shopworn*, but Mr. Venture is willing to overlook a few defects in the interests of civil intercourse."

Then Joy wished she had bitten her tongue, for she could hear the rage quivering beneath each contemptuous syllable she had spoken and was afraid that the others could hear it, too. Gabe certainly had. But despite the answering anger in his eyes, his touch remained gentle on her wrist and arm, wordlessly reassuring her that she wouldn't push him to physical retribution again. She felt a wild impulse to tell him that she understood, that she knew he never would have grabbed her arm last night if he had seen the bruise, but there were too many people around to make such personal explanations.

And those people were looking at her rather speculatively right now.

"Well, Gabe," she said, "I'm afraid our secret is out." She rushed on before the surprise in his hard green eyes could translate into words. Forcing a wry smile, she looked over her shoulder at the other three people. "You see, the Great Gabriel Venture and I struck sparks off each other six years ago. Obviously that hasn't changed. But we didn't let it get in the way of caving then, and it won't get in the way now." She looked back at him. "Will it, Gabe."

It wasn't quite a question, nor was it a demand. There was a hesitant overture in the softness of his name on her lips, a silent, not quite defiant apology implicit in her offer of half truth and truce.

"Struck sparks," murmured Gabe, his smile off center, hard. "Yeah, I guess you could say that. In bloody spades." He looked past her at the three people watching him. "The good doctor and I will probably fight like hell on fire. When we do, just take cover," he said, looking directly at Davy, "and no one else will get hurt." Gabe held Davy's eyes for a long hard moment before the older man looked back down at Joy. "Right, *Joy*."

There was the same ambivalence in Gabe's soft-voiced, hard-eyed offer of truce that there had been in Joy's, but his eyes were unflinching. She hadn't realized until that moment how angry Gabe had been with Davy for his teasing remark about Maggie not being decorative. Perhaps it might be a good idea to keep the two men on separate ropes for awhile. Davy didn't need to be distracted by the kind of icy male anger Gabe projected effortlessly, devastatingly.

"Right, Mr. Venture," Joy said crisply.

"Gabe. Just Gabe." The threat was soft and very clear, as hot as his fingers stroking her captive palm.

"Gabe," she said, her voice husky.

"That didn't hurt, did it?" he asked, smiling coldly at her. He caressed the softness of her palm and inner wrist until he felt the wild beating of her pulse beneath his fingertips. "Think of it as a little practice in the fine art of civil intercourse. You need it, doctor," he said, contempt in his voice and in the line of his mouth. "You need it bad."

Joy hated herself for the betraying race of her pulse beneath his touch. Part of her response was anger, pure and hot. But not all of it, and Joy was honest enough to admit it. She flushed, jerking away from Gabe's too-knowing touch.

Davy swore and took a quick step toward Gabe, only to collide with the even faster Fish. "Think it's time to take cover, children," Fish said, deftly using Davy's momentum to head him out the door. "Lots of room to hide in that old cave." He turned and gave Joy a direct look. "Unless you changed your mind, Dr. Anderson?"

Joy knew that he was asking if she felt safe with Gabe. Gabe knew it too, and it infuriated him. He turned on Fish with a poised speed that the combat-trained mechanic noted and understood. Even so, Fish didn't back up.

"Just take all the blunt instruments with you and we'll be fine," said Joy quickly, her voice determined and light. "We'll catch up with you in the Voices in ninety minutes."

Fish nodded. He herded Maggie and Davy out the door, laden with equipment. As he passed Gabe, the mechanic said in a low voice that Joy couldn't overhear, "Luck, man. You'll need it. In the five years I've known her, ain't no man been able to get next to her. Damn shame, too. That's a whole lot of woman going to waste."

Whistling, Fish let the porch door slam behind him. Too surprised to do more than let the parting shot sink in, Gabe watched the mechanic walk to the Land Cruiser. Then Gabe turned and looked at Joy speculatively. *Five years. Did my leaving hurt her so badly that she had refused to trust any man after me? Had she really meant it when she cried out her love in my arms?* Even as the thoughts formed, Gabe rejected them. He had learned long ago that you can only trust what people do, not what they say. A woman in love doesn't casually have an abortion. Joy had done just that.

Joy saw the speculative expression on Gabe's face give way to the contempt for her that she was learning to dread. Abruptly she felt exhausted, unable to continue the battle. It was hurting her too much. She spoke before he could, for she knew that she couldn't take any more verbal shots without revealing how very vulnerable she was. All the emotions she thought she had controlled—love, hate, fear, fury—came boiling up with each cutting remark he made. She had felt like this after her parents had died and she had found out she was pregnant, abandoned by Gabe with no more notice than a check to pay for an abortion. Not even a few gentle lies about how he was sorry he couldn't be with her to help her. Nothing.

She had been all but devastated by his cruel indifference. Then the false comfort and strength of hatred had come, driving out love. Finally she learned to put aside the hate which threatened to corrode her very soul, for she had wanted her unborn child to know only love. She had never regretted her choice. Kati had been worth every agonizing moment of Joy's ordeal. Rightly or wrongly, in love or in lust, Gabe had given Joy a beautiful child. If for no other reason than that, she had to stop tearing at him and at herself. In the end it would be Kati who would lose more than anyone.

"Truce," Joy said raggedly, rubbing her arms as though she were cold. "Either that, or go caving with Fish right now. I'm not as cruel as you Gabe. I can't survive this kind of battle."

Gabe's face hardened even more. He opened his mouth, a harsh retort on his lips. The words died as he saw the shadows of exhaustion and lines of strain on Joy's face, emotions she could no longer conceal. She had never looked less like the name he had given her—Joy.

"Please," said Joy, hating the tremor in her voice but unable to control it. "No more." She turned away swiftly, appalled at the tears she felt closing her throat and burning behind her eyes. She hadn't cried since she had looked at the tiny, perfect scrap of life that was her baby and realized that Kati would never have a father to tease and love, cherish and protect her.

"Which is it, Gabe? Cutting me or going caving?" she asked, her voice raw.

"Are you going to stop clawing at me," he asked, keeping his voice even with an effort, "or is this a one-way truce?"

"It hasn't been deliberate," Joy said carefully, sorting through her caving gear, unable to meet his jade-green eyes. "I guess there's more of the betrayed nineteen-year-old left in me than I realized."

"Betrayed?" asked Gabe, his voice as harsh as his face. "I never promised you anything!"

"I know," she said instantly. "I'm sorry. You're right. There was no betrayal. You delivered exactly what you promised."

Nothing.

Though neither one spoke, the word hung between them like a water drop suspended from a stalactite, shivering before the moment of release.

Gabe swore softly, violently, a single word that slipped past his control.

"I'm sorry," began Joy helplessly, "I didn't mean—"

"Shut up," he snarled. "Your so-called apologies are worse than your insults."

Despair darkened Joy's eyes. It wasn't going to work. They couldn't say three words without slashing at each other. And what would happen when Kati returned? When she grew up and Joy told her who her father was, would Kati's only memory be of a man who loathed her mother? "Gabriel," she said desperately, "what do you want from me? What can I do to make you hate me less?"

Gabe's first thought was of the hunger that still swept through him, memories of what it had been like to feel Joy moving in his arms. Then he remembered the I-love-you lies, the baby she had refused to have. He wanted to strike out at her, to wound her as deeply as she had wounded him by refusing his child. And then he saw Joy's despair and knew that somehow he had hurt her more than he had ever realized, just as she had hurt him. Despite the fact that he had never said he would stay with her or marry her—had in fact never even said that he loved her—despite the lack of promises, when he had left Joy he had cut her to her soul. Was that why she had aborted his baby? Revenge? Without knowing it, had he taken a young girl's love and twisted it into hate?

Abruptly Gabe felt old, stained, spent. The despair in Joy's clear eyes was echoed in his own. "What happened is in the past," he said, his voice hoarse. "There's nothing either of us can do about it now. Except live with it."

Joy wanted to cry out *What have I done to make you hate me?* but she didn't have the strength to argue with him anymore. It was enough that for a moment he had looked at her with sadness rather than contempt in his eyes.

"Then let's see if we can't create something now that's better than the past," she said wearily. "No matter what did or didn't happen between us, I respect your ability to share new worlds with people through your writing."

Gabe looked into Joy's bleak gray eyes and felt an impulse to comfort her despite the fact that rage still made his heart beat hard and fast. "And I," he said softly, "respect the expertise that has made New Mexico's Dr. Anderson one of the foremost speleologists in the U.S."

Surprise showed clearly on Joy's delicate face.

"Oh yes," continued Gabe. "I finally did what I should have done the instant I accepted the assignment—my homework."

If I had done it sooner, I would have known who Dr. Anderson was, and you wouldn't have been able to get past my guard so quickly, so easily. And if I hadn't come early, I'll bet I wouldn't have been able to get past yours. It would have been easier that way. For both of us. But he didn't say that, because it would have shredded the tenuous overtures they both were making toward a truce.

"The package my editor sent me was very impressive," Gabe continued quietly. "You've had articles published in the most prestigious scientific journals, including a monograph on the effects of differing ratios of carbon dioxide on solution rates in New Mexican limestone that's causing a substantial revision of former estimates of how long it takes caves to develop. Then there's the treatise you did on deducing paleoclimates in the southwest through analysis of Lost River Cave's formations. That, I'm told, is rapidly becoming known as the definitive work on cave formations and ancient climates."

Gabe looked at her as though she were an undiscovered territory which had just opened in front of him. And, in many ways, she was. The younger Joy of his memories had been bright, yes; that was part of her appeal to him. She hadn't had the maturity to apply herself to such sustained intellectual efforts, though. Nor had she shown any real inclination to do so, except for her fascination with the process of cave formation.

"Very impressive," repeated Gabe. "Your parents must be proud of you."

The pain that darkened Joy's eyes lasted only an instant, but it was long enough for Gabe to see it.

"My parents are dead," said Joy, turning back to her caving equipment.

"I'm sorry. I didn't know." He hesitated, wondering if their deaths had been recent, if that was what had taken the laughter out of Joy. The death of his own father had shaken Gabe, even though they had never been very close. So much of childhood died with a parent, and Joy had no brothers or sisters to share her memories with. "It must be very hard for you. Was it . . . recent?"

"They died ten days after you left Cottonwood Wells," said Joy, fighting to keep her voice level but not succeeding. "Helicopter crash."

The sound of Gabe's quick intake of breath was loud in the silence. Unbidden, his hand stretched out to touch Joy's cheek. "I'm so sorry," he whispered, regretting more than the deaths of two people he had respected and liked. *My God, to lose your first lover one week and your parents the next. No wonder she had felt abandoned, betrayed. Life had turned on her and knocked her flat—and then had rolled over her again for good measure with a pregnancy she wasn't mentally or financially equipped to survive.*

"Why didn't you write me?" he asked tightly. "I would have helped you." Yet even as he heard his own words he wondered how he could have done anything. By the time mail would have reached him on the Orinoco, her parents would have been dead for months and the abortion an accomplished fact. "Somehow," he whispered as much to himself as to her, "I would have helped you."

Joy's only answer was a short, harsh laugh as she remembered the check for an abortion. "I'd had all of your brand of 'help' that I could survive just then," she said. She sensed Gabe's anger in the sudden clenching of his hand and the stiffening of his body. She looked up and saw rage darkening his face and making his eyes glitter like cut glass. "The truce won't work if we talk about the past," Joy said bluntly. "Somehow we both feel we were wronged. Well, tough. We'll just have to pull up our socks and go on. Or we'll have to call it quits on Lost River Cave. Take your pick, Gabe. I won't talk about the past if you won't."

"Just a mutual professional love feast?" he said sardonically. "I admire your work and you admire mine?"

"Love feast?" retorted Joy mockingly. "*Love?* The Great Gabriel Venture? Ain't hardly likely, cowboy," she drawled. "Would you believe an armed truce?"

"Would you believe a bridle on the bitchy repartee?" he shot back, grabbing her, careful to avoid her bruised arm this time. "Or would you like me to put on the bridle?" he asked coolly, looking at her mouth.

A recent memory quivered between them—Joy trembling with something more than anger as he stroked her soft wrist and palm.

Joy flinched away from both the memory and the man. She took a deep breath, trying to damp down the rage that had come when Gabe had used the word *love*. The sensual threat in him was vivid, as hot as her own rage. Too many memories whispering to her, telling her that she had responded to this man before. He had been the man who explored the secrets of her virginal body.

Perhaps she could still respond to him. Perhaps she could finally escape the numbness in her core, the absence of passionate response that had doomed the possibility of her loving another man and ensured that Kati would always be what her mother had been—a lonely only child.

Yet even as it came, the thought of succumbing to Gabe frightened Joy. She knew that she could no more survive his sensuality than she could his contempt. But somehow she had to get along with him. She had endured too much to get where she was today. She wouldn't let it all go to hell simply because she couldn't control either her antagonism or her response to Gabe.

"You don't want me, so please don't play this kind of power game," she said quietly, her voice shaking slightly as she looked into the green eyes that were too close, too familiar. "No matter what you do to me, or I do to you, it can't change what happened when you left Cottonwood Wells. What we do can only affect this instant, now, and the future of a place that is very special to me."

She drew a long ragged breath and made the only offer she could to placate Gabe, although even the thought of missing out on the last weeks of Lost River Cave made tears gather in her eyes.

"I'll leave Cottonwood Wells," Joy offered huskily, "and I won't come back until you're gone."

Gabe saw the tears that Joy fought so hard to hide and knew how much the offer had cost her.

"Christ! You really hate me, don't you?" he asked hoarsely, releasing her. "Lost River Cave is your life, yet you'll walk away from your last chance to explore it just to avoid being around me."

"And you," she said, "can't look at me without wanting to hurt me."

Joy's voice was as empty as her eyes. She waited silently for Gabe's decision, too spent to say or do anything more. He saw the soul-deep weariness in her and knew that it was an accurate reflection of his own. Whatever he had hoped for when he flogged himself halfway around the world to come back to Cottonwood Wells, it hadn't been what he had found. Fury. Hatred. Despair.

Regret.

Well, fool, what now? And don't bother bitching about life's little surprises. The men who screamed for two thousand feet before hitting bottom would be glad to trade surprises with you. Besides, look at it from her point of view. You seduced a virgin and left without knowing if she was pregnant. Ten days later her parents died. Then she found out she was pregnant and you were way beyond reach. For this you expected her to throw roses at you when she saw you again?

Yeah, and she flushed my kid and lied about loving me. For this I'm expected to throw roses at her when I see her again?

What would you have done in her place—pregnant, nineteen, parents dead, nowhere to go, no one to turn to, no money and no way to earn any?

It was the first time Gabe had asked himself that question. It wasn't one that he wanted to answer. He hadn't meant it to turn out this way. He hadn't meant to leave her alone in a world that cared not one bit whether Joy survived. He hadn't known her parents would die. He hadn't meant to hurt her like that.

Right, fool. You just took what you wanted and left. No hard feelings and no regrets, right? Fool.

But she didn't love me!

And you didn't love her. I'd call that even all the way around. You dumped her and she dumped your baby. Just one of life's little surprises, like a landslide and a grave two thousand feet deep.

Broodingly, Gabe looked at the woman who waited in front of him, all her laughter quenched, not even a glimmer of hope to ease the exhausted lines of her face or soften the bleak clarity of her eyes. The girl-woman he had made love to so long ago was dead, killed by time and circumstance and a lover who hadn't meant to be cruel. If he had come halfway around the world to try to resurrect the sweetness and innocence of a past affair, then he was indeed a fool.

And if he made this woman pay for his foolishness a second time, he would never be able to call himself a man again.

"Stay," said Gabe, his voice flattened by the same emptiness that had flattened Joy's. "If I had known that your parents had died so soon after I left..." He let the words trail away into silence, feeling almost sick at what he had inadvertently put Joy through. He regretted the abortion deeply, bitterly; but he no longer hated her for it, no longer felt quite so completely betrayed. "We'll explore Lost River Cave together, and we'll leave the past where it belongs. In a grave two thousand feet deep."

Joy shuddered visibly, caught as much by the echoes of pain in Gabe's voice as she was by his last brutal words.

"We'll have to start all over," said Gabe, looking at Joy. "I haven't been in a cave since I left here six years ago. Treat me like a novice and you won't go far wrong. Can you handle that?"

"Yes," she said huskily. Then, so softly that he almost didn't hear. "Thank you, Gabriel."

"For what?"

"Letting me stay. I know you don't understand, but—"

"I think I do," he said tiredly, watching her with eyes that were almost opaque, like jade, translucent without being clear. "Lost River Cave is all you have left of your childhood, your innocence. Life has taken everything from you except the cave's beauty, its mystery, its dreams condensed into extraordinary, living stone."

"How did you know?" she asked, searching his face as though a stranger had appeared in place of the Gabe she thought she knew so well.

"Because I feel the same way about Lost River Cave," he said simply. "But I'm damned if I know why."

For a moment silence gathered between them, as though they had both discovered themselves lost in the same place at the same moment. Joy had an irrational desire to comfort Gabe, as though he had never hurt her, never abandoned her, never taught her to hate.

And perhaps he hadn't. Not this Gabriel Venture, this tall, weary, jade-eyed man who radiated questions and pain and . . . loneliness. This was a man she did not know, just as she was a woman he did not know.

Perhaps he never had known her. Perhaps she had never known him either, never loved him. Perhaps she had simply loved a young girl's dream of love.

"Maybe you'll find out once we're down there," said Joy.

"What?" asked Gabe.

"Maybe when we're down there you'll discover why Lost River Cave is special to you."

Gabe's off-center smile was as unexpected as his words had been. It was the smile of a man who had stopped running and only then realized that he had run himself almost to exhaustion. "That would be too much to expect of life," he said softly. "I'll settle for finding the same kind of beauty there that I remember. Just that. A memory that isn't a lie."

Chapter 5

Joy parked the Jeep next to the dusty white Land Cruiser just beyond the mouth of Lost River Cave. Gabe got out and began unloading caving gear.

"You're sure you want to act like you've never been caving before?" she asked dubiously. "You're going to get awfully bored hearing what you already know."

Gabe's off-center smile tugged oddly at Joy's emotions. "I've learned that I don't know nearly as much as I thought I did," he said, watching her with an intensity that was new.

I didn't know your parents had died. I'm sorry, Joy. For so many things. But Gabe's words went no farther than his mind. He had promised to leave the past in a grave two thousand feet deep. He would try very hard to keep that promise. It was the least he could do for the woman who watched him with shadows and no laughter in her clear gray eyes.

The regret in Gabe's voice made Joy ache. No matter how hard she searched his eyes, his face, the nuances of his voice, she could find none of the contempt he had shown for her. Bitterness, yes, but not focused on her, not completely. Somehow the knowledge of her parents' death had taken away Gabe's hatred of her. She wanted to ask why that had made such a difference to him, but she knew she would not. She had no more desire to stir the ashes of their mutual past—and burn her fingers—than he did.

A grave two thousand feet deep.

"All right," said Joy, drawing a deep breath. She pulled out her own supplies. "Let's go through the checklist. Helmet?" she asked, holding out her hand.

Gabe dug his helmet out from under a pile of wool clothes and placed it in her hand. She saw the dents and scars on its surface and looked up at him, her eyes wide.

"Landslide," he said. "Peru."

"My God, Gabe," she said in a husky voice, unable to control the trembling of the hand holding the helmet. "You're lucky to be alive."

He shrugged. "The helmet's still good, anyway. If the dents bother you, I'll hammer them out."

Joy checked the helmet with fingers that showed a marked tendency to quiver from time to time. Despite the dents, the helmet was in good shape. Nowhere did the interior metal impinge on the network of straps and padding that cushioned the wearer's skull. She looked thoughtfully at the leather chin strap.

"I've got an extra elastic strap," she said, rummaging in the glove compartment of the Jeep. "I'd rather you use it. That way if you get jammed descending a tight chimney, you can tip your head out of the helmet and there's no chance of strangling yourself."

"Elastic it is," murmured Gabe, taking the strap from her fingers. "Can you really strangle yourself on a helmet strap?" he asked.

Joy almost smiled at the change in Gabe's voice. This was the man she remembered, asking questions, assembling facts, making of them a coherent whole that crackled with insight and intelligence. She had meant it when she told him that she respected his work. She did. Despite the pain it caused her, she had read everything he had done in the years since he left her.

"Someone accidentally strangled himself a few years ago when his helmet wedged in a narrow slot during a descent," she said. "That's when elastic chin straps started becoming popular."

Gabe eyed the new strap with respect.

"Helmet lamp?" asked Joy.

He dug out his electric lamp and battery pack. The lamp was new, almost startling in its polish against the battered helmet. The bulb fit snugly and the filament was intact.

"All right?" asked Gabe.

"Fine," she said absently, prying into the battery pack. As she had suspected, the pack, too, was new. No one had modified it for caving. "This will be okay for today, but tonight you'll want Fish to put some masonite spacers in. Otherwise the batteries will slip away from the contacts and you'll be—"

"Left in the dark," finished Gabe dryly, peering over Joy's shoulder into the battery pack.

She made a muffled sound of agreement and began laying out the contents of his rucksack on the Jeep's hood. "Flashlight, extra batteries, extra lamp bulb, waterproof matches, candles—oh good, you have the chemical light sticks, too," she said, referring to the slender plastic tubes that, once twisted, began to glow with a surprisingly strong light. As long as the chemical reaction inside the tube lasted, usually twenty-four to forty-eight hours, the light stick was an all but indestructible source of illumination.

"Where's your pocketknife?" she asked.

Silently, Gabe reached into his climbing shorts and produced the knife. Joy put it with the rest of the equipment on the hood.

"Nice compass," she commented, admiring it before setting it aside. "Mmm, Swiss chocolate. Better not let Fish see that. He has a passion for the stuff. Raisins," she muttered, moving aside a plastic packet with her index finger. "Yetch."

Gabe smiled slightly at Joy's sound of disgust, remembering that she hated raisins despite their usefulness as emergency food. No matter how you packed, smashed, drowned or otherwise mistreated raisins, they remained pretty much the same in taste and texture.

"Peanuts," she continued. "Soon to be peanut butter, compliments of Gotcha. Tablets to purify water. First aid kit." Her eyes widened as she opened the small kit. It was like a deftly miniaturized surgery, everything in place from sutures to disinfectant. "What a beauty," she said, closing the tiny case reverently.

The canteen was all it had to be: tough, waterproof and small enough not to be in the way more than half the time. Gabe also had a compact survival kit that was a miracle of modern advances in materials to keep a human being warm and relatively comfortable under conditions that were neither.

"Space blanket, extra wool socks, shoelaces, change of clothes, paper clips and safety pins—" She looked up suddenly, almost smiling. "Useful little devils, aren't they?" Before he could answer she was concentrating on the equipment again. "Ensolite pads for knees and seat, more batteries, peppermint hard candies. Oh, oh, you're in trouble. Better hide those."

"Fish has a thing for them, too?" guessed Gabe, amused.

"Nope. I do. After a few hours down there, peppermint is like having sunshine dissolve on your tongue. Problem is, I like them when I'm on top, too. Can't keep the darn things around." She gave everything on the Jeep's hood a final, quick look. "That's it for the personal gear. On to the climbing stuff."

While Gabe refilled his backpack, Joy opened his canvas rope sack and began pulling things out. She was satisfied with everything until she came to his climbing rope. It was designed for mountains, not caves. It was nearly one-half inch thick and had never been used.

"We should have washed this last night. It would have been much easier to handle. Then there's the stretch factor." She frowned and mentally went through alternative routes down to Lost River Cave's third level. She shook her head. "Won't work. This rope is great for belaying the leader on a mountain, but it's too stretchy for caving. We've got one vertical descent of nearly a hundred and fifty feet—if you fell using this rope, it would stretch so much before it stopped you that it would be like having no rope at all. You'd end up ten feet wide and an inch thick at the bottom of Surprise."

"Surprise?"

"That's our name for the slot. It had what looked like a floor fifty feet down. It wasn't a floor. It was a very thin cave formation that had closed the slot partway down." Joy smiled crookedly, remembering. "Good thing Fish was belaying me. I don't weigh much, but I didn't even have time to call out a warning when the floor gave way. He didn't let me slip more than six inches."

Gabe pictured Joy standing on a fragile sheet of rock more than one hundred feet above the true bottom of the slot and then going through, falling, her life dependent on her rope and the skill of the person belaying her. Even though he knew that Joy was a careful, experienced caver, the image of her falling left a hollowness in Gabe's stomach. He had learned that no matter how carefully life or an expedition is planned and executed, things go wrong. What looks like a floor is really a fragile ceiling, and what looks like solid mountain is really a lethal slide just waiting to be triggered. And ropes, even the best, contain flaws that can't be found short of the ultimate instant of testing, when a human life dangles over a bottomless void.

"Anyway," said Joy, shrugging, "there's too much stretch in this rope for the longer descents. We'll use my backup rope for you."

"May I see the rope," asked Gabe, but there was no real question in his voice. He would inspect the rope very carefully before he trusted his life to it.

"Sure," Joy said, looking up quickly, catching the steel beneath the polite request, wondering if he really distrusted her that much. *If he's that worried about my judgment, maybe we shouldn't go down in the cave alone.*

"Nothing personal," he added in a quiet tone, reading her thoughts in the sudden uncertainty of her question. "I check my own ropes. Always."

She searched his face but found only the contrast between his dark, thickly curling lashes and the luminous green depths of his eyes. "It's in the gray canvas bag," she said.

Joy went back to sorting through Gabe's rope sack. She found another rope, this one thinner, a rope for emergencies. There was the usual assortment of backup equipment such as webbing loops and spare carabiners. Then she pulled out a piece of rope that was less than a foot long. Both ends had been neatly cut, as though this were a segment removed from a longer rope. But the segment itself was useless. The outer surface of the nylon rope was badly abraded, almost furry looking. In one place the structure of the rope itself had been frayed until all but a quarter inch of the inner core was worn through. She stared at the ruined rope, wondering why Gabe bothered to carry it with him.

"It reminds me how narrow the margin between survival and death can be," he said, watching her, "and how important a good rope is. That was new, top-of-the-line, and I used it only once. In Peru. If it had been cheap or worn, I'd be dead."

Joy looked at the horrifyingly frail strands that had been all that had held together the rope and Gabe's life. "This?" she said. Then, "How far?"

"Did I fall?"

"Yes," she said, her voice dry.

He shrugged. "Not far. Under twenty feet, for sure, or the force of the rope stopping me would have broken my back. But," he added grimly, "I fell far enough to bounce like a yo-yo on an elastic string. Far enough for the chest harness to break and part of the Swiss seat to give way and leave me dangling by one leg and a chicken loop. But the piton held during all the time that landslide broke like a stone wave over the cliff we'd been climbing. My rope held, too. It tore hell out of my hip and leg, but I survived."

Joy closed her eyes and drew an unsteady breath as she envisioned Gabe dangling helplessly at the end of a rope while a landslide ripped through piece after piece of his safety equipment. The strain on his leg must have been horrible. "No wonder they thought you might never walk again," she said, her voice ragged. "It's a miracle you survived, Gabe."

His eyes narrowed as he saw the depth of Joy's response to the knowledge of his past danger and injury. She hated him, but the thought of him dangling at the end of a fraying rope, battered by falling rocks, brought her no pleasure.

Joy looked up at him, her eyes as clear as spring rain, searching. "Does your leg still bother you?" she asked softly.

"Not as much as the questions."

"The questions?"

"Why me? Why did I live? Why did other men die? Why—" He made an abrupt gesture with his hand. "Questions without answers."

"Yes," she said, ruefully, sadly. "The questions we all ask on the way to growing up."

Instinctively Gabe knew that Joy had asked those same questions of herself after her parents had died in a helicopter crash. "The questions were a little late coming to me," he said sardonically. "I'm nearly thirty."

"Some people never ask those questions at all, no matter how long they live," said Joy with a shrug.

"And the answers? When do they come?"

"There's a world full of answers. The trick is to find one that satisfies you."

"Have you?" he asked, emotion rippling beneath his voice.

"Sometimes. And sometimes...not. Some nights are longer than others."

That, thought Gabe grimly, *is the understatement of the century.*

Joy looked at him for a moment, seeing the restless urgency beneath his controlled exterior. Whatever was driving him was deep, all the way to his core. It was this same intensity that had drawn her initially to Gabe, the instinctive knowledge that here was a man who thought and felt deeply, who would always seek beneath the surface to the enduring truths beneath, who would demand a response as intense as his own. She had never met another person like him. No one combined his intelligence and sensuality. No one shared her eagerness and consuming wonder in the world around her as he did. No one had been able to release the primal response of her body and mind as he had.

And no one had hurt her a tenth so deeply as Gabriel Venture.

"We'd better get going," said Joy, looking from him to the watch on her wrist. "I want to have plenty of time for you to get used to being in a cave again."

Silently Gabe reassembled the contents of his rope bag and climbed into his thermal underwear. The same clothes he had worn for mountain climbing would serve for caving. The underwear combined with desert sun made him eager to be within Lost River Cave's coolness. He pulled on his pants quickly and left his wool shirt unbuttoned. He put on the battery pack and helmet. The coveralls he had bought six years ago still fit. He put the pads in the seat and knee pockets and pulled on the loose garment, leaving it unzipped. The wire leads from battery pack to helmet stayed beneath the coveralls, protecting the wires from snagging on rocks during a tight crawl. Wool socks, jungle boots and leather-palmed cotton gloves completed his outfit. He tested the lamp. It worked. He was ready to go.

Getting hotter by the instant, he shrugged into his backpack and followed Joy to the mouth of the cave. At the entrance there was a doubled loop of rope with a carabiner attached. The loop was slung around a huge boulder, which would serve as an anchor. A rope attached to the loop trailed down like a bright narrow tongue into the cave's beckoning darkness. Cool air stirred caressingly, whispering of the moist cave hidden beyond the reach of the searching desert sun. Joy reversed the specialized harness she wore, called a Swiss seat. Reversed, the seat was an ideal restraint for anchoring a belay. She checked that the rigging around the boulder hadn't frayed or become displaced before snapping herself to the anchor.

"I'll belay you into the cave," said Joy. "It's a steep pitch over loose rubble, nearly two hundred feet down. Holler to make sure no one's on the way up."

Gabe went to the cave's mouth, yelled "Yo!" and waited. No answer came up. No one was below.

Carefully Joy retrieved the rope that went into the cave, automatically examining it for fresh cuts or abrasions as she wound it into a neat coil. Gabe checked the rope, too. She didn't object. After seeing the wretched segment of rope he carried in his pack, she wouldn't have protested if he had insisted on going over every inch of every rope with a sixty power magnifying glass. In fact, she had an impulse to do just that herself. Instead she sat down facing the mouth of the cave with her legs partially extended. The newly coiled rope was at her left. One end of the rope went around her lower back, and from there to Gabe.

Gabe put on his Swiss seat and attached himself to the rope in such a way that he would be able to climb without restraint unless he slipped. Then the rope would spring taut under Joy's hands, preventing Gabe from falling. Joy herself would be anchored against the pull of his weight by her own attachment to the massive boulder. Although Gabe could clearly see that Joy was in position to belay him, he went through the necessary ritual of voice signals—necessary because he wouldn't always be able to see her, and then communication would be critical.

"Belay on?" he said clearly.

"On belay," answered Joy in an equally carrying voice.

"Ready to climb," said Gabe, poised on the brink of the cave, his helmet lamp looking very pale against the blaze of desert light.

"Climb!" responded Joy.

"Climbing!"

Gabe began his descent into Lost River Cave, his life quite literally held by Joy's hands. He didn't hesitate, a fact which astounded him when he realized it. Despite all that had happened, despite the violent emotion he had seen lurking within Joy's gray eyes, he knew at some visceral level that she would not deliberately harm him. It was one of the few certainties that had remained with him after the accident in Peru, and he hadn't even discovered that certainty until the instant he stepped off into blackness with nothing more between him and the possibility of a brutal fall than the rope playing skillfully through Joy's small hands.

The last of yesterday's stiffness had left Gabe's hip. He climbed quickly, smoothly, his body supple and sure. As he felt the reassuring tension of the rope move with him, neither too tight nor too loose, he had an impulse to call up his praise to Joy's expertise through the deepening well of velvet darkness folding around him. He kept silent, though. Only a few words were used when on belay, and *You're doing a great job!* weren't among them.

Lost River Cave's seamless night enveloped Gabe coolly, caressingly. For a moment memories spun out of the darkness like immaterial ropes attaching him to anchor points in the past. The first time he had come down to the cave alone with Joy, they had turned out their lights and stood hand in hand, adrift in the limitless, magic night of Lost River Cave. With sight gone, every other sense leaped into razor focus. The subtle lemon-and-rose scent of her perfume. The warmth of her breath washing over his lips. The heat and peppermint taste of her tongue. The exquisite textures of her mouth revealed to him in a kiss that had no end.

The memory sliced through Gabe while his body moved more deeply into Lost River Cave. His breath came in sharply, then settled into its former rhythms as his muscles responded to the demands of the moment. Soon he was at the end of the steep pitch, looking up toward the brilliant spot where the mysterious cave world ended and the New Mexican desert began. He removed the rope and stepped back.

"Off belay!" called Gabe.

"Belay off!" came Joy's response, carrying easily to him on the damp air.

He buttoned his wool shirt and zipped up the coveralls against the increasing coolness of the cave. The rope shifted and slithered, responding to movements beyond the reach of his cone of light. He looked around quickly, then walked to a point where he would be protected against any rubble disturbed by Joy's descent.

On the surface Joy finished connecting the rope to the boulder once more. She reversed her seat harness, positioned the climbing rope so that she could in effect belay herself down the steep pitch, and stepped off backward into Lost River Cave's welcome darkness.

"Coming down!" she called.

"Yo!" answered Gabe.

Moving rhythmically, Joy fed rope across her body, using the friction of rope against her clothes to slow and control her descent. Gabe could have descended in the same way, but if he had fallen—and if she herself fell now—the shock of landing against a static anchor such as the boulder was enough to break bones, even if the fall was only a few feet. With a belayer the shock of hitting the end of the rope was softened by the inevitable slippage of rope through the belayer's hands. The slippage was only a few inches, but it was the difference between an abrupt, brutal stop and a much more gentle end to the fall.

Joy came to the bottom of the rubble slope, released herself from the rope and put it aside. They would use it to climb out of the pit in a few hours.

"Ready?" asked Joy, carefully avoiding stepping on the rope, for the only thing worse than walking on a rope was hacking at it with a knife.

Gabe turned slowly, letting his light play over the room in which he found himself. "Ready," he said absently. Then softly, almost gratefully, "This hasn't changed."

Joy looked up where collapsed ceiling had broken through to the ground above, revealing the presence of Lost River Cave. She and Gabe stood at the base of a huge rubble mound which had once been ceiling. The breakdown contained blocks of stone as big as houses that canted every which way. Smaller rocks of all sizes filled in the cracks. Debris had sifted down from the surface, sand and dirt and pieces of desert plants, even a few white bones from animals that had ventured into the cave and not found their way out. Though beautiful, Lost River Cave was not a place for the foolish or the weak.

The path deeper into the cave was little more than smudge marks from previous cavers' boots pointing the direction over the immensely jumbled floor of the cave. The floor was dry, as were the walls and ceiling. There were no formations visible, no fantastic stone decorations to make a person stand and stare in disbelief.

"Not what most people expect of a cave," said Gabe.

"The highest level is often like that in a limestone cave," said Joy. "Without water, caves die. In this area the groundwater level has been fluctuating for millions of years. At one time this was all below the water table. Hidden rivers and streams and lakes moved slowly through the limestone, dissolving it away."

She looked up, directing her helmet lamp at the ceiling of the cave. "As the water table sank, rooms and passages were left behind."

"Why haven't any new formations built up since the ceiling fell? Not enough time?"

"Probably. Not enough rainfall, either. It's a lot drier today than it was a few hundred thousand years ago." Joy turned and spotlighted the nearby cave wall with her headlamp. Carefully she began picking her way over to the wall. "Watch it. A lot of stones are loose."

Gabe followed, curious. He could see no other tracks, no other sign that anyone had ever walked on this particular stretch of cave floor before. Joy stopped near a knee-high boulder, shining her light on the surface of the rock. The angle of the light revealed a stalagmite no bigger than a fingernail. The stone growth was dry, almost powdery looking.

"I don't know how old this tiny stalagmite is," said Joy. "In the years I've come here, I've never seen a drop of water on this stone. Maybe some year it will rain and rain until the ground is too full of water for it to be carried down into the cave in the usual ways. Then the ceiling will drip here, and water will fall on this little nubbin, calcium carbonate will precipitate out on impact, and the stalagmite will come to life again."

"I thought that evaporation was what caused stalagmites, not precipitation."

Joy almost smiled. It was good to hear curiosity instead of hostility or regret in Gabe's voice, good to sense his quick mind fastening onto words and phrases and facts, shaking them until a new insight fell into place.

"That's what speleologists used to believe," admitted Joy. "We've all seen the salt formations left when one of the local rainwater lakes dries up. We thought it was the same when groundwater broke through to a cave: water evaporated and left its mineral content behind as a layer of new stone. Very logical. Very neat. Except for one little fact.''

"What's that?" asked Gabe, both curiosity and challenge implicit in his voice.

"Evaporation isn't possible down here. The humidity is one hundred percent all day, every day, year after century after millennia," said Joy, letting her helmet light sweep across the jumbled room for a moment. "The air simply can't hold any more water. Which means that water drops can't evaporate into water vapor. And if water can't become vapor, then all the lovely cave decorations we'll see farther down had to have another source."

The sidelight from Joy's lamp washed over Gabe's face, highlighting his thoughtful frown.

"Okay," he said, "water percolates down, gets to a cave ceiling—and then what?"

"Read my thesis," suggested Joy dryly.

"Translate it into layman's English," challenged Gabe, a smile in his voice.

She laughed softly, not knowing that the sound went through Gabe like an exquisite knife, opening up areas of memory that he had spent years burying.

"You drive a hard bargain," said Joy. "I don't know if I can translate. That's your department, isn't it? Taking new worlds and translating them into universal experience for everyone to share? And doing it beautifully."

The compliment was like Joy's laugh, bringing Gabe both pleasure and pain, memory and regret. He felt at ease with and understood by Joy as he had by no one else. And yet—and yet—the past was always there, like the shattered beauty of the underground room they stood in, beyond hiding, beyond healing.

"Without being too technical about it—" she said.

"Thank God," murmured Gabe.

Joy ignored him and continued, "The amount of dissolved limestone that water can hold is directly related to the amount of carbon dioxide that is already dissolved in the water. Are you with me so far?"

"So far, so good," said Gabe cautiously.

"Okay. Now imagine that you're a water drop sliding down through the earth. You're stuffed with dissolved limestone and gases like carbon dioxide and you're hanging onto them with everything you've got. You pass through the ceiling of a big hole in the ground. Instead of being surrounded by water-impregnated stone, suddenly you're surrounded by air."

"Still with you," said Gabe when she paused.

"Great. Get ready for the moment of truth. The carbon dioxide you've been holding in your arms escapes into the air. Suddenly you can't hold onto the dissolved limestone, either. It falls out of your arms and becomes a very thin coating of limestone on the ceiling—the beginning of a stalactite. And then," amusement shimmered in Joy's voice, "much lighter, you fall to the floor and help to build up a stalagmite."

"But if limestone has already precipitated out of my water drop to make a stalactite, how can there by any left over for stalagmites?"

"Because when you hit the floor, your hands and arms fly open, allowing even more carbon dioxide to escape. Which means—"

"More limestone precipitates out," finished Gabe thoughtfully, sweeping the floor with his helmet light as though seeking evidence of what Joy had been describing.

"Yes," she said. Her voice changed subtly as she added, "And after hundreds of thousands of years, millions of years, stone is built by tiny increments into shapes more fantastic than any man's dream, a creation as incredible as anything in art or nature."

Gabe's headlamp shifted from side to side almost impatiently, searching.

"Oh, we're about a million years too late for this chamber's glories," said Joy. "If there were any cave formations here, they're buried beneath the breakdown. You see, all that water percolating down, dissolving stone happily as it goes, widens natural joints and joins in the bedding planes of the limestone itself. Eventually there's not enough structural integrity left in the limestone to hold up the ceiling against the pull of gravity. Sometimes that happens as soon as the water table drops, draining the room, leaving the ceiling unsupported. Sometimes the ceiling doesn't fall until much later, and then it all comes crashing down, burying the beautiful formations that have been built drop by drop."

"Pity," said Gabe, imagining what the room might have looked like with fantastic spires and columns and draperies of multicolored stone. "So much beauty destroyed."

"In some ways, yes. In others..." Joy hesitated, trying to find words to make Gabe understand that in the natural world there were no absolute beginnings and endings. "It's simply change, not destruction," she said quietly. "The water is still at work below the original chamber, leaping from ceiling to floor across a bridge of air, creating new beauty. And below the level of cave decoration is the saturation zone, where the chambers themselves are actually formed. Maybe only one level exists down there, filled with water. Maybe there are as many levels as there are beds in the limestone to form chambers. We don't know. We only know that a cave is there, now, forming beneath our feet. Not destruction. Simply change. And, often, creation. In an eerie, magnificent way, caves are alive. Like us."

Gabe played his helmet light over the ceiling and down the wall, trying to imagine the room filled with water in an era of great rain. Then the coming of drought, the water table shifting down, down, taking with it the power to dissolve stone. And then the dripping of ground water on its way down, the slow, slow creation of beauty within a stone hollow; and the eventual collapse when the ceiling fell, smashing everything that had been so painstakingly built through time spans incomprehensible to man.

Like life, changing in an instant, rearranging everything. A sudden roar as a mountain gave way, and a grave as deep as time. A helicopter crash that devastated a young girl six years ago—and a man sixteen hours ago. Did the cave feel like that? Did the smashing instant of change reverberate through time, reshaping everything, even the cave's perception of itself?

The fanciful thought both amused and saddened Gabe. He found himself quietly hoping that Lost River Cave was not alive. He would not wish a million years of questions and regrets on anything, even stone.

Chapter 6

As Gabe followed Joy deeper into Lost River Cave, the rock surrounding him closed down. The chamber became a twisting, ever contracting passage. Before, his helmet lamp had been lost in the immensity of the collapsed chamber. Now, pale limestone walls threw back his light. Soon he could touch stone on both sides simply by raising his arms. The ceiling, too, pressed down, even as the floor began to slowly slant downward.

"Watch your head," called Joy, tilting her head back just enough to highlight the ragged ceiling. "It goes down to five feet four real quick."

Within moments Gabe was crouching to avoid the ceiling. Ahead of him Joy walked on untouched, for even with the added height of a helmet, she could move normally.

"You're enjoying this, aren't you?" grunted Gabe, quickly feeling the effects of walking bent over at such an awkward angle.

"You bet," she said enthusiastically. "Up on top I have to buy my clothes off the kiddy rack and stand on my tiptoes to see over everything except jack rabbits. But down here the world has to bend and look at things my way."

Gabe chuckled despite his discomfort. "I'm going to take you to see the Sequoias some day. You'll get a crick in your neck looking up."

"I get a crick in my neck looking up at Davy," said Joy dryly. "Going down," she added, suiting action to words and bending over.

Gabe doubled over, resting his hands on his knees, his elbows bent. It worked for a while, and then he and Joy were both forced down on their knees while the passage sank deep into the earth. The walls showed stains of black or brown or orange, depending on which minerals had been dissolved within the water. Here and there patches of moisture showed through, glistening in the lamplight.

"I don't remember this route from six years ago," said Gabe, his breath coming easily but more deeply than normal.

"New," said Joy succinctly.

"Who discovered it?"

"Me."

"Figures," grunted Gabe, banging his head and elbows on the shrinking passage. The helmet and clothes protected him, but he took the warning and slowed down slightly.

"How so?" asked Joy.

"Small," he muttered.

"Yeah? Just wait until you try Gotcha. Had much practice crawling lately?"

"Does six miles down a mountain trail count?" he retorted.

"It's a start," she conceded, but her voice wasn't as light as she wanted it to be. The thought of Gabe injured and crawling down a mountainside made her feel almost physically ill. "Going up."

"Thank God," said Gabe a few moments later when Joy stopped and directed her light up, telling him wordlessly that he could straighten. He stood up and stretched muscles that were complaining from the unaccustomed stress. "And I thought rock climbing used every muscle in your body from every possible angle."

"Caving is a lot like rock climbing," said Joy. Then, quietly she added, "In the dark."

"No rain, though."

"Nope. Ever climbed up a waterfall, though?"

"Can't say as I have," admitted Gabe. "Sounds cold."

"It is. Bell Bottom is one of the few caves I've met that I didn't like. You go in via a waterfall, which ensures a wet, cold time until you come out."

"At least you don't have wind tearing at you."

"Don't bet on it. Some caves literally breathe, with air flowing in and then out at rhythmic intervals. Winds up to thirty miles an hour have been clocked in caves."

"Really? What causes it?" asked Gabe.

"I told you. Caves are alive," said Joy, a smile rippling through her words. Then she continued more seriously, "No one knows. Lots of theories, though. Most of them have to do with the movement of warm air replacing cold and vice versa, or differing air pressures below ground compared to on the surface."

"Any waterfalls or wind in Lost River Cave?"

"Waterfalls, yes, somewhere. We can hear them but we can't find them," said Joy, exasperation clear in her voice. More than anything else, she wanted to find the waterfalls that gave the Voices its murmurous music. "As for wind, not really. Oh, from time to time you get a small breeze through some passages, but nothing to worry about."

"Worry?"

"Windchill factor," said Joy, turning away and leading Gabe farther into the cave. "Hypothermia. When the body gets too—"

"Cold to survive," interrupted Gabe, walking behind her. "A common problem for explorers everywhere but the tropics."

"Was it cold that day on the mountain?" asked Joy. The words were hesitant, her voice almost husky.

"Not really. That was the only thing that didn't go wrong. That and a quarter inch of rope."

"Have you climbed since then?" This time the question was obviously hesitant, for she added quickly. "I'm sorry, Gabe. I don't mean to pry. It's just that if you don't climb any more, there will be some places in Lost River Cave that—"

"It's all right," said Gabe quietly, cutting across her apology. "As soon as I could, I went up on that mountain again. It had taken a lot from me and given me only questions in return. I didn't want it to take my self respect, too."

Even as he said the words, Gabe knew that was why he had come back to Lost River Cave. Somehow, in some way that he didn't understand, he had lost or left behind something of himself here. He didn't know what it was or if it could be regained. He did know that he had to find out.

Joy wished she could see Gabe's face, for she sensed that he was thinking of something that had little to do with the cave around them. She wanted to ask what his thoughts were. She wanted to *know* him with an intensity that shocked her. When she had been with Gabe six years before, she hadn't felt the necessity of sharing his mind, his fears, his hopes. The mere presence of him had been over-whelming, like the moment when she had pushed through the tight crawlway called Gotcha and had found herself within the murmurous beauty of the Voices.

That instant had so saturated her senses that she hadn't been able to think at all. She had simply felt the immensity of the room, seen its beauty shimmering in her light, heard the eerie, extraordinary voices whispering in the velvet darkness. She hadn't thought of the forces that had shaped the chamber, or the explorations awaiting her, or the dangers and the sheer hard work and unexpected rewards of surveying the chamber, or the possibility that the room would lead to other rooms, other passages, other instants of overwhelming discovery. Those thoughts had come later, when she had absorbed the Voices into her daily experience, growing and changing to meet the challenges of her discovery.

There had been no "later" for her when it came to Gabe. There had been no chance to absorb and grow and change to meet his challenges. There had been only the incredible rush of discovery, the sweet, hot, secret moments within his arms and the endless chill of his loss. Losing him had been like being caught within Lost River Cave with no light and no hope of it. That had happened to her once. As part of her training in cave exploration she had been left alone, without light, in one of Lost River Cave's smallest rooms. She had managed to grope her way back to the entrance as required, but she had never forgotten how unfamiliar the cave had become, how distorted by darkness and fear. The lesson had been well learned. Never again did she enter a cave, no matter for how short a time, without thoroughly checking her light sources.

In the same manner she had groped her way out of darkness and fear after Gabe abandoned her and her parents died. She had learned from that, too. Not once in the days and weeks and years since then had she allowed herself to trust another human being enough that his absence would cast her adrift in darkness with neither light nor hope of it. Only Kati had slipped inside her guard. Only Kati, Gabe's daughter, a little girl whose smile was like her father's, lighting up any darkness.

For an instant Joy wanted to tell Gabe about Kati, about the life that he had so casually spurned. It wasn't the first time that the impulse had come to Joy. Many times in the last five years she had wanted to send pictures to Gabe, to share with him the trivial and the sublime moments of raising his child. She had never given in to the impulse in the past. She didn't now. The Gabe she had given herself to six years before hadn't been interested in anything but the sensual moment and the long-term of his career. He had had no room in his life or his mind or his heart for the woman who loved him. How much less would he have been interested in a child who in the beginning had needed rather than given love?

If, after he met Kati, Gabe asked who her father was, Joy would tell him the truth. No man was Kati's father, except in the briefest, most tangential sense. The instant of conception was not the enduring relationship known as fatherhood. When Kati was eighteen she would be told about Gabe. Until then Kati would have no father except in her own dreams. It was better that way. Dreams were kinder than reality. It would crush Kati to know that her father had never wanted her to be born.

As for Gabe . . . he had made his choice six years before. Joy had lived with it. He had no right to complain.

"The next part starts out easy," said Joy, turning away from Gabe, leaving him in darkness. "There's a steep scramble down, about a hundred feet of stooping, and then the ceiling pitches way down. Thirty feet later you're into Gotcha." She hesitated. Never in the time she had known

Gabe had he displayed any hint of claustrophobia. That might have changed, like the change from a Gabe who rarely noticed other people's feelings to the man who not only saw Maggie's hurt but tried to ease it. In Gotcha Passage, claustrophobia could be fatal.

Joy turned back toward Gabe. "Are you uneasy in tight places?" she asked bluntly.

"No."

"You're sure? I found another way into the Voices, but it takes forty-five minutes and involves a vertical drop of two hundred feet."

"I'm sure. If you're worried, though, take me the long way around."

That surprised Joy. Six years ago he would have insisted on going through Gotcha just to prove that he could. And he would have been able to. Then, as now, Gabe was both supple and powerful.

There was silence while Joy moved her light thoughtfully across Gabe's body as though measuring him against both her memories of the past and the needs of today. He wasn't as thick as Davy, but Gabe was very wide across the shoulders. Wider than she had remembered. The years of living outdoors, on the edge, testing himself against the land, had left a legacy of strength and assurance about Gabe that was both reassuring and—exciting. That hadn't changed. He was an exciting man. He would still be exciting when he was sixty.

Abruptly Joy turned away. "Gotcha it is. I'll go through first, taking our equipment. Then I'll come back and follow you through."

"So if I get stuck you can pull me out?" asked Gabe, amusement in his voice.

"Don't laugh. I pulled Davy out once."

"Impossible," Gabe said, amusement rippling just beneath the words. "You're too small."

"You'll laugh up the other sleeve after I yank you out of the third curve and get you headed straight again," said Joy crisply.

"Small but tough," answered Gabe, yet there was no laughter in his voice now. He was remembering what she had gone through when she was nineteen. Yes, she was tough. He had known grown men who had gone under carrying less of an emotional load than she had carried through her nineteenth year. "I'll try not to get stuck on you," he said. Then he heard the echo of the words in his head and he realized that they had another meaning, too. Before he could say anything more, Joy did.

"Don't worry," she retorted instantly. "I'm a champion unsticker and you're a champion eel. Gotcha's little games should be no problem at all for us."

Joy walked off quickly, picking her way across the uneven, downward slanting floor with the ease of long experience. It was harder for Gabe but he didn't complain. He followed her at his own pace, moving with both strength and coordination, knowing that it was futile to push himself when going through undiscovered territory. Accidents happened that way, and regrets. He had made enough mistakes in the past to know that it was far easier to do it right the first time than to try to undo errors amid a storm of if-onlys.

"Pit ahead," said Joy.

"How deep?"

"Bo Peep's just a middling drop," she said. "Under one hundred feet. Straight down, though. Doesn't go anywhere useful, either."

They skirted the pit's black mouth. The farther down they went, the more signs of moisture there were—dampness on the walls, patches of mud between rocks, the vague glistening of stone surfaces that indicated the cave was alive, limestone dissolving and regrowing drop by drop. Gabe wanted to stop and examine some of the cave decorations that occurred with increasing size and frequency, but Joy showed no signs of slowing down. Gabe made no objection. There would be time later to understand the fine details of Lost River Cave. For now it was more important to get some idea of its broader outline.

Joy's light stopped, then swept back over the cave floor to Gabe's feet. When he stood next to her, he could see the steep scramble that lay just a few yards behind her. As before, there was a sling anchorage for the belayer and a rope waiting that had been used by the three cavers who had gone ahead to the Voices. Unlike the first descent into the cave, this pitch was narrow, water-smoothed, with few hand and foot holds. Here, belaying was not only a safety precaution, it was a necessity. The chance of someone slipping—especially a person unfamiliar with the cave—was close to one hundred percent.

Silently Gabe and Joy prepared for the descent. She snapped herself into the anchor sling, settled in for the belay and waited for Gabe to announce his readiness.

"Belay on?" asked Gabe.

"On belay," responded Joy.

"Ready to climb."

"Climb!" said Joy, bracing herself subtly.

"Climbing!"

There was silence for a time, broken only by the whispering sound of rope moving over Joy's clothing as she fed out more of the coil with each downward motion of Gabe's body. He was invisible to her. Only the changes in tension on the rope sliding through her hands told her that she was not alone. She felt the sudden lurches as he lost his footing for an instant, but each time he regained it. Not before her heartbeat raced, though. She found herself straining to hear the least noise, sense the tiniest change in the pressure on the rope.

"Falling!" shouted Gabe, warning her of the jolt to come, his voice ragged as he felt his body slipping from his control.

For an instant he was back on the mountain again, falling, falling, the landslide and the screams of men battering him in the horrible instants before the rope sang taut, ending the fall. It took him a moment to realize that he was in Lost River Cave, that he was dangling from Joy's hands rather than a piton hammered deep into unyielding stone, that there was a steep, smooth slope rather than a two thousand foot drop beneath his feet. He felt the sweat bathing his body, the adrenaline sweeping through him, his chest a hot cage that both demanded and resisted breath. With the discipline that had kept him alive more than once in the past, he brought his body and mind back under control. He turned until he was facing the smooth rock again. Within moments he was supporting his own weight.

"Climbing!" he called.

"Climb!" called down Joy, hoping he couldn't hear the relief in her voice. It wasn't just that Gabe hadn't hurt himself—as long as the belay held, he was in no real danger. But she knew that he must have a horror of falling after what had happened in Peru. To feel himself falling again, even for an instant, must have been terrifying. Yet he had kept his head, collected himself and resumed the climb as though nothing had happened.

Joy knew the kind of courage and discipline that was required. The day Kati had wandered alone into the desert picking wildflowers, Joy had discovered just how much she loved her little daughter. The discovery had been terrifying, for deep within herself Joy had hoped never to love again, not like that, hostage to another life which could be taken in an instant, leaving her alone once more.

The rope went slack in Joy's fingers.

"Off belay," called up Gabe.

Joy answered, flexed cramped fingers and prepared for her own descent. The light from Gabe's helmet washed over both the smooth, steep pitch and the small, gliding figure of Joy moving in and out of light and darkness with dream-like ease. When she touched the cave floor beside him, she gave him a quick glance and a reassuring smile before she led him deeper into Lost River Cave. As he followed her, he found himself at first intrigued, then fascinated by her grace and assurance. He had been with many men in many wild places, but he had never met anyone who so completely accepted the land for what it was. She didn't so much conquer the cave as slide between its spaces, its unique probabilities. It wasn't her strength that gave her access to the cave's secrets, but her finesse. She knew herself, knew her equipment, knew her own possibilities and limitations. At nineteen she had been more impulsive, less accepting of the impossible. When she was nineteen he never would have stepped off backward over a slippery stone lip while she held his life in her hands. It had always been the reverse. He had belayed her. She had trusted him.

The insight all but paralyzed Gabe. Like the moment when he had first seen Joy's delicate features in the shadow of Davy's naked strength, Gabe felt as though he had taken a blow to his diaphragm.

Why should she trust you now, fool? asked the sardonic part of his mind that hadn't let up on him since he had crawled off the mountain in Peru.

But I never meant to hurt her.

Bloody wonderful, retorted his mind. *Bet that just comforted her no end at her parents' funeral. Bet it helped her all to hell at the abortion clinic, too!*

Gabe stumbled and nearly went full length on the cold stone.

"Gabe?" asked Joy, hearing the scrambling sound behind her.

"I'm fine," he said curtly, controlling his thoughts and his body with a savage inner curse, focusing his attention on the demands of Lost River Cave's uneven surface.

"Ceiling's coming down," she warned.

Within moments Gabe was duckwalking again, grateful for every one of the viciously painful exercises the physical therapist had given him after the mountain had nearly killed him. Now, despite the strain of the awkward movements, his left side was no worse off than his right. It was small comfort, but better than no comfort at all. The farther he went, however, the more he understood why Joy didn't use a backpack. His kept snagging on the ceiling every time he tried to shift position.

"Sit here," said Joy.

Gabe sat on the cold stone, thankful for the insulating pad that fitted into the seat of his coverall. Joy shrugged out of her equipment sling and tied it to her ankle. The sack holding her rope she positioned so that she could push it along in front of her.

"Give me your backpack," she said.

Gabe stripped off his backpack and watched her tie it just behind her own rucksack.

"Now," she said, "Davy swears that Gotcha is only six inches across at one point."

"Can he get his helmet through?" asked Gabe dryly.

Joy smiled, remembering the old caver axiom that if you can take off your helmet and push it through a passage, your body can follow. Surprisingly enough, that was often true. Not always, though. Especially for someone with as much bone and muscle as Davy—or Maggie, for that matter.

Joy pulled the wire leads to her helmet lamp, separating helmet and battery pack in order to prevent the leads from becoming hung up on rocks as she crawled. Without being asked, Gabe directed his helmet lamp toward the discouragingly small opening to the crawlway that Joy had named Gotcha. He watched while she flattened onto her stomach and eeled into the passage, pushing the rope bag ahead of her and dragging two compact sacks of equipment behind. His helmet light became almost useless to her, for her body blocked the tunnel, leaving room for little more than random fragments of illumination as she moved into the constricted crawlway. The sounds of cloth rubbing over stone, boots scrabbling against mud to find the rock beneath, and Joy's soft grunts of effort faded, leaving Gabe in Lost River Cave's immense silence.

The darkness within Gotcha was complete as soon as Joy jackknifed through the first of Gotcha's seven major twists. The lack of light didn't disturb her. She had done Gotcha so many times that she could, and usually did, take it on touch alone. Besides, it was very hard to get lost when there were only two ways to go—forward or backward.

Joy rested for a moment after the fourth twist in the tortuous tube. Despite the fact that Gotcha had been formed by water seeping through joints and seams in the limestone bed, and subsequently widened by becoming the conduit for an underground stream, the walls of the crawlway weren't even. The thin layer of fine silt called cave mud was deeper in some places than in others. The ceiling pitched down in some areas and up in others and the walls pinched in according to ancient weaknesses in the limestone bed. On top of that, moving water always had currents, and currents wore away stone unevenly. The scalloped pattern that remained in Gotcha's confines snagged clothes, helmets, equipment bags and boots. The scallops also made great leverage points for elbows, hips, knees and feet. Even so, getting through Gotcha was a workout that never failed to leave a caver slightly breathless and sweating.

Voices came above the sound of Joy's breathing, voices whispering, voices murmuring, liquid songs teasing her mind. By the sixth twist in the tortuous tube, she was immersed in ghostly sound. The first time she had forced her way through the unknown crawlway the voices had almost terrified her. Her parents had been dead less than a week, Gabe had been gone sixteen days—and she had heard her mother and her father and her lover whispering to her, calling her name softly, tearing her heart and mind with claws of memory and need. By the time she had emerged into the Voices' immense room, she had been crying too hard to see anything within the cone of her light.

Today Joy wriggled out of Gotcha with fine silt and memories clinging to her. She stood quickly, searching for lights weaving among the unearthly voices. She saw nothing. Automatically she connected the wire leads to her helmet lamp. A cone of light sprang forth, revealing the cave's muted shades of cream and rust, oyster and tan. She walked left, then right in a thirty-foot zigzag that led around a drapery of solid stone and into the room itself.

From her new perspective she saw a diffuse glow of light somewhat to the right and below her. There were no other light sources that she could see. Either Davy, Fish and Maggie had stayed together, thus showing their three combined lights as a single source of illumination, or someone was hidden among one of the hundreds of deep alcoves and overhangs that lined the room. The Voices was four hundred and six feet long, three hundred and fifty-three feet wide at its widest point, and so irregularly shaped in between that at first the cavers had thought it was three rooms rather than one. It was easy to get lost among the Voices until you learned a few landmarks.

"Davy!" called Joy.

"Yo!" came the response, a single syllable that carried with amazing clarity over long distances.

"I'm—going—back—for—Gabe," she called, spacing the words carefully so that they wouldn't become lost in the Voices' eerie acoustics.

"Yo!"

Joy peeled off equipment, stacked it neatly to one side and hesitated as she remembered the impact of the Voices on her the first time she had heard them six years ago. She didn't know the names of the ghosts who would whisper to Gabe. She knew that he had them, though. She had seen them in his eyes. That was new, different; the Gabe of her memories had no shadowy ghosts, no dark regrets, nothing but the bright future calling to him.

With a decisive motion Joy untied her rucksack and plunged her hand in. After a few moments of rummaging, her fingers closed around one of her emergency light tubes. She brought it out, twisted it sharply and was bathed in pale green light as the stick came to life. She propped it against a stalagmite growing a few feet beyond the hole that marked Gotcha's beginning—or end, depending on which way you were going. The light would serve as a beacon for Gabe, a piece of reality to hold onto while the Voices sang to his soul in Lost River Cave's unutterable darkness.

Joy unplugged her light again and went back into the water-smoothed, twisting passage. When she emerged there was only darkness. Hurriedly she plugged in her helmet lamp.

"Gabe?" she called, her voice frayed.

"Here," he answered from her right.

Reflexively she snapped her head around, bathing him in light. He winced and closed his eyes.

"Sorry," said Joy, tilting her light away. "You startled me. I didn't expect to find you sitting alone in the dark."

"Just getting reacquainted with an absolute absence of light," he said. "Better here than when I'm wedged in Gotcha."

"Are you," she hesitated, then continued, "all right?"

Joy heard the smile in Gabe's voice even though she couldn't see it on his face. "I'm fine," he said softly. "I find the blackness very... peaceful. It makes all my other senses come alive."

"Yes," she said, her voice subtly vibrant as she remembered a time six years ago when she had turned out both their helmet lamps in order to let Gabe experience the total absence of light. He had kissed her then, deep within Lost River Cave's night, and she had been all but overwhelmed by sensations that had nothing to do with sight. It was the first time she had truly appreciated the strength in his lean body, the heat, the hunger.

The memory went through her like the Voices, calling to her in ways that she could neither fight nor understand.

"Give me your rope," said Joy, her tone almost husky.

Silently Gabe handed over the canvas sack with his rope in it.

"At about the fourth twist of Gotcha," she said quickly, tying the bag to her ankle, "you'll hear voices. You aren't going crazy. It's just flowing water and the chamber's odd acoustics coming to you through the crawlway. Hold that thought and keep wriggling."

There was a quality to Joy's voice that made Gabe wish his helmet light were plugged in so that he could see her face.

He thought it was the same concern that had been in her when she had looked at him at the bottom of the last belay after he had fallen. It was as though she sensed at some level the caustic interior dialogue going on in his mind as he sought to accept and understand insights about himself and the past.

"Spooky, huh?" he asked curiously.

"Very. When I forced the tube the first time, I thought I had finally gone crackers."

"When was that?"

"Six days after my parents died."

Gabe said nothing more. Joy's clipped voice did not invite comment or comfort. Using the illumination from her helmet lamp, he lined himself up with Gotcha's small mouth.

"Like most vadose waterways—those are the ones formed below the water table, where there's no air," explained Joy, "Gotcha is essentially circular. People aren't. If the going gets too tight, take off your helmet and push it ahead of you. If that doesn't change your profile enough, back up until you can pull one arm down along your side and lead with the other arm. That will give you a more circular profile."

"If Davy can make it," said Gabe dryly, "I should slide through Gotcha like grass through a goose."

"Don't bet on it. He has more meat, but you have the same width in the shoulders," said Joy. "It's the shoulder bones that get stuck on a man."

"And on a woman?"

"Pelvic girdle," she said succinctly.

"Poor Maggie," murmured Gabe, laughing softly.

Joy said nothing. The thought of Gabe noticing Maggie's firm, lushly rounded bottom irritated Joy even as she told herself that she was being foolish. Nothing had changed

Gabe's sensual nature in the last six years, and Maggie had a body to tempt any man. Grimly Joy hoped that Maggie kept her usually level head when Gabe's charm started to work dissolving her barriers like groundwater working on limestone.

As Gabe had dissolved Joy at nineteen.

"I'll be right behind you," she said in a clipped voice. "Don't try to stay on your stomach all the time. Use your side, your back, whatever gets it done. Make your body conform to the passage, because it sure won't conform to you. Don't fight it. Flex with it, because that stone is stronger than any man. If you get stuck, either holler or thump your foot three times. When you feel me grab your ankle, relax and *breathe out*. You'll be unstuck in no time at all. Okay?"

"Gotcha," said Gabe.

Joy groaned.

He gave her a triumphant smile and began slithering into Gotcha's mouth. Joy waited until he was at least four feet in front of her before she unplugged her helmet lamp and began to wriggle slowly after him. She paused from time to time, gauging his progress by the soft grunts and not-so-soft curses that punctuated his efforts. There was no problem with the first three twists, although Gabe had to back up on the second and try a different angle of approach. As near as she could tell, he ended up on his back coming out of the turn. That didn't surprise her; Davy had the same problem with the second twist and solved it in the same way.

Silently Gabe kept mental track of the twists and turns of Gotcha's unforgiving stone tube. Somewhere on the way through the fifth turn, the aches and scrapes and complaints of his straining body dissolved in a susurration of sound, spectral whispers washing over him, calling to him. Despite Joy's warning he froze in place with his heart hammering, knowing that it was his mind that was giving flesh and names to impossible ghost voices from his past—knowing and yet not believing it.

I love you, Gabe. I love you! Don't leave yet. Stay for another week, a day, a minute. Oh, Gabe, I love you so much! Stay with me, love me, let me love you. Please!

He didn't hear his answer. He didn't have to. Woven through the ghost-Joy's words, dissolving them, came the soft cries of a baby that had never been born.

Chapter 7

Even days later, in late afternoon's pouring light, the memory of that moment down in the cave was as real to Gabe as the hot water pouring over him while he stood beneath Joy's shower. The first aches of cave crawling's unaccustomed exercise had vanished, but the uncanny cries had not. He relived again and again that instant and the instant five years before when his brother's much-forwarded message had finally reached him. *Your latest cutie settled for a check and an abortion.*

Only now did Gabe question the white-hot rage that had consumed him as he had held the letter that had waited for him for eleven months. Only now did he acknowledge that if it had been any other woman but Joy who had had the abortion, he would have felt little except a determination never to be so careless again. He certainly wouldn't have felt betrayal, contempt and a rage that had known no end until Joy had told him that her parents had died within days of his leaving. Whatever else, he now knew that she hadn't had the abortion casually.

After five years of rage, the knowledge that Joy truly had been as loving as she had been innocent was a balm easing a raw spot on Gabe's soul that he had never before admitted to having. He didn't know why he hadn't questioned his rage before or why he was seeking the truth of the past now. He did know that he was doing just that. Each time he thought of the past, the certainty that what he had known with Joy wasn't a delusion or a lie gave him a bit of peace. Like a fantastic decoration forming deep within the earth, Gabe sensed something precipitating within himself, moment by moment, memory by memory, something of unearthly beauty growing where only darkness and emptiness had been.

He turned off the water and began toweling himself dry. The long, livid rope burns that had marked his leg so badly a year ago had faded to dense maroon shadows which he didn't notice. He had a few odd scrapes and bruises here and there, legacies of Lost River Cave's hard and slippery surfaces, but nothing of any importance. Despite the strenuous days of cave crawling he had put in with Joy and the others, he was none the worse for the wear. In fact, he hadn't felt as alive in years.

With a quick glance he checked the time on the watch he had left on the bathroom sink. Quarter of five. It was Davy's turn to cook dinner for the camp, which meant tacos and refried beans. Sighing softly, Gabe wished that it were Joy's turn to cook. Apparently she was the only one in camp besides Gabe himself who knew how to bake biscuits or toss a salad, fry a chicken or barbecue a succulent rack of ribs. But Joy was working on some esoteric estimates of the importance of phreatic versus vadose water in Lost River Cave's formation. Normally she would have done the work at night, but Kati Something-or-other was coming back to camp and Joy wanted to have time to spend with her.

From what Gabe had gathered the few times Kati's name had come up, she was a camp favorite who had taken a week's vacation nearby. Beyond that, nothing much had been said, which didn't surprise Gabe. Most camp conversation revolved around speleology, Lost River Cave, government grants and the latest advances in cave exploring equipment. People were rarely mentioned, unless they were one of the early, almost legendary cave explorers. Until the ride back to camp today, Gabe hadn't even known that Fish had a wife, much less two kids in high school and a live-in brother-in-law he couldn't stand.

Gabe stretched until the ligaments in his neck and shoulders shifted and popped. He pulled on underwear, a pair of walking shorts and sandals. There was no need for any more, and a case could be made for wearing a good deal less if modesty weren't mentioned. The New Mexican summer was an endless cauldron of dry heat. Gabe enjoyed it, just as he enjoyed the contrasting coolness and moisture of Lost River Cave. He had even come to love the Voices once the first shock had worn off. He knew now that the cries had been in his own mind, not in the whispering darkness.

But he still wondered what voices Joy heard, what ghosts called to her, rending her peace of mind. He knew that there must be some, for how else would she have guessed that emotional shock would overtake him in Gotcha? How else could she have known to leave a light burning at the tube's black exit, giving him a luminous bit of reality to hold onto while the Voices broke over him in an immaterial, overwhelming wave.

Once they must have broken over her, too. Had she heard a baby cry then?

Did she hear it still?

That was one question Gabe would never ask. Just as Joy had known that he would be emotionally disoriented and had left a light to help him, he knew that the abortion must have left a psychic wound on her that would never heal. A wound he had helped to inflict and had done nothing to soothe. A wound that had now, too late, become his.

If only—began the familiar thought.

If nothing, fool, came the equally familiar rejoinder. *Time runs forward, not backward.*

Gabe walked swiftly to the back porch, opened the front door of the washing machine and pulled out a rope. He looked at it critically before deciding that it would benefit from another rinse and a second dose of fabric softener. When the rope was awash again, he checked the clothesline to see that nothing had come off in the desert's playful wind. After that there was no further excuse to delay going to the cottage next door and putting it back together. The fact that he had to haul his water in a bucket because the plumbing was defunct didn't wholly excuse sloppy housekeeping.

On the other hand, what was the point in straightening out a sleeping bag only he would see or use and knocking mud off boots that would only get muddy again in a few hours? If he were going to be sharing his sleeping bag, on the other hand...

With a harsh word Gabe reeled in his thoughts. It was bad enough to have Joy haunt his dreams as thoroughly as water haunted the Voices. If he allowed her into his waking thoughts as well, he would walk around in a permanent state of arousal. Which wasn't all that far from the truth as it was. The more he saw Joy, the more his memories welled up, overflowing the barriers of his will, filling him. He could remember all too vividly the contrast of her small hands against the dark hair of his body, the pleasure of her touch so great that it was nearly agony, the incredible feeling when she caressed him as intimately as he had caressed her, the gentle heat of her lips and mouth teasing him, and the even softer, hotter sensation when he became a part of her.

The worst of it was that he knew she was remembering, too, and the memories were a fire burning beneath her calm surface. He could see it in her eyes, in her expression, in the fact that she was reluctant to touch him in even the most casual way. At first he had told himself that it was hatred which made her avoid touching. Then he had found himself doing the same thing, drawing back rather than touching her because if he touched her once he didn't think he could stop. She filled his dreams the way whispers filled the Voices, irrevocably, part of the very fabric of reality itself.

In that instant Gabe decided he would have Joy again, know once more the incredible satisfactions of her response, hear again her wild cries as he brought ecstasy to her. He would no longer allow her to evade his touch as she had the past week. The next time she looked up at a man's naked shoulders, it would be Gabe bending over her, not Davy Graham.

The sound of a car driving past the front of the house pulled Gabe out of his thoughts. Whistling softly to himself, he went to the living room and looked out at the sun-drenched brilliance of the dusty driveway that joined the ramshackle cottages of Cottonwood Wells. Joy was standing next to the car, laughing, her face alive with pleasure. It was a face out of Gabe's dreams, a happiness that he had not seen in her since he had come back to Lost River Cave. Gabe felt a slicing instant of envy for the person who had the ability to transform the cool, restrained Dr. Anderson into the laughing Joy of his memories.

Two children climbed out of the car and began running toward the cottage. The first girl was dark-haired, quick, unremarkable. The second girl sent the ceiling of reality crashing down around Gabe, irrevocably changing everything in one explosive instant. He made a hoarse, harsh sound like a man who has been hit from behind. He forced himself to take a deep breath, control his wild thoughts and look rationally at the little girl who was taking the front steps two at a time despite her short legs.

Red hair. Slanting eyes. High cheekbones. Triangular chin. Dimple on the left side. A way of looking over her shoulder with her right hand on her hip.

Stunned, Gabe watched the girl romp up onto the porch and call gaily over her shoulder. The closer she got the less he felt there was a chance that he was mistaken. He didn't know this child's name but he had a picture that looked just like her, a picture more than a half-century old, a picture of his mother celebrating her sixth birthday with a cocker spaniel panting at her feet and a new doll under her arm.

"Laura!" called the driver of the car. "Get back here, honey. You promised to help me with dinner!"

The dark-haired child stopped, pouted momentarily, then turned and went back to the car.

"Kati, say goodbye and then help me bring in your stuff," said Joy, halting her daughter's headlong rush back to the car after her friend.

"Aw Mom—"

"Kati—" began Joy.

After token resistance Kati danced back around the car toward Joy, overflowing with energy and life. The little girl stood on tiptoe at the driver's side of the car, kissed the woman who was driving, accepted a sleeping bag and a ratty stuffed animal from Laura and headed for the house.

Gabe's chaotic thoughts settled into new awareness, new insights, new truths reshaping his understanding of himself and Joy, the past and the present. Joy had loved him. She had loved him enough to bear his child with no one to help her, no one to advise her, no one to comfort her, no one to share the burdens and the rewards and the responsibility. She had loved him more than he had believed possible, more than he had deserved.

And then she had hated him enough to tell him that she had had an abortion when she had not. She had hated him enough to raise his child in silence, telling him nothing, not even that his daughter was alive. Love might have dulled, but hatred had not. Even when they worked alone in the cave, Joy had given not one hint that she hadn't had an abortion.

If we talk about the past, Gabe, it won't work.

Joy's words came back to him out of the seething darkness of his emotions, whispers that had new meaning. Hatred. She hated him more than he believed possible, more than any man deserved. It was a miracle she hadn't dropped him down one of Lost River Cave's deepest pits and tossed the rope in after him.

It would be a miracle if he didn't do the same to her at the first opportunity.

The front screen slammed and a little girl raced into the house, only to stop abruptly when she saw Gabe standing very still in the living room. "Who are you?" she asked.

Gabe looked at the girl with a hunger he wasn't aware of, an intensity that had been born of years of rage and regret. Nothing he saw made him believe that his first impression was wrong. This was the image of his mother all those lost years ago. The eyes were gray rather than green, but the rest was like seeing a picture come to life.

"I'm Gabriel Venture," he said, his voice rich with emotions held in check. "My friends call me Gabe. Would you like to?"

"Sure," Kati said casually, trotting past him, her arms full. "I'm Kati. Are you a caver?", she called over her shoulder as she dumped the sleeping bag on the sofa.

Gabe closed his eyes, caught among too many emotions to name them. Kati hadn't recognized his name. Joy hadn't told her child who her father was.

"I'm a writer," said Gabe.

"Oh, you're the one Mommy told me about."

"What did she tell you?" asked Gabe. His voice was too sharp, too demanding, but there was nothing he could do about it any more than he could control the adrenaline that had poured into his body when the ceiling of reality had caved in and he had recognized his own daughter dancing among the rubble.

"You're gonna write about the cave and then maybe we can come back here someday," said Kati, emerging from the tiny room that Gabe had assumed was a den.

"Back?" asked Gabe carefully, holding his voice as though it were very fragile. "Are you leaving?"

The girl shrugged with a maturity far in advance of her years and her size. "Sure. When the cave closes, Mommy's got to get a job somewhere or we won't have any money."

For the first time Gabe thought—really thought—about what would happen to Joy when Lost River Cave closed. Where would she go? What would she do? She hadn't mentioned anything to him, so he had assumed that she was going to stay on with the university. Apparently he had been wrong about that, as he had been wrong about so many things.

But then, it was easy to be wrong when you're blindfolded and left to stumble through darkness. Anger curled through him, hot and eager. Before he could ask any more questions, he heard the car out front start up, then drive by in a subdued cloud of dust.

Kati trotted past him to the back porch. He heard the screen door slam and the girl's high, excited voice as she spotted someone.

"Gravy-bear! Catch me!"

Gabe got to the kitchen window just in time to see Kati throw herself into Davy's arms. Laughing, shrieking, she was lifted and whirled over his head in a game that was obviously familiar and much enjoyed by both participants. Maggie stood at the sidelines, calling encouragements and laughing as hard as Kati.

Joy walked into the kitchen, expecting it to be empty. She didn't expect to see Gabe leaning against the counter, staring out of the window with hunger in his eyes, in his face, in the very tension of his body. At first she thought it was Maggie that had called such depth of feeling out of Gabe. With the thought came a tearing emotion which Joy was forced to acknowledge as jealousy even as she told herself that the reaction was totally irrational. Then Gabe turned as she set a bag of groceries on the counter. There was hatred and contempt in his expression as he looked at her, jade-green fury in his eyes.

"Tell me, Dr. *Anderson*," said Gabe, giving a sardonic emphasis to Joy's maiden name, "was yours a long marriage?"

Abruptly Joy knew Gabe had discovered that Kati was his child. Conflicting feelings swept through Joy—relief and anger and curiosity. She was the only living person who knew the truth of Kati's parentage. How had Gabe known? Kati didn't look anything like her father. She was fair where Gabe was dark; her eyes were gray rather than green; she had a dimple and he had none; her hair was red and she had golden freckles where Gabe tanned darkly, smoothly. Kati didn't resemble Gabe at all, except in the subtle ways that tore at Joy's heart at odd moments—Kati's wide-ranging

You know the thrill of
escaping to a world of
Love and Romance as it
is experienced by
real men and real women...

Escape again...with
4 FREE novels and

**get more great Silhouette Intimate Moments® novels
—for a 15-day FREE examination—
delivered to your door every month!**

Silhouette Intimate Moments offers you romance for women...not girls. It has been created especially for the woman who wants a more intense, passionate reading experience. Every book in this exciting series promises you romantic fantasy...dynamic, contemporary characters...involving stories...intense sensuality...and stirring passion.

Silhouette Intimate Moments may not be for everyone, but if you're the kind of woman who wants more romance in her life, they will take you to a world of *real* passion, *total* involvement, and *complete* fulfillment. Now, every month you can thrill to the kind of romance that will take your breath away.

FREE BOOKS

Start today by taking advantage of this special offer—4 new Silhouette Intimate Moments romances (a $10.00 Value) *absolutely FREE,* along with a Cameo Tote Bag. Just fill out and mail the attached postage paid order card.

**AT-HOME PREVIEWS
FREE DELIVERY**

After you receive your 4 free books and Tote Bag, every month you'll have the chance to preview 4 more Silhouette Intimate Moments novels *—as soon as they are published!* When you decide to keep them you'll pay just $9.00 (a $10.00 Value) *with never an additional charge of any kind and with no risk* You can cancel your subscription at any time simply by dropping us a note. In any case, the first 4 books, and Tote Bag are yours to keep.

EXTRA BONUS

When you take advantage of this offer, we'll also send you the Silhouette Books Newsletter free with each shipment Every informative issue features news on upcoming titles interviews with your favorite authors, and even their favorite recipes.

Get a Free Tote Bag, too!

EVERY BOOK YOU RECEIVE WILL BE A BRAND-NEW FULL-LENGTH NOVEL!

Escape with 4 Silhouette Intimate Moments novels (a $10.00 Value) and get a FREE Tote Bag, too!

Silhouette Intimate Moments®

Silhouette Books, 120 Brighton Rd., P.O. Box 5084, Clifton, NJ 07015-9956

Yes, please send me FREE and without obligation, 4 new Silhouette Intimate Moments novels along with my Cameo Tote Bag. Unless you hear from me after I receive my 4 FREE books, please send me 4 new Silhouette Intimate Moments novels for a free 15-day examination each month as soon as they are published. I understand that you will bill me a total of just $9.00 (a $10.00 Value) with no additional charges of any kind. There is no minimum number of books that I must buy, and I can cancel at any time. The first 4 books and Cameo Tote Bag are mine to keep, even if I never take a single additional book.

NAME _____
(please print)

ADDRESS _____

CITY _____ STATE _____ ZIP _____

Terms and prices subject to change. Your enrollment is subject to acceptance by Silhouette Books.
SILHOUETTE INTIMATE MOMENTS is a registered trademark.

CT8865

intelligence, her physical courage, the way she had of looking over her shoulder with her hand on one hip and her eyebrow half-raised.

"No," said Joy, her voice husky.

"No what?" demanded Gabe. Then, in a low voice that vibrated with warning, he added, "Don't lie to me, Joy."

"I've never lied to you."

"Like hell you haven't!" snarled Gabe. "Who is Kati's father?"

"No marriage. No father." Joy's voice was under control again, as cold as Gabe's was hot.

"That's not what I meant and you damn well know it!"

"Then what did you mean, Gabe?" asked Joy, setting aside the groceries that Susan had picked up for the camp.

"Kati's my daughter."

Joy shrugged. "Technically, yes. In any meaningful way, no."

"Meaningful? *Meaningful!*" he retorted, his voice increasing in depth and volume until it was just short of a shout. "It's damned hard to have a meaningful relationship with a child I thought you'd flushed as soon as you found out I wouldn't be supporting you!"

It was Joy's turn to be shocked. "What are you talking about?" she asked, her voice shaking. "I never asked for a penny from—"

"I'm talking about abortion," Gabe interrupted harshly, overriding Joy's words without hearing them. "I'm talking about a lying little bitch who told my brother she had an abortion, then went and had my baby and never told me about it. For five years I thought my baby was dead—but she was alive and growing and I didn't even suspect it. My God, I didn't know you had that much hate in you."

"You didn't know a damn thing about me except that I was a good lay," shot back Joy, feeling a searing flash of temper unleashed and not even trying to control it. "All you cared about was a hot time in the sheets and no strings attached. I gave you just what you wanted, everything you asked for. Don't come whining to me if you don't like what you got! I paid the price of your precious freedom, not you!"

"You didn't even tell Kati about me," said Gabe, his voice controlled, savage, like a whip curling out, hungry for flesh to tear.

"What should I have told her?" snapped Joy. "That her father didn't even want her to be born? That he gave me $5,000 for an abortion? That when I told him to take the money and go to hell, he never even bothered to write and find out whether I'd had a boy or girl?"

Gabe made an inarticulate sound. His shoulder muscles bunched as his fist crashed onto the counter with enough force to make dishes in the cupboard leap. In the charged silence the sound was like an explosion.

"You never wrote to me about money or anything else," said Gabe finally, his voice flat.

"Where would I have sent the letter—to the Great Gabriel Venture, care of the Orinoco River?"

Gabe's eyes narrowed to jade slits. "Dan had my address."

"Dan refused to give it to me. He told me to take the check and forget about you and your money." Joy's smile was like a knife sliding out of a sheath. "I took part of his advice. I forgot about you. As for the money, I told him to sit on it and spin until he threw up."

"He wrote and told me he sent the money to you."

"And I sent it right back."

The gray blaze of Joy's eyes told Gabe as much as her words. She was telling the truth. She had been telling the truth six years ago. She had wanted him, not his supposed wealth.

"I'm sorry," said Gabe, thinking of how difficult it must have been for Joy with no parents, no money, nothing.

"For what—that I didn't have the abortion?"

"Damn you!" snarled Gabe. "You know I didn't want—"

But Joy was still talking, years of rage honing her voice until it was as cutting as her smile had been. "You made your choice, Gabe. You seduced a nineteen-year-old virgin who was dumb enough to fall in love with you. You knew when you left that I might be pregnant, and you left anyway. But before you left you made arrangements for me to have an abortion, just in case I might need one. Any rights you might have had to Kati ended that instant. You're not her father, Gabe. You're nothing."

"I didn't want you to have an abortion! I left the money so that if you were pregnant you'd have something to pay the bills until I could send you more! When I found out that you'd flushed my baby I wanted to—"

Abruptly he realized that his fists were clenched so hard that his knuckles were white. Rage was a bitter taste in his mouth, a wild flush across his cheeks. He took a deep, shaking breath and was appalled at the depth of his fury. It had lived within him for five years, eating away at him in unexpected ways—and then it had exploded. It was still exploding. Very carefully he relaxed his hands.

"It was eleven months before I got Dan's letter telling me about you and the money and the abortion he thought you'd had," said Gabe wearily. "After that, there wasn't much point in writing to ask you about the sex of your baby, was there?"

As Joy saw through the dissolving veil of Gabe's rage to the regret beneath, she felt her own fury slipping away. He hadn't wanted her to have an abortion. He hadn't wanted to kill the only thing that she had left to remind her of how it had felt to be alive and in love and at peace within his arms. He hadn't wanted to destroy her.

Nor had he wanted to cherish her.

"Let's be honest with ourselves," said Joy, the words almost a sigh, her voice as weary as his. "Neither of us wanted an abortion. Neither of us wanted a child. You chose your course. I chose mine."

"I didn't know you were pregnant," Gabe said urgently, crossing the kitchen in two strides and pulling Joy into his arms. "Sweetheart," he whispered against her hair, her cheek, the corner of her mouth, "I didn't know!"

Gabe kissed Joy with consuming tenderness, his lips trembling as they brushed over hers, his whole body trembling when he felt her hands frame his face. Then he lifted his head and her sad smile splintered through him, telling him that he was only beginning to measure what he had lost, what he would yet lose.

"Gabriel, Gabriel," she murmured, shaking her head slowly, feeling the warm, remembered silk of his hair slide between her fingers, her body trembling against his. "Let's be as honest with each other now as we were six years ago. If you had known that I was pregnant, you still would have gone away."

Once Gabe would have brushed her words aside with the easy assurance of youth. He wanted to brush them aside now, but the attempt died in his throat. He was older, wiser, with the kind of self-knowledge that came from hanging head-down over a void and measuring the depth of his own grave. Even as he folded Joy closer to him, he remembered vividly how he had felt six years ago at the thought of staying with her, giving up the siren call of all the places he had never seen, would never see, a man trapped by desire in a life he had never expected.

"Joy—" he said, but could say no more.

She understood. Gabe saw the instant of knowledge move through her, the pain darkening her eyes. Despite her calm statement that he would have left anyway, part of Joy had always hoped that if he had known she was pregnant he would have stayed with her. Part of her had always hoped that he had loved her.

"I was too young, too ambitious," said Gabe bleakly, rocking Joy gently against his chest. His arms tightened for an instant when he felt her hands pushing against him, silently asking to be released. "Joy," he said urgently, "it was nothing against you. It was simply too soon for me."

She stepped away from him, her face pale. "I know."

"I'm not the same as I was six years ago," he said, taking her hand.

"I understand," she said. And even as she spoke she withdrew her hand from his.

"Then why are you turning away from me?" he asked, his voice husky, urgent.

"Because you don't understand."

"What?" he asked, searching the crystalline shades of darkness in her eyes. "What don't I understand?"

"Me. I've changed, too, Gabe."

He remembered the black emotions he had seen staring out at him from her eyes. "You don't really hate me," he said. "Don't try to tell me that, Joy. I don't believe it. You were trembling when I kissed you."

"No," she said softly, "I don't hate you." She looked up at him, her eyes as bleak as winter. "It was too soon for you to love six years ago—and now it's too late for me."

. "Why?"

"Love requires trust," she said simply, meeting his eyes without flinching. "Trust requires innocence. I'm not innocent anymore, Gabe."

"I took that from you when I left," he said, his voice raw. "Is that what you're saying?"

"Yes." She smiled gently, sad and accepting at once. "Abandonment is very educational. And—" she paused, closing her eyes for a moment, concealing the pain of her own self-knowledge "—there's the fact that even if you had stayed, it wouldn't have worked." Her eyes opened, clear and certain. "You would have resented me and Kati. Instead of simply not loving me, you would have ended up hating me. As you said. Too soon."

"And now you think it's too late," he said grimly.

"Not for you, Gabe," said Joy, turning away, her expression taut, hidden. "All you have to do is find someone innocent enough to trust you. Like Maggie. And then, of course, you have to have the guts to follow through."

The back porch door slammed. "Mommy? What's for dinner?"

Joy turned toward the young voice and held out her arms. "Hi, punkin. Hungry?"

Kati leaped up just as Joy's arms closed around her. Joy settled the child's legs around her waist and looked eye to eye with Kati.

"I missed you, Mommy," said Kati, giving Joy a noisy kiss.

"Even with the whole Childer family around you?" teased Joy.

"Uh-huh. I still want brothers and sisters and a daddy, but no one is as good as you."

Joy hugged her daughter close for an instant, then lowered her to the floor. Though Joy couldn't see Gabe, she felt the intensity of his attention like a hot sun pouring over her.

"Bath before dinner," said Joy, seeing the streaks of dust on Kati's fair skin.

"Fried chicken, huh, please?" asked Kati earnestly.

"Tacos and refried beans," countered Joy.

"Uh-oh, Gravy-bear is cooking again, isn't he?"

"Yes, but don't hurt his feelings."

"Oh, I won't," said Kati solemnly. "Gravy-bear is soooo nice. Are you sure he isn't my daddy?"

"I'm sure, punkin," said Joy, controlling her voice with an effort.

"Do you think he'd like to be?" asked Kati, her eyes and voice wistful.

"I think your Gravy-bear couldn't love you any more if he were your very own daddy," said Joy, her voice teasing, her face terribly strained.

"Yeah," said Kati matter-of-factly, chewing on her lower lip. "That's what he said. But then why doesn't my own daddy love me?"

Joy felt her emotions slipping away from her as she swept up Kati in her arms and turned so that the child's back was to Gabe. Joy fervently wished that Kati had chosen a better moment to air her desire for a father. It was a conversation Joy was used to, along with her daughter's wheedling, teasing pleas for siblings. But Joy wasn't used to conducting the conversation with Kati's father standing two feet away, his body taut, his eyes like green ice, his face fierce with a truth that no one had spoken to Kati.

Oh, God, don't say it, Gabe, pleaded Joy silently, giving him a look as fierce as his own. *Please. Don't let Kati find out like this. She isn't ready for it. I'm not ready. And you're not ready, either. Don't you see? She can handle the reality she knows. But if you tell her, then when you leave she'll feel rejected all her life. Don't do that to her, Gabe.*

"I'm sure your father does love you," said Gabe quietly, his face aching with the strain of controlling his expression. If he had never meant to hurt Joy by leaving, he had never dreamed in his deepest nightmares that he had also hurt his own child.

"You really think so?" asked Kati, turning her head so fast that her hair flew out in a fiery cloud.

"Yes."

There was a certainty in Gabe's voice that cut through Kati's doubts.

"Do you know my father?" she asked, watching him with transparent eagerness.

Joy closed her eyes and waited for Kati's innocent world to be destroyed.

"I don't know any man who deserves a little girl as special as you," said Gabe honestly, his voice husky.

For a moment Kati measured Gabe with unflinching gray eyes that reminded him very much of Joy. Then Kati gave him a breathtaking smile.

"You want to help me make tacos with Gravy-bear?" Kati asked Gabe.

"Bath, young lady," said Joy quickly, carrying her daughter out of the kitchen.

"But Mommy—" began Kati.

"Mr. Venture has a lot of work to do," Joy said calmly, overriding Kati's objections.

"Gabe," retorted Kati. "He told me to call him Gabe."

Joy's lips flattened. "Bath," she said curtly.

Kati accurately read the danger signals in her mother's voice and resigned herself to losing this round. "Then I get to help with tacos," said the little girl in a firm voice.

"Depends on how fast you take your bath, doesn't it?"

Kati frowned. She loved taking long baths. Gabe listened to the voices floating back from the bathroom, the muted thunder of water filling the old, claw-footed tub and Kati's peals of uninhibited laughter. He visualized the ritual from his own childhood, his mother bent over the tub, washing him and his brother while they did their best to splash water over everything in the room. Sometimes things had gotten out of hand. Then his father would come into the bathroom, lift his wife out of the fracas and begin sudsing squealing young bodies with equal parts resolution and resignation. When that happened Dan and Gabe had looked at each other and laughed secretly, glorying in their power over their parents.

The memory made Gabe smile in the instants before he realized that Kati had never known that delicious childish collusion with a sibling against a parent. Nor had she had the sweet certainty that if one parent got exasperated, there was a fresh one just down the hall. And if both parents were out of sorts, the siblings could ride out the storm together, secure in their attachment to a co-conspirator.

Kati was alone, except for Joy. And Joy was alone, period. No one to lean on. No one to take her place when her child's needs exceeded her own resources as a parent. No one to relax and curl up with at night. No one to reassure her that she was doing a fine job under difficult circumstances.

No one.

Because that, too, was obvious. Kati might be actively seeking out a father among the world's unattached males, but Joy was not seeking out a man in any capacity. Clearly she had meant exactly what she had said to Gabe. She loved no man because love required trust and she no longer trusted. From her reaction when Gabe touched her—the reflexive flinching, the surprise in her eyes—he would bet that she rarely allowed anyone close to her but Kati.

Yet Joy had trembled when he held her, shivered when his lips brushed over her mouth, sighed when her hands had sought and found the warm thickness of his hair. He might have killed her ability to love, but her body still responded to him. The shimmering sensuality he had once discovered in her was there still, waiting to be released.

And he would be damned if "Gravy-bear" would be the one to do it.

Chapter 8

The voices closed around Gabe, murmuring endlessly, spectral phrases from his past and his present. No matter how many times he heard them, he knew that they would never fail to move him. At least now an unborn child never called to him through the cool darkness. He heard cries, yes, but they were from Kati's living lips, a child's questions as she tried to understand why a father she had never known didn't love her.

There was no way for Gabe to tell the Voices to be still, that he regretted the past as he had never expected to regret anything in his life. There was no way to tell Kati that it wasn't her fault she didn't have a father. There was no way to explain that he hadn't suspected that Joy was a virgin until he was too gripped by passion to believe that any moment would ever exist except the one consuming moment when he found himself deep inside Joy. The fact that she had wanted him as much as he had wanted her, the fact that he hadn't known her innocence, the fact that the Orinoco

assignment was accepted long before he ever came to Lost
River Cave, the fact that he had done all he could for her by
leaving her every bit of money he had—those facts de-
scribed but didn't relieve him of his responsibility to her.
And to himself.

Love requires trust. Trust requires innocence.

What did forgiveness require? Was it simply a need and
an overwhelming ache, a tearing certainty that life lived this
way was not life at all? Did Joy ever wake up in the bleak
hours before dawn and wish to hell that she could live the
past all over again?

Like him. Wishing. Asking questions that had no answers. Feeling loneliness and regret like a cold, hidden river
dissolving away his soul while darkness closed around in a
seamless shroud.

"Gabe?" asked Joy softly, seeing the unmistakable lines
of pain in his face. She touched his shoulder in the instant
before she controlled herself and snatched back her hand.
Since she had found herself trembling in Gabe's arms, she
had been very, very careful not to touch him. "What's
wrong? Did you hurt yourself coming through Gotcha?"

His brief smile tore at Joy, for it revealed a defenseless
agony that she knew too well from her own experience. She
made a sound of protest and touched him again. "Gabe?"
she whispered, one voice among the Voices swirling around
them in darkness.

"Have you ever been lonely?" he asked, hearing the
words as though someone else were speaking them, hearing
the pain and the emptiness and the searching hunger. Then,
even as his words sank beneath the murmurous sounds of
the room, he said bitterly, "Christ, listen to me asking you
about loneliness."

As Gabe moved off into the room, his bleak laughter
stabbed through the Voices. Joy made a small sound and

turned away, shaking with a sudden storm of emotions, torn apart by discovery—and anger.

What right does he have to be lonely? He's gotten everything he ever wanted—fame, respect, adventure, discovery. He is the Great Gabriel Venture. He explored the world while I explored the depths of abandonment. It cost me too much to care about him in the past. I won't make the same mistake again. I can't. So what if I sense loneliness in him, a hunger and a need that are like my own? It isn't enough. He hasn't changed in the most important way. He still cares more about his career than about anything else, including his loneliness. He proved it when he agreed without argument to leave the past alone so that he could do what he came here to do—another article about Lost River Cave.

Gabe hasn't changed, not really. I have, though. I'm immune to love, to him. Be as lonely as you like, Gabe. It won't touch me.

"Coming through," grunted Davy.

Suddenly Joy realized that she was blocking Gotcha's exit. She stepped aside and watched as Davy wriggled out of the impossibly small hole, pushing his wadded-up clothes and helmet ahead of him and dragging a string of equipment from his ankle. Wearing only his underwear, Davy stood and stretched thankfully.

"Gonna freeze," said Joy, nudging his clothes with the toe of a muddy boot.

"Nah," said Davy, whacking himself on his stomach with a broad hand. "Too much natural insulation."

Maggie emerged from the hole in time to hear Davy's comment. "Gravy-bear, you don't have a spare ounce of fat on you and you know it."

"Do tell," he said, bending over and scooping her to her feet as though she were no bigger than Kati. "Can't say the same about you, can we? You got a license for that trailer?"

he asked, swatting Maggie on the rear as he reached for his clothes.

Joy didn't need to see Maggie to know that Davy's casual comment stung.

"Tell you what," said Joy to Maggie. "You hold him and I'll cut his throat."

"Sold," said Maggie, with enough emphasis to cut through Davy's thick hide.

He looked injured. "What did I do?"

"Got an hour?" retorted Joy.

"For you, Dr. Anderson, I have more than an—"

"Would it be possible to get on with this bloody exploration?" asked Gabe's voice coldly from the darkness, cutting across Davy's half-serious flirtation. "Or are you waiting for your audience to tuck dollar bills in your jock strap?"

"Tsk, tsk," chided Davy, reaching for his clothes. "Flattery will get you nowhere."

"Gravy-bear," said Maggie sweetly, "did anybody ever tell you that you have enough mouth for another row of teeth?"

Davy laughed and stuffed his shirt in his pants, completely unselfconscious as he dressed. "Just you, Maggie, and you're too young for me to take seriously."

"Then you're a fool," said Gabe quietly, turning away, remembering a nineteen-year-old woman whom he had been too young to take seriously.

"Whew," said Davy, looking from Maggie to Gabe. "Looks like you have yourself a champion. You got something going that I don't know about?"

"Brains," said Fish succinctly, emerging from Gotcha. "Not to mention heart, guts and a body that doesn't quit."

"Fish," said Maggie, "would your wife mind horribly if I kissed you?"

Fish laughed and stood up as he plugged in his helmet light. "She'd mind like hell. You see," he said, winking at Maggie, "she knows I'm too old *not* to take you seriously."

"Old!" said Maggie indignantly. "You're not a day over thirty-five."

"You're right," gibed Davy. "He's hundreds of days over. Thousands."

"Davy," said Maggie, "sometimes you're a real pain in the butt."

"Shut up, children," said Fish amiably, turning toward Joy. "What's on the program today?"

"I want you to referee while Maggie helps Davy with his survey," Joy said dryly. "Begin at the breakdown on the north quadrant of the Voices. I'm going to try to find a path through the Maze."

Fish laughed softly.

"Yeah," said Joy, sighing. "I know. But I can't help believing that there's a passage from the Voices into a whole new area of the cave. The water we're hearing has to come from somewhere and go to somewhere else."

"No argument from me, boss," said Fish, smiling. "Who's keeping time?"

"You."

He looked at his watch. "How long?"

"Call out the hours. And make sure Maggie drinks," said Joy. "She keeps coming back with her canteen half full. Just because it's cool doesn't mean your body isn't using up a lot of water."

Joy walked toward the pool of light cast by Gabe's helmet lamp.

"Is Maggie all right?" he asked quietly, following Joy as she walked deeper into the Voices.

"Yes."

Joy's answer was quiet, yet it slid among the murmurous cascading whispers like a knife.

"Davy's a fool," said Gabe.

"Maybe," said Joy, her voice low and crisp as she tried to focus on the cave's uneven floor rather than on her own uneven emotions. It was hopeless. Her feelings were too strong to be ignored. Hearing Gabe champion Maggie was like forcing an unknown passage through the cave; it scraped and bruised her in unexpected ways. "And maybe Davy's just smart enough to know that Maggie is too much woman for him."

"Do you really believe that?"

"Maggie has never had a lover, and it's not for lack of offers," said Joy, stopping, turning on Gabe. "Her first man will be her last. Do you think Davy's ready for that?"

"I wasn't," said Gabe.

"Tell me something I don't know," said Joy, making her tone matter-of-fact with an effort that left her throat aching.

"I'm ready now."

"Then what are you waiting for?" she retorted, her voice strained. "Get moving before Davy wakes up and realizes he's letting a fantastic woman slip through his thick fingers. Of course, you might have a small problem," added Joy, her voice slicing through the room's murmurous sounds, each word distinct, icy. "One or all of Maggie's brothers will do their best to kill you when they find out you've seduced and abandoned their sister. They just wouldn't understand how writing a new article about the ragged end of nowhere is more important than their little sister's innocence."

Joy heard the harsh intake of Gabe's breath but she didn't see his expression. She was already turning away, regretting both her quick tongue and the emotions eating through her control as surely as water ate through limestone. She knew that if Gabe took her advice and pursued Maggie, she would hate him, hate Maggie, hate herself. The thought that Gabe might have learned enough to find and recognize love in another woman was terrifying. She had felt nothing like it since the moment she had doubled over the steering wheel of the Jeep with labor pains and realized that she had started toward town too late; she would have her baby in the desert with no one to help her.

Gabe saw Joy stumble as she turned away from him. He caught her, turned her toward him and then wanted to cry out in protest at the strain he saw in her face. Instinctively he knew that she had been thinking about the past, a past that she refused to talk about with him. As for the future—it did not exist for her, for him, for them. Gabe refused even to think about it. There was only the time he would spend at Lost River Cave, exploring the earth and himself and the past Joy would not acknowledge despite the small, red-haired tornado dancing through their lives.

Very carefully Gabe released Joy, for even through the multiple layers of clothing he felt the warmth of her beckoning to his senses. If it were only desire twisting through him, he would have seduced her, satisfying both of them, relieving a torment that had begun six years ago and had no end in time. Yet the longer he was with Joy, the more he knew that he wanted more than her body. He wanted what he had once had from her. All of her: mind and body and soul. The laughter and the tears, the heat and the silences, the luminous reflection of himself in her eyes. He wanted her love with a savage force that taught him how little he had ever wanted anything before in his life.

"I think," said Gabe distinctly, "that you had better restrict your lectures to the nature and formation of limestone caves. Because if you keep chipping away at me, something's going to happen that we'll both regret. Do you understand?"

Numbly Joy nodded, appalled at the cruelty of her own words. Ten days ago she had forbidden Gabe to talk about the past, yet she had kept alluding to it herself, nicking at his civilized exterior, trying to discover what feelings lay beneath.

"I'm sorry, Gabriel," she said huskily. "It isn't fair of me to keep prying beneath your surface, trying to find out how you really feel. I already know. I know how important your career is to you. I understand. You've made a life for yourself that is very exciting, very fulfilling, a life that anyone would envy."

"Do you?"

"What?"

"Envy my life."

The question shocked Joy. Her eyes widened despite the intense illumination of Gabe's helmet lamp washing over her. The answer came to her, and it was as shocking as the question itself.

"Yes," she admitted hoarsely. "Part of your fascination for me," she continued, her voice halting, "was the wild places you had been to, places you had made a part of yourself. I wanted those places, Gabe. I wanted them as deeply as you did. I wanted them and—"

Joy's voice broke. She made no attempt to speak again.

"And I knocked you up and took off for the very places you would have cut off your hand to see," finished Gabe softly. A shudder moved over him as he realized that he had delivered Joy into the very fate that he had fled from—the baby trap, life closing down around you in a cage that had no key. "I didn't know you wanted the wild places," he whispered, one voice among the many Voices in Lost River Cave. "Believe me, sweetheart, I didn't know."

"How could you?" she asked. "I didn't know myself, until this instant. I couldn't let myself know because there was nothing I could do about it except break my heart over it." She drew in her breath and released it in a long, ragged sigh. "But it's all right. I had Lost River to explore. And Kati." Joy smiled through trembling lips. "She's a miracle, Gabe. She trusts so easily, loves so beautifully, lives so completely." Joy laughed shakily. "She's also a stubborn little witch, but that just reminds me that she's real, that she'll grow up, that someday she'll love a man and—" Joy bowed her head against the ache in her throat. *"Oh God, let her love wisely,"* she whispered beneath the liquid sounds pouring through the darkness.

But Gabe heard. He closed his eyes against the naked pain on Joy's face, yet nothing could close out what she had said. He knew that her agonized prayer would come to him again and again in the bleak hours before dawn, and would be whispered endlessly among the Voices in the darkness of his soul.

"Joy," he said huskily, reaching for her, needing to comfort her and himself.

His fingers closed on emptiness. He opened his eyes. Joy's light was retreating from him silently, farther away with each breath, each heartbeat. He pulled back his hand, saw it was trembling and swore deep within his own silence. Grimly he followed her, moving quickly over the uneven cave floor, closing the distance between himself and Joy.

"We'll begin here," she said, hearing him come up behind her. "Do you recognize that drapery?" Her voice was controlled, professional, as though she had never prayed that her daughter would be wiser in love than her mother had been.

Gabe turned his head in the direction of Joy's helmet lamp. Growing down from what had once been a sinuous crack in the ceiling was a huge sheet of limestone. Joy had told him that it was variations in the impurities of the groundwater that caused the striping that had given this type of formation the nickname of "cave bacon."

"Wait here," she said. "When I call out, turn off your lamp."

Silently he waited while she picked her way around the drapery. As always, she was meticulous in her care of the delicate formations that grew among the more robust decorations. She placed her feet only where the floor was the ancient limestone bed itself rather than the newer, unique sculptures precipitated out of clear water.

"Off," she called out.

Gabe shut off his light—and then sucked in his breath in wonder. For all its massive weight, the limestone drapery was translucent. Joy's light pervaded the stone until it glowed with an unearthly beauty. Subtle colors rippled sinuously, silently, a dream frozen in the mind of a nameless god. Graceful folds of stone shimmered with moisture. The drapery was vital, alive, growing, and he had seen nothing to equal it in any of the places on earth he had explored at such great cost to himself and others.

Joy's light moved across the drapery, then away, leaving it in primal darkness once more. Gabe made a sound of protest that went no farther than his mind. He tried to tell himself that the drapery wasn't a miracle, that it was the result of simple, rational physical processes working over long periods of time. A water drop zigzagging across the slanting ceiling, the slow seepage of more water, the even slower precipitation of stone, more seepage flowing over the new stone, more precipitation, until the result was an extraordinary limestone drapery so delicate that light could slide through it in a subtle blaze of radiance.

Silently Gabe turned toward the woman who was standing beside him once again. He realized that she had been watching him, absorbing his reaction. And then he understood that she had given him those moments of beauty in a silent apology for the prayer that would haunt his dreams.

"Thank you," he said simply, wanting to touch Joy, afraid that if he did she would withdraw again. "What do you call it?"

"You mean like Gotcha or Surprise or the Voices?"

"Yes."

Joy hesitated. "No one else knows about the drapery. It's not on Davy's survey," she said in a low voice. "I discovered it a few days ago when we got lost in the Maze," she said, gesturing toward the massed growth of cave formations that all but filled the Voices just ahead. "I turned back to see if you were following, and your light was shining through stone. I couldn't move; I couldn't even speak. It was the most impossible, most beautiful things I had ever seen."

The knowledge that Joy had shared with him what she had shared with no one else transformed Gabe as surely as light transformed the sinuous stone. He saw the same knowledge come to her, changing her. She stepped back from him quickly, fear plain in the tight lines of her face.

"We'll have to be sure that Davy surveys it," said Joy, her voice uninflected.

"What will you call it?"

"Deception," said Joy.

Gabe thought of the beauty, the impossibility, the light pouring through stone. "Why not call it Love?"

"Same difference," she said flatly. She continued speaking quickly, her voice precise. "There are four areas on the perimeter of this room that haven't been thoroughly explored. They're our best hope of finding a passage through to the cavern that is producing the water sounds."

"Like Honeycomb?" asked Gabe.

Joy thought of the section of limestone that had been dissolved away until all that was left was a lacework of stone that very much resembled a honeycomb. From that honeycomb issued an endless murmuring of voices and a faint breeze, telling Joy that there was an opening, a large opening, on the other side of the hall-sized formation of lacy stone.

"Yes, like that. But to get through there would mean destroying the Honeycomb itself. No matter how much I want to find the source of the Voices, I won't do that. Lost River Cave has been growing for thousands and thousands of years," said Joy. "I couldn't bear knowing that I'd destroyed part of it in a reckless search for its deepest secrets. The cave will either yield to me in the time I have left, or it won't."

Once Gabe might have disagreed with her, but no longer. He knew now the many ways regret haunted ambition's deepest caverns, like a cold black river running through layers of dissolving stone.

"I want to attempt the Maze again," said Joy. "I'm sure we can find a way through it if we just keep trying."

"And don't get lost again," he said quietly, remembering the last few times they had tried the Maze. In the end they had been forced to find their way out by listening carefully for the sounds the other three cavers made as they went about helping Davy with his survey.

"Oh well," she said, "it won't be the first time Fish has pulled me out of a hole."

There was a quality to Joy's voice that told Gabe she was referring to more than being belayed up a steep pitch by

Fish. But she was still talking, giving him no opportunity to ask questions about anything except the exploration itself.

"Damn," she muttered, frowning over her own compass, then snicking its face against her watch, jogging loose the stubborn needle.

Gabe reached into his backpack and brought out the compass that Joy had quite frankly coveted at first glance. "Trade you," he offered.

"Yours is five times better than mine," she protested.

"Guess I'll just have to stick real close so you can't lose me," he retorted, switching compasses with her.

"I'll only borrow it for the Maze," said Joy firmly. "And I brought a handful of extra light sticks too. We'll use them as markers."

She reached into her rucksack and pulled out a notebook containing the crude map that she and Gabe had expanded upon each time they attempted to unravel the Maze's secrets.

"We're here," said Joy, pointing to a sinuous line on the paper that represented the translucent drapery.

Gabe moved until he was behind Joy, looking over her shoulder, standing so close that each time he exhaled, his breath washed warmly over her cheek. She breathed in sharply, trying to control the shiver of awareness that went over her when she realized how little distance separated them. Gabe reached around her, took the notebook and pencil from her hands and began to write, but all Joy noticed was the pressure of his chest against her back. She tried to move away, only to fall prey to an odd weakness that made her want to lean against his strength instead of withdrawing from it.

You have got to be crazy, she told herself wildly. *You haven't been able to let a man touch you in six years. Gabe killed that part of you when he left, and you proved it when*

*you tried to date other men. Don't kid yourself that you've
changed. You've just got a bad case of memories, that's all.
That's the only way you can respond—in memories. That's
why Kati will be a lonely-only the rest of her life. If Gabe
made a real pass you'd freeze solid and you know it. So quit
tormenting yourself and teasing him. That kind of revenge
is despicable.*

And then she saw that Gabe had labeled the stone drapery "Love" on the crude map.

"Naming is the prerogative of the one who discovers, isn't
it?" asked Gabe softly, seeing the sudden tension in Joy's
face. "As you pointed out, it was my light that picked out
the formation first."

"Yes," said Joy in a faint voice.

She took a deep breath, but with it came the warmth and
scent of Gabe's body, triggering an extraordinary burst of
memories. For a timeless instant she was in the desert rather
than in the cave, and the Voices were Gabe's love phrases
caressing her as he merged with her for the first time, making both of them whole. It was a moment that had often returned to her in dreams and memories, the exquisite sliding
instant when his body first moved within hers.

"Joy?" murmured Gabe, steadying her as she swayed.
"Are you all right?"

*No! I'm going crazy! Don't stand so close to me. Neither
one of us can deliver on what you're promising, so just back
up!* But the wild words went no further than her mind. She
shook off the hands that were burning through layers of
cave clothing to the vulnerable flesh beneath.

"I'm fine," she said curtly, moving away from him. *Or I
would be if you and my damn memories would just quit
teasing me, reminding me of what it's no longer possible for
me to feel.*

She found a light stick and twisted it harshly. Eerie green illumination pooled in her hands. With a shoelace from her pack she looped the light around the slender tip of a head-high stalagmite. She tried to take a reading from Gabe's compass on the beacon of light, but her hands weren't steady enough. Silently he took the instrument from her. When he called out the numbers she wrote them on her map.

Together they moved into the Maze, pausing frequently to describe cave formations on the map, take readings on the compass and stack bits of natural debris into direction markers. Twice Joy added new light beacons, leaving behind unearthly glows as she and Gabe pushed deeper into the Maze.

Once, after Fish's second "Yooooo!" came to them from the Voices' immense darkness, Joy called a halt. They lingered only long enough to eat a handful of high-energy food and drink from their canteens. There was no way of telling how wide the Maze itself was, how long it would take to find the wall of the cave and work their way along it, searching for passages that might lead to other rooms. It was a time-consuming task, and two hours below ground had already passed.

"Ready?" asked Gabe, twisting to shrug into his backpack again.

Joy murmured something as she groped through her rucksack for some hard candy. Her fingers closed around several circular, paper-wrapped shapes. She didn't remember packing anything like them. She pulled out her hand and looked. Pink-and-white peppermint pinwheels shone on her palm. Gabe's candy, the candy she once had told him to hide before she stole it from him. He had given it to her and she hadn't even known.

"Thank you," said Joy, looking up suddenly, sensing that he was watching her.

"My pleasure," he said, his voice deep, remembering how much better peppermint once had tasted from her lips.

Joy looked away quickly. She unwrapped the mint with clumsy fingers, put it into her mouth and tucked the wrapper deep within her rucksack. Walking carefully over the uneven, often slippery floor, Gabe followed Joy deeper into the Maze. It was a veritable forest of cave formations, a beautiful obstacle course composed of draperies, flowstone, glistening stalactites, rugged stalagmites and the columns that were formed when the latter two kinds of cave formations met and grew together.

Sometimes the columns were so thick that they made an impenetrable barrier. Then Joy could only stand on tiptoe and shine her light longingly through the small openings that remained between columns. In the moving cone of her light were revealed more parts of the Maze, hidden parts, passages that could only be reached by destroying them. Sometimes the stalactites growing from the uneven ceiling had no stalagmites beneath them. Then the formations hung down like a fantastic, subtly colored fringe. In other places the stalactites were no larger than soda straws and far more delicate.

"Gabe, look," said Joy, her voice wondering. "Be very careful," she continued, stepping backward, easing around his body in the narrow gap between two slender columns. "You'll never see anything more fragile, more beautiful."

He felt the sweet, changing pressures of Joy sliding by him and wanted to cry out at the stolen pleasure of the instant. Silently telling himself that nothing he would see could be half so beautiful as Joy, he walked carefully toward the grotto that she had just abandoned.

Gabe's breath came in audibly as his light swept ahead. Within the grotto were incredibly slender crystals that reflected light in tiny glittering fragments. The formation grew neither up nor down, but had a spiral orientation, as though the laws of gravity were magically suspended deep within Lost River Cave. The least current of air, including his breath, caused hair-fine curves to quiver and sway. Gabe backed up a step, afraid that an incautious breath would destroy the eldritch beauty shimmering in the circle of his helmet lamp.

Slowly he turned toward Joy. "What are they?" he whispered, as though the impossibly thin crystals were alive and could be frightened by the sound of his voice threading among the eternal murmurings of the Voices.

"Helictites," she said, her voice as hushed as his.

"How are they formed?" Then, quickly, "Wait. I'm not sure I want to know. I don't want to spoil their mystery." Gabe made a disgusted sound and grimaced. "Listen to me. I'm the guy who makes a living taking the mystery out of the unknown for others."

Joy's gentle smile made Gabe's breath thicken in his throat. It was a smile from his memories, when two lovers had looked at each other and shared something silently yet just as completely as though they had spoken aloud.

"Your writing enhances what you describe," said Joy softly. Her hand briefly touched Gabe's arm. "Knowledge, real knowledge, always enhances. It's ignorance that destroys."

"Then enhance me," said Gabe, memorizing the elegant lines of Joy's face, remembering what it had been like to have the right to bend down and taste peppermint from her mouth.

"The latest theory is that helictites are formed by water squeezing through solid stone," she said. "If the water finally reaches an air pocket, the drops that emerge on the interior hollows of the bedrock are so tiny that they aren't affected by gravity. The crystals form without reference to

up or down or sideways. They follow their own imperatives, their own internal logic.''

"And they do it with extraordinary beauty," murmured
Gabe.

"Yes. But it isn't free or easy," Joy pointed out, her voice
both whimsical and serious. "Those crystals spend a long
time suspended within bedrock, waiting for just the right
circumstances to allow their beauty to be born."

"I must be part helictite," he said, searching Joy's luminous grey eyes. "I know how they feel."

Joy looked down, avoiding the hunger in his look as she
trained her light on the notebook opened between her
hands. She braced the notebook on her thigh and wrote
quickly.

"What are you calling them?" asked Gabe.

"Gabriel's Grotto," she said, her voice muffled.

"People will think you mean something Biblical."

"Good. Names should have as many levels as caves do."

Gabe laughed softly. "You know, I'd almost forgotten
what it's like to be around someone whose mind is as quick
and curious as mine."

"As in warped?" she suggested wryly.

"Definitely. Like helictites. Shaped by our own spiral
imperatives in a world where most people only recognize up
or down."

She glanced up and smiled as though it were six years ago.
"It seems like that sometimes, doesn't it? Maybe it comes
from exploring caves. Most people only live in two dimensions. Caves live in three."

"Or four."

She waited, her eyes intent, her heart beating oddly.
"Four?"

"Time," Gabe said silently, watching Joy. "Time changes
everything."

Joy didn't know how much time—and how much change—passed before she looked away from Gabe.

Working slowly, they found a new part of the Maze extending from the twisting path that had brought them to the helictites. Gently, inexorably, Joy insinuated herself between columns and around the broad bases of stalagmites. Flowstone formed by water seeping over the cave's uneven surfaces was everywhere, making it nearly impossible to move forward without walking on some type of cave formation. She pressed ahead anyway, knowing that it was inevitable that some marks of human passage would be left upon Lost River Cave. In time, those faint marks would be covered in flowstone, invisible.

In time, everything changed.

A cool breath moved across Joy's face. With the faint breeze came an almost imperceptible increase in the sounds of falling water. She stopped instantly, removed her glove and licked her finger, holding it upright. The left side of her finger felt distinctly cooler from the movement of air over it.

"Joy." Gabe's voice was urgent, excited. "Can you hear it?" he whispered.

She spun around and saw him turning his head slowly, helmet held in his hands as he caught the direction of the new sounds murmuring among the old Voices. In her helmet lamp his eyes flashed like green gems.

"To the left, I think," murmured Gabe. Like her, he had pulled off his glove and licked his skin, knowing it was one of the most sensitive organs of his body for weighing subtleties of temperature and pressure.

"Yes," said Joy breathlessly. "I felt air moving. Wait," she added, holding onto his arm when he would have walked on. "Mark this point with a light stick. It may be the only place in the whole Maze where we can really feel a distinct current of air.''

Gabe pulled out a slender tube, twisted it, and was bathed in pale green light. A spare piece of cord served as a harness for the stick. Gently he looped the light over a stalagmite as thick as his body. While he worked, Joy took a compass reading off the other two light sources she could still see and made notes on her crude map.

When Joy looked up again, Gabe was watching her.

"Ready?" he asked.

As he spoke, he held out his hand to her.

"I—" Joy felt her bare hand resting on the hard warmth of his palm and didn't even remember reaching for him.

"Lead the way," he commanded softly.

Chapter 9

The Maze was all around them now. Only compass readings and the light sticks they had left behind kept Joy from becoming totally disoriented as she followed the vague stirring of air among an endless variety of cave formations. The air current was baffling, coy, elusive. It breathed out from glittering stalagmite forests and curled among columns of golden stone three stories high. When Joy finally lost the vital breath, Gabe came to stand behind her, listening intently, holding himself with the stillness he had learned in the wild places of the world.

"There," he murmured. "To the right."

As he spoke he turned Joy, hands on her shoulders. She held herself as still as Gabe and half-closed her eyes, trying to reach into the Maze with primitive senses that were more useful than sight within Lost River Cave's mysteries. After a moment she sensed a tiny, trembling current of air caressing her face.

"Yes," she breathed, feeling Gabe's warmth and his presence behind her and the rich mystery beckoning ahead.

Hands squeezed Joy's shoulders and she thought that she felt the brush of his cheek against her helmet just before he released her. Her head tilted back, seeking the vertical dimensions of the section of the Maze that they were in.

"Ceiling coming down," she said, her voice oddly taut, almost breathless.

Gabe's only answer was a soft sound that could have been her name.

Joy walked forward, seeking pathways through or around crowded formations. When she was stymied, Gabe's helmet light moved forward to sweep the cave alongside hers, probing the darkness. The unusual twin-sourced illumination made formations leap into high relief. For the first time Joy noticed that there was a tantalizing hint of pattern to the cave floor in front of her and the stalagmites beyond, as though they were signposts on a loosely curving road cobbled by smaller, younger cave formations.

"It's a piece of Lost River," said Joy, her voice excited.

"What?"

"Lost River. The one the cave is named after. A river flowed through here once, long after the cave itself was formed. The Voices has parts of the river channel, but I've never been able to trace it this far before." She looked up and saw from Gabe's face that he didn't understand yet. "The cave's levels have been dried out and decorated and inundated repeatedly. A river flowing from room to room, cavern to cavern, will carve out connecting passages. All we have to do is—"

"Find out where Lost River went," finished Gabe, excitement kindling in his green eyes. "But it's flat here. How can you tell which way is upstream and which is down, or doesn't it matter?"

"It matters," said Joy. She dropped to her hands and knees and pushed forward into the narrowing confines of the Maze. "We want to go downstream. But there's no problem. All we have to do is follow the channel markers."

"Glad to," said Gabe dryly, crawling along behind her. "Just point them out."

"The scallops," said Joy, shining her helmet light at the point where the cave's wall joined the floor. There, Lost River's ancient flow had hollowed out a long shallow curve, like the side of a tunnel. Smaller curves overlapped along the wall, making a scalloped pattern that was repeated on the far side of the channel. "They're caused by moving water. In limestone the upstream end is rounded and the downstream end is more pointed."

"The things you learn in school," said Gabe, his voice both teasing and admiring.

Joy laughed quietly. The ceiling came down until the overhang became a slit barely three feet high and twenty feet deep. She knew that vadose stream channels such as this one rarely contained pits like Surprise, but rarely was not the same as never. She moved slowly, literally feeling her way, alert for a downward slant in the floor or any pool of shadow in her helmet light that could signal the mouth of a pit.

"Wait," said Gabe.

Joy heard the sound of canvas scraping over rock and knew that Gabe was having trouble with his backpack.

"Stuck?" she asked.

Gabe's only answer was a grunt and the sound of air being expelled forcefully.

"Back up, take off your backpack and loop your elbow through a strap," she said. "Or tie the backpack to your ankle. You can try pushing the pack ahead of you, if you can handle both it and your rope sack," added Joy, follow-

ing her own advice. With careful contortions she managed
to secure the rucksack to her ankle.

"Does it get smaller ahead?"

"Count on it," said Joy dryly.

Gabe's muttering was lost among the increased strength
of the Voices. The breeze hadn't increased though. It was
still a fine, almost imperceptible exhalation over their faces.

"Ready," said Gabe after a few moments.

Joy crawled forward again, hearing little except the sound
of her own clothing rubbing over stone and the occasional
muted thump of her helmet on an unexpectedly low por-
tion of the ceiling. The farther she went the more the passage took on the aspect of a true tunnel rather than simply
a long narrow strip gouged out of the Voices' overhanging
wall. The floor pitched down slightly; the passage narrowed even more; and the ceiling came down. Joy's heart
beat faster in sudden exhilaration. There was little doubt
now that this channel would lead to another room—unless
the passage had been closed by debris or the breakdown of
the ceiling. Those things happened depressingly often. All
cavers knew that for every passage that went somewhere,
many more dead-ended at a natural, utterly impassable obstacle.

The sound of Gabe's occasional blistering curses came
above the heightened murmur of the Voices. The passage
twisted sinuously, a riverbed carved through solid stone,
complete with bends and deposits of stony debris swept
from the huge room behind Joy and Gabe. Both of them
were moving along on their stomachs or their sides or their
backs, depending on the nature and orientation of the
opening. Their progress was limited to eel-like motions that
were tiring. Neither of them noticed, though. They were
gripped by the possibility of a discovery just around the next
twist or turn, for even above the sound of their exertions,

the multiple voices of falling water came to them, a siren song that grew louder with each movement forward.

Joy's light rarely revealed more than the next few feet of the passage, and as often as not the plugs leading to the battery pack were pulled out as she wiggled around. Several times she came to a place where the limestone had been more easily dissolved. There the passage widened enough to allow them to rest. Each time Joy checked her watch, not wanting them to stay long enough for the chill of the bedrock to seep into their bodies or for them to miss answering Fish's hourly call.

"Ready?" she asked after a few minutes.

"After you," said Gabe gallantly, giving a sidelong swipe of his arm toward the muddy tunnel that awaited them.

A few minutes farther into the passage, Joy found herself confronted by a barricade made up of debris deposited by Lost River when it had flowed through long ago. Although there was no water in the passage now, everything was damp, slick and muddy, as infused with moisture as the air itself. Cursing silently, Joy began to dig. She said nothing, saving her oxygen for work and avoiding the thought that the fill might be too deep, too thick and too well packed for her to dig through it all.

"Problem?" asked Gabe.

His voice came from behind Joy and to her right. Though the ceiling was no more than twenty inches from the floor, the tunnel itself was nearly four feet wide at this point.

"Clastic fill," said Joy, the words clipped.

"Dirt," said Gabe. This time his voice was nearly beside her.

"Not to a biologist," retorted Joy. "No worms."

"For these small things, Lord, we are grateful," Gabe muttered as he wriggled alongside Joy and began digging.

"Don't like worms?" she asked.

He made a throaty sound of disgust. "Give me a good dry snake any day of the week," he said with feeling.

Joy smiled to herself at the discovery that the Great Gabriel Venture, a man who had proved his physical courage many times over, was more than a little put off by worms.

With Gabe helping it wasn't long before they had scraped aside enough silt and water-rounded pebbles to allow their bodies to squeeze through between ceiling and floor. Joy forged ahead once more, making encouraging noises to Gabe who was just behind her heels. The passage closed down, forcing her to work very hard to eel between floor and ceiling, making her wonder if Gabe was going to have to turn back—or worse, if he would get stuck. Then she realized that she wasn't hearing him behind her anymore.

"Gabe?" she called, her voice breathless from more than exertion. "Are you all right?"

The answer was a hot curse and the sound of cloth ripping. "Just bloody fine, thanks," he said a moment later. "Emphasis on the *bloody*."

Joy hesitated, then wriggled around until she could bring her wristwatch in line with her eyes. The face of the watch was muddy. Automatically she rubbed it against her chin. That didn't work, for her chin was also muddy. Her nose wasn't, though. She rubbed and peered at her watch again. They had been in the passage twenty minutes. They had thirty-seven minutes before Fish would hail them again.

"Maybe we should head back," she said reluctantly.

"Not on my account. Blood makes a great lubricant," said Gabe in a wry voice.

"We're running out of time."

"That's not all we're out of."

"What?"

"Room," he explained succinctly. "I'd have a bitch of a struggle wriggling out of this place backward."

"It's not as hard as it sounds," she said in a reassuring voice. "Davy can do Gotcha nearly as fast backward as he can forward."

"Davy's mother must have been a python," retorted Gabe.

Joy laughed, relieved that Gabe wasn't frightened by the thought of being so tightly held by the earth that he couldn't even turn around. "You'd only have to do the first few minutes feet first. After that we'd come to the wide spot where we rested and you could turn around."

There was a moment of silence before Gabe spoke quietly. "I'd rather go forward, Joy. If you want to."

She hesitated only an instant. "Five minutes. Seven at most. All right?"

Gabe's response was a low laugh that ruffled her nerves. "Get moving, beautiful. There's a whole new world waiting to be discovered by us."

"Beautiful?" she retorted, knowing full well that by now she was as muddy as swamp puppy. "Turn on your lamp, Mr. Venture. You're hallucinating in the dark."

He laughed again with an excitement that was contagious. Joy attacked the next section of the tunnel with high spirits, feeling as though it were six years ago, when she and Gabe had explored together just a few of Lost River Cave's secrets. It was good to laugh with him again. For a few precious instants he had not been the man who had suspended her between yearning and hatred for long, long years.

There was no warning. One instant Joy was snaking forward on her side. The next instant constriction vanished and much of her upper body was touching nothing at all. She had only enough time to snatch at her falling rucksack, barely saving it, before she froze in place.

"Gabe! Grab my feet and hang on!"

Instantly Gabe's powerful hands clamped around her ankles.

"Don't let go," she said, her voice urgent.

"Not a chance," he said reassuringly. "Not a chance in the world."

Slowly, Joy let out the breath she had been holding in order to wedge herself into the tunnel more tightly. The leads to her helmet lamp had come unplugged a few minutes back, so she could see nothing at all. She could be in a small expansion of the tunnel or she could be suspended over a drop hundreds of feet deep. There was no way of telling without light.

But there was a sense of air moving subtly over her hands and a thousand liquid voices calling to her. As soon as her heart stopped pounding, she began to separate out the sounds and sensations. Distance. Space. Moisture. A beautiful, rushing sigh. Somewhere ahead, clothed in darkness and diamond mist, water was leaping from one level of the cave to another, a river shattering itself on stone and then flowing back together, healing itself, curling down and down into the limitless earth.

Cautiously Joy connected the leads to her lamp. Light flared out into blackness, light both defining darkness and being itself defined in turn. For an instant she saw nothing but the two stark contrasts. Then, slowly, a world condensed out of the void, a place of fantastic golden shapes, inky shadows, impossible spires and draperies and columns; a vision of flowing stone condensed out of water through time spans so great that they could only be numbered, not understood.

"Oh, Gabe," she said, her breath rushing out. "It's so beautiful! I wish you could see it."

Relief swept through Gabe. Joy was all right despite whatever danger had made her demand that he hang onto her ankles. Relief was followed by a fierce elation that her first reaction had been a desire to share the instant of discovery with him. Then came the more pragmatic concerns of a man who had spent his life in wild places.

"Are you safe?" he asked urgently. "Shall I pull you back from the pit?"

"As long as you don't let go, I'm safe," she said almost dreamily, her eyes focused on the astonishing room ahead. The knowledge that no other human being, ever, had seen this subterranean landscape sent currents of awe through her. Yet she wished Gabe were beside her, seeing it as she did, sharing it with her. There was too much beauty for one person to hold alone. It overflowed, nearly drowning her. "It's not a pit, exactly," she said in a husky voice. "It's a high entrance to another room. I think water once poured out of here into the cavern below."

Gabe visualized a tunnel in the sheer face of a cliff, an opening suspended between an invisible ceiling above and an equally invisible floor below.

"I'd feel better if I had a rope on you." Gabe heard his own words and smiled rather grimly to himself. He realized that he would feel better if he had Joy roped and tied, all right—to himself, permanently. Failing that, he'd settle for the usual methods—safety harness, carabiners and anchor points.

"I'm going to wiggle forward a bit so I can see if there's a way down," she said. "Ready?"

"Joy—"

"It's all right, Gabe. If you don't let go and I keep my center of gravity within the tunnel, I'll be safe."

"But—" Even as he objected, he remembered that a woman's center of gravity was usually in her hips, whereas a man's was usually about twelve inches higher. In this case Joy could get a better, safer look than a man could. "All right. But first I'm going to put a half-hitch or two around your ankles."

While Gabe worked over her feet, Joy surveyed as much as she could of the space ahead. Everywhere light fell there were flowing formations of stone, stone sculptures both massive and delicate, turrets and naves and walls, columns that tapered in the middle like an elegant woman, flaring above and below into the velvet darkness. Joy didn't know how big the room was, for her light reached neither ceiling nor floor nor walls. She did know that the cavern was a place of extraordinary beauty. It sang with water, a chorus murmuring musically amid fantastic shapes, a three-dimensional poem composed out of confinement and space, limestone and water, darkness and light.

And time. Immense time, eternity dreaming in stone.

"Be careful, sweetheart," Gabe said, his voice deep, almost harsh. "I didn't come all this way to go back alone."

"I'll be careful," she promised, her voice husky, hearing the word *sweetheart* echo in her mind and her blood as it always had in her dreams. "I'm going to stuff my rucksack alongside my body as a wedge, then inch forward. Ready?"

"Ready."

Joy felt Gabe cinch the rope more tightly around her ankles. She twisted about until the rucksack was alongside her. As she inched forward the rope resisted, then gave slightly, no more. Gabe was keeping a pressure on her that was just short of painful. It was also very reassuring, for as her headlamp swept directly over the lip of the stone, she saw that there was nothing at all beneath but a velvet darkness that looked heavy enough to walk on.

"Gabe, go back down the tunnel at least ten feet," said Joy quietly.

"Overhang?" he asked in a clipped voice, but he was already making a very rapid retreat, not waiting for the answer.

"Yes," she said, grateful that he understood the danger instantly instead of hanging around and waiting for a long explanation.

Gabe went back down the tunnel as instructed—and took Joy with him at the end of the rope whether she wanted it or not. She started to protest but the words died in her throat. In Gabe's place she would have done the same thing. If the limestone overhang on which she had rested for a moment was faulted or cracked by water, the stone could give way at any time, leaving her dangling by her heels over nothing at all.

"Enough," said Joy.

The tugging on her ankles stopped.

"I'm going forward again," she said.

"Like hell you are."

"Someone has to do it, and I'm the lightest one."

A long silence answered her, followed by a single, succinct curse. While Gabe chewed over the inevitable, Joy reached into her muddy rucksack and withdrew a slender tube.

"I'll check for cracks as I go," she said.

Grudgingly Gabe played out enough rope to allow her to move forward again. This time Joy looked carefully at the surface she was crawling over rather than at the opening beyond. The stone was chill, smooth, homogenous and unmarred by cracks or seams or joints. It stayed like that right up to the brink of the cavern.

"It's solid all the way," said Joy.

She hesitated for an instant before she twisted the light stick and threw it into the void, counting beneath her breath. Pale green illumination washed over stone, throwing a nearby fluted drapery into fantastic relief. The light arched down and down, shimmering like a comet across unknown skies before it struck a thick column and ricocheted. Finally the light lay unmoving, a green glow calling to her. She ached to answer it, to explore every bit of the mystery opening before her, but she knew she could not. Not yet.

Joy eased backward as Gabriel pulled in the rope behind her.

"How far down?" he asked, moving backward as he spoke.

"Roughly—very roughly—seventy feet straight down," said Joy, retreating even as Gabe did. "I couldn't see, but I assume that there's some sort of talus pile before you get to the floor of the room. If this was once a waterfall, the bottom of the wall would have been undercut, leaving a pile of fallen stone where the floor meets the wall."

They came to a widening of the tunnel. Joy looked at her watch and calculated quickly.

"Want to take a look?" she asked.

"You bet your sweet bottom," said Gabe, the electric excitement of discovery in his voice.

Joy laughed softly. "Then make like a snake and slither on by," she invited, putting her arms above her head and rolling onto her side with her back to the tunnel wall, giving him all the space she could.

He didn't wait for a second invitation. Facing her, arms above his head, his body turned partway on his side, he began his snake act. There was barely enough room. He was compressed between stone and the much more forgiving surface of Joy's body. Even through layers of gritty clothes he felt both the resilience and the softness of her. He sensed the laughter rippling through her and the sudden, hot instant when she went utterly still, feeling him pressed against her from her forehead to her toes.

"Joy," he breathed.

She couldn't move as his mouth closed over hers, for she was trapped between the chill of the stone and the warmth of his body. But even if she could have moved, she wouldn't have. As his tongue teased her lips she felt sensations that she hadn't known in years except in her memories and dreams, fire blooming through her so hotly she felt must be radiating like a light tube twisted in his hands.

The knowledge that she could still respond to a man was as overwhelming to Joy as the instant when she had found herself half dangling over darkness with nothing but Gabe's hands to anchor her. She made a sound that could have been his name as he teased open her lips, asking for further exploration, a deeper intimacy.

Joy didn't deny Gabe, or herself. The heat and taste of him swept over her senses. She forgot where she was, forgot that he was the man who had seduced and abandoned her, forgot that he was the man who had left love behind in order to pursue the lure of discovery throughout the world. She forgot everything but the sweet, hot presence of him within her mouth. With an inarticulate sound she pressed against him, giving herself to the kiss, regretting only that she could not put her arms around him and know him as completely as she had in her dreams.

After the first few instants of mutual exploration, Gabe felt control slipping away. He wanted to do so much, feel so much, share so much; and he couldn't even put his arms around her. His mouth bit into hers, straining to be closer still to her warmth. She made a tiny, soft sound in the back of her throat and he felt the stone shatter into flames around him. He called her name hoarsely, demand and apology at once. He hadn't meant to come to her like this, half wild, control slipping away with each small movement of her tongue over his, his mind reeling and his body shaking, starved for her. Slowly, sinuously, his whole body caressed Joy as he searched every texture of her mouth with his tongue.

Joy felt the strength and urgency of Gabe's passion in every movement of his powerful body. She made a sound of frustration and hunger, wanting to be able to touch him, to feel the heat and hardness of him. She needed his skin sliding against hers to reassure her that this wasn't a dream, that she was awake and wholly alive for the first time in six years. With a low moan she moved against him, returning the sinuous caress of his body, withholding nothing of her response, for she had never been able to deny him, even in her deepest dreams.

"Oh, God," gritted Gabe. "Tell me I'm not dreaming." His teeth ravaged her lips delicately. He murmured her name repeatedly in a litany of joy as he licked her mouth with tiny, hot strokes, savoring and caressing her. "I used to wake up shaking after I'd dreamed of you," he whispered. "I'm shaking now but I'm not dreaming. Tell me I'm not dreaming."

Reality broke over Joy in a cold wave. She shuddered convulsively and would have withdrawn, but there was nowhere for her to go.

"Joy?" he asked, sensing her withdrawal even though there was no possibility of physical retreat.

"I—" Her voice broke on another shudder.

Gabe kissed her mouth with ravishing delicacy, sipping at her lips and tongue as he wanted to sip at the tips of her breasts. And then his tongue took hers, filling her mouth as he wanted to fill her body, stroking her slowly, deeply.

"Gabe," she groaned, feeling rings of pleasure expanding through her, shimmering, threatening to burst. She had been wrong, so very wrong. She was capable of responding sensually to a man—so long as that man was Gabriel Venture.

Somehow she managed to turn her head aside. "Gabe, don't," she said, her voice shaking. Her breath caught as his body moved over hers again and rings of pleasure burst into shimmering light within her. "Ahhh, Gabe," she moaned. "Don't. You don't know what you're doing to me."

"I hope it's half of what you're doing to me," he said, his voice intense, husky, resonant with the extraordinary pleasure of touching Joy again.

"Please," she said urgently as his hips moved sinuously, hotly, caressing her. "Don't. Don't! Stop teasing me, Gabe! I haven't been with a man since you left me!"

Gabe froze, unable to believe what he was hearing. He had never touched, ever, a woman half so sensual, so responsive as Joy. It was unbelievable that she had denied herself the physical pleasure she so clearly hungered for.

"Why?" he said, his voice hoarse.

Joy wondered how she could tell Gabe that a man's touch, any man's touch, hadn't moved her, even when she had been determined to go out and get pregnant, to give Kati the sibling she so desperately wanted. "I tried—God how I tried!—but I couldn't respond," she said dully. "When a man touched me, I would miss you even more. It was like rope running through my hands, out of control, burning me. Finally I just—gave up."

Emotion speared through Gabe like light through darkness, changing and defining him. He remembered all the times he had taken a woman in the hope of filling the void expanding within him, a hollowness where nothing existed. And each time it had been worse, the void deeper, wider, taller, more complete, growing until he sensed it would devour him and he would live forever in the echoing emptiness.

Then he remembered what he had thought as he had taken Joy the first time: *He would match her sensuality with a perfection that no other man could ever equal. He would melt her to her bones, and when she re-formed again in the aftermath of passion, she would never be touched again without remembering him.*

And it had been just like that. Hot. Perfect. Enduring.

Only it had worked both ways. He had never again touched another woman without remembering Joy, regretting her loss deep within his soul, emptiness growing.

"I'm sorry," he whispered, brushing her lips with his breath, his tongue. And then, in a ragged rush. "No, I'm not. I should be, but I'm not. I've missed you in ways you'll never know, in ways I'm only just discovering."

Joy said nothing. She could not, anymore than she could pull back from Gabe. She was suspended between the passionate present and the bleak pain of past betrayal. She was falling, and the regret in Gabe's anguished voice was a safety rope burning against her body as she fell. She didn't know if he could hold the rope, stop her fall. Or if she wanted him to, if she wanted her life held within his hands once again.

Her watch alarm cheeped urgently, startling both of them. She felt Gabe draw a deep breath, pinning her intimately between his hard flesh and the stone wall of the tunnel.

"Time to go home?" he asked quietly, trying and failing to make his voice calm.

"There's still time for you to have a look at the new cavern," said Joy, controlling her breathing with an effort. "A very fast look."

"How much time?" he asked in a low voice.

"A minute. Maybe mo—"

The word was never finished. Gabe tilted his head and took Joy's mouth again, blending their bodies together in the only way he could within the confines of the moment.

It was different from the kisses he had given her before. There was flaring passion, yes, but there was something more, something both gentle and enduring, apologies and promises spoken in silence, a warmth that transcended the cold stone passage wrapped around them.

After more than a minute Gabe slowly, reluctantly, released Joy's mouth. In stunned silence she felt him slide past her, moving back toward the Voices, away from the newly discovered room. Automatically she followed him, her body progressing by reflex and experience, for her mind was still spinning around a fact more incredible to her than the discovery of her own renewed capacity for passion: Gabe had stayed in the tunnel to kiss her rather than going on to measure the wholly undiscovered territory that beckoned just beyond the stone overhang. He would never have done that six years ago.

She could barely believe that he had done it now.

Chapter 10

Wearily Joy climbed up to her screened porch, her arms loaded with gritty caving gear. Behind her the desert's hot, brilliant sunlight filled the air to bursting. Gabe held open the screen door and followed Joy inside, letting the door swing shut behind him.

"Sure you don't want to change your mind?" asked Joy, looking at her watch. "I could belay you down and you could help the others look for a shorter way into Small Favors. In fact—"

"Small Favors," repeated Gabe, chuckling and shaking his head.

"The new tunnel," Joy reminded him.

"As in thank the Lord, no worms?" he asked, watching her with luminous jade eyes. His smile was as wide and warm as the sun itself.

"That's the one."

"Small Favors leading to Joy's Castle. Now," he said quickly, "don't object. Fish, Davy, Maggie and I agreed that even though you had found it, you'd never name it for yourself. And it should be named for you. Joy."

She started to object, then shrugged, accepting the name. She dropped her equipment and stretched, enjoying the freedom and dryness of the desert day with as much pleasure as she would enjoy the mysterious passages and moisture of Lost River Cave when she returned. "Okay. Joy's Castle it is. People will think it refers to the emotion, anyway."

"To tell the truth, I'm having a hell of a time separating them myself."

She gave him a startled look.

"You have the most beautiful smile I've ever seen," said Gabe simply, tracing her lips with his eyes. "That hasn't changed, Joy. Not in all the years, all the memories, all the dreams. I didn't know it then, but I used to measure how empty I was by remembering your smile."

Joy's lashes dropped over her transparent gray eyes, concealing them for an instant. "Gabriel," she said, her voice taut, strung between the past the present.

"Yeah, I know. Nearly two weeks ago I promised you that I wouldn't talk about the past." He put down his equipment and dirty clothes, sighed and ran silt-stained fingers through his dark hair. He remembered the flash of hatred that he had seen more than once in her eyes during those first few days. Yet he no longer believed that she hated him. She felt fury, yes. A hot desire for revenge, perhaps. But hatred? No. When he touched her, currents of hunger had run through her like a river seething through darkness. She couldn't hate him and still respond like that, no matter how long it was since she had been with a man. "But it's damned hard not to talk about the past," he said, watching her, wanting her. "There are things we have to settle, Joy."

"There's nothing to settle," she said, turning away, putting her helmet on its shelf. Automatically she pulled the batteries out of the pack and plugged them into the recharger as she spoke. "The simple truth is that the past is gone. Period. Nothing can affect it in any way."

"And the future?" he asked softly.

For an instant Joy's body stiffened, then she continued caring for her equipment. "The same," she said, her voice bleak. "Out of reach."

"I'm Kati's father," he said bluntly. "That began in the past and will go on forever. How's that for a simple truth?"

She spun sharply, forgetting everything but the challenge implicit in Gabe's jade eyes. "While you're passing out simple truths, try this one on for size," Joy said icily. "When this assignment is over you'll go on to the next assignment, leaving your daughter behind, rejecting her, breaking her heart."

Anger flashed through Gabe, a need to hurt as he himself was being hurt. He hadn't expected her to attack after the intimacy of the cave. "What do you want me to do?" he snarled. "Stay here in New Mexico with Kati while you get your revenge playing international globe-trotter?"

"Didn't we have this conversation almost two weeks ago?" asked Joy, her voice ragged, her eyes the color of winter. "We know all the answers, Gabe. They haven't changed."

"And just what are those answers?" he asked.

His soft voice should have warned her; but like Gabe, Joy was in the grip of a rising rage that was every bit as deep as her passionate response to him had been. It was the same for him, passion and rage intermingling hotly.

"They all boil down to the same thing," said Joy. "Nothing means as much to you as your career. You don't know how to love," she said flatly, her voice aching with emotions more enduring than anger. "Haven't you learned that about yourself yet? That's why I'm not going to tell Kati who her father is until she's eighteen, when she'll be old enough to handle it. Tell her sooner and you'll destroy her. You won't mean to, but you'll do it just as surely as you almost destroyed me."

Rage ripped through Gabe, rage and something more, a twisting anguish that he couldn't express. He could express anger, though. That was easy. He had had a lifetime of practice at that. "Are you saying that *you* know how to love?" he asked sardonically.

"Yes," she whispered.

"Oh, really?" he asked. "Funny, I always thought forgiveness was the hallmark of love."

Joy went pale beneath the streaks of rich silt smeared across her cheeks. "Is that why you were so *forgiving* when you thought I'd had an abortion?" she retorted. "Did your *love* just overflow with the understanding that you'd put me in the position of having to choose between an abortion and my own sanity?"

Gabe flinched and knew a wrench of pain that surpassed his anger. He didn't want to hear any more. He didn't want to hear Joy's rage and anguish. He didn't want to confront himself and her and the past.

"But you didn't think of that, did you?" continued Joy relentlessly. "You just thought that—"

"I just thought that you'd lied when you said you loved me," interrupted Gabe bleakly. "I was wrong. You loved me. If I'd known that six years ago, I'd have—"

He stopped speaking because he didn't know what he would have done. He hadn't believed that she loved him, because if he had believed, he would have been trapped. The Gabriel Venture of six years ago couldn't have borne that captivity, for he hadn't been capable of returning the kind of love that increases rather than decreases the possibilities of life.

"You would have left me just the same," said Joy, her voice flat and unflinching as she finished Gabe's sentence for him.

"I came back," he said softly.

"But you didn't come back here for my love or even my forgiveness, did you?" she asked, her voice low, trembling. "You didn't even know I was here. You came back because the Lost River Cave article was the best piece you'd ever written and your editor wanted another one like it. Work, Gabe. You came back here because of your damned career. Forgiveness and love had nothing to do with it!"

"Do you really believe that?"

"Don't you?" she retorted swiftly.

"I might have, once. But I haven't known what to believe since I watched my life peeling away with each strand of rope." Anger drained out of Gabe's voice. "That's the real reason I came back here, Joy. I spent a long time in that filthy hospital thinking about life. My life. I thought about all the mountains I'd conquered and the ones I hadn't, the wild places I'd known and the places I'd never know. And through it all Lost River Cave was like a light burning in an overwhelming darkness, calling to me in ways that I still don't understand. It . . ."

Gabe hesitated, understanding part of himself for the first time. The discovery was bittersweet, a knowledge of his own past limitations. "It frightened me," he said simply. "I ran. Everywhere. Mountains, oceans, jungles. A year. I ran until I was too exhausted to fight my obsession with Lost River Cave. So I came back here. And I saw you. Joy."

She looked at Gabe's eyes, startled by the hesitations and emotions resonating within his voice. He was a man who had always known what he wanted, what he thought, what was or was not worthy of his time and consideration. Self-confident. Sensual. Joy closed her eyes suddenly. That, at least, hadn't changed. He was still as sensual as she had remembered and dreamed. More sensual.

And, oddly, much more fundamentally intriguing. When she had been nineteen, Gabe's lack of philosophical questions about himself and the world had excited her. In retrospect she realized that a man without questions wasn't exciting to anyone but a girl. She was a woman now. Gabe still appealed to her, for in many ways he was more of a man than ever before. His searching, aching, questioning intelligence was infinitely more alluring than his narrow, static self-confidence had been. And he was stronger. His mind had grown, shedding old and confining certainties, flexing against the intimate unknown that was himself, beginning an interior exploration that equaled in danger and fascination any that he could have found in the exterior world.

She knew what such interior explorations were like, the danger and the excitement, the risk and the reward and the despair. She knew how vital it was to explore and accept yourself, your limitations and strengths, your fears and hopes, your ability to love—and to hate. If she hadn't begun to know herself she wouldn't have survived the loss of Gabe and of her parents, or raising a fatherless child. She had finally stopped asking old questions and begun searching for new answers.

So had Gabe. It was there in his eyes as he watched her, waiting for her decision.

"I don't understand what brought you back to Lost River Cave," admitted Joy huskily, "any more than I understand why you left. I do know that each of us has to do what is necessary, what we can live with. Hatred isn't one of those things, Gabe. I can't live with it." She took a deep shaking breath. "As for forgiveness—you're right. It's a part of love. And love—" Her voice broke. "Love like that just isn't a part of me anymore. So if you came to Lost River Cave to be forgiven, you came to the wrong place. I've never forgiven myself for being such an innocent fool. How can I possibly forgive the man who took the innocence and left only the fool?"

"Joy," Gabe whispered, but his voice fragmented into silence. He swallowed against the emotion closing his throat. "You weren't a fool. Your love was the most beautiful thing I've ever known. I was the fool. I left you."

She smiled sadly, trying to keep her tears from falling. "No, Gabriel. I was the only fool. I loved the wrong man. But it was a long time ago. Please—oh God, please—can't we just let go of it?"

"No," said Gabe softly, bending over, kissing the long, honey-colored lashes that were infused with tears. "Only a fool would let go of love. I'm not a fool anymore." His lips both soothed and incited Joy's, and his tongue was a hot moist flame licking over her. "It will be good, sweetheart," he promised in a low, husky voice. "It will be unbearably good."

Joy trembled between Gabe's hands, knowing only her need for him. Remembering too many things, she was suspended between passion and fear. He had promised nothing but the satisfaction of the hunger that raged through her, shaking her.

What did you expect—a promise to spend the future with you? she asked herself wildly. *He's being honest with you this time. No. He was honest before. He never promised a damn thing. Why should it be different this time?*

And then a thought came, a thought both sweet and savagely triumphant. *Yes, why shouldn't it be the same? Why shouldn't he make love to me while he's here and then leave me as he did before? Pregnant. Why shouldn't I give him the passion that's all that he wants and take from him all that I want—passion and another child?*

There was no answer but the liquid heat of desire uncurling between her thighs. With a moan she gave herself over to Gabe's touch, saying nothing, asking nothing of him beyond the hot, sensual glide of his flesh over hers. His hands tightened almost painfully on her shoulders as her response swept through him. She felt him try and fail to control the urgency driving him, felt his kiss go in a single instant from tender to devouring. The unbridled strength of his arms should have been painful to her, but she was straining against him just as harshly, her body burning with demands.

When Gabe pulled his mouth from hers, Joy protested with an inarticulate, throaty sound. He laughed shakily and watched her with hungry green eyes.

"If I don't slow down," he said, his voice almost harsh, "I'm going to hurt you. I'd never forgive myself for that. It's been so long for you. And—" His breath caught as discovery raced through him, illuminating a part of his inner maze that he had never known. He kissed her with an aching hunger that was new. "In all the ways that matter," he said huskily, "it's been just as long for me."

Joy arched into Gabe's kiss, wanting to be closer to him, wanting nothing between them but the endless, passionate present. Her fingers moved futilely over the mesh of the body-covering underwear Gabe wore. No matter how she probed, she couldn't feel the smooth heat of his naked skin or the rough silk of the hair that she knew curled across his chest. She had loved playing with that hair, had teased him and tantalized him mercilessly, using the tip of her tongue to comb through the dense mat to the tiny nipples hiding beneath. She wanted to do that again, to know again every texture of him, every taste, everything.

"Are you going to take off that damned underwear," she asked huskily, "or am I going to get out my pocketknife?"

"Funny, I was just thinking of making you the same offer," he said, his eyes black except for the brilliant rim of green circling the enlarged pupil.

Joy started to ask Gabe what he was waiting for, but the clean line of his lips distracted her. She stood on tiptoe and traced his mouth with the moist tip of her tongue. His fingers kneaded hungrily down her back and hips, pressing her against his body, letting her feel the hard length of him. She responded with a sinuous movement of her hips that made his breath come out in a deep groan of need.

"I want to kiss you like this," whispered Joy, tracing his lips again, nibbling, "everywhere."

He threaded one hand into her short, silky hair and pulled her head back until she was arched like a bow, her thighs taut against his. She smiled and moved slowly against him, watching the need that made his face tight, dark, exciting. His hand ran urgently down her body in the instant before his mouth closed over hers, stifling her gasp of pleasure as his fingers found and caressed the heat between her legs. His tongue thrust into her until she had no room even for breath. With tiny, teasing nips, his teeth tormented her soft mouth while his palm cupped her intimately, hungrily, and he groaned when he sensed the welcome waiting for him.

A shudder ripped through Gabe as he knew again the overwhelming need to sink into Joy, transforming her, loving her so perfectly that she would never again look toward another man. With an effort of will that left him aching, he stepped back from her and began stripping off the maddening clothes that kept her flesh from his touch. Yet even when she was naked he simply looked at her, almost afraid, for he hadn't known he could want anything as much as he wanted Joy.

"Gabriel?" she asked, her voice like his eyes, almost afraid, for he was shaking as he looked at her.

He closed his eyes. "Get in the shower," he said, his lips thinned with the effort of controlling himself.

"But—"

"*Go*. Or I'll take you right here, right now, on the floor, because I've never wanted anything so much, even my own life when it was hanging by a thread." His eyes opened hot and green. "Do you understand?" he asked violently.

He saw the wild blaze of response in her, felt her hands touching him, seeking him, shaping his hot, rigid flesh in a caress that made the air hiss out from between his clenched teeth.

"Joy—" he grated. "I meant it!"

"Good," she said, her voice shaking as badly as her hands. She tugged at the mesh underwear separating her from Gabe, stripping it from his powerful body. "I want it like that. I want to watch you take me and know that you've never wanted anything more than you want me now!"

Gabe stripped off the last of his clothing with careless strength, ripping the tough mesh and taking Joy down to the floor in the same continuous motion. She moved sensually beneath him, opening herself to him without restraint, watching him want her.

He tried to stop, to ask her if this was what she really wanted, but the hungry softness of her parted legs brushed against him, searing him with a promise of pleasure so great it was almost overwhelming. With a groan he slid into her and then cried out with the sweet agony of being alive within her again. The liquid heat of her body enclosed him tightly, completely, and the tiny cries she made as she felt him once again inside her were like crystals glittering in darkness. He felt the instant, deep ripples of her ecstasy tug at him and knew that she had wanted him as unbearably as he had wanted her. The discovery exploded through him, bringing heat and a release so great he could only arch against her sweet, clinging body, pouring himself into her as she cried out his name.

For long moments there was no sound but their ragged breathing as Gabe rested his head on Joy's breast and felt the world slowly re-form around him once again.

And then he realized that he had not protected her. He swore painfully, savagely.

"What's wrong?" she asked, her gray eyes searching his.

"I didn't protect you," he said. "It's the past all over again. I get close to you and nothing else is real, especially tomorrow."

Joy smiled crookedly. "Don't worry Gabe," she said, kissing him lightly. "I know the risks of sleeping with a man like you."

"What's that supposed to mean?" he asked, rolling aside so that he could see her face clearly. He saw the unspoken protest that tightened her lips when he left her body. And then he saw the smooth mask of Dr. Anderson descend, veiling the vivid sensuality of Joy.

"It means I'm not nineteen anymore," she said, standing gracefully as she spoke, walking into the kitchen. "This time I'm an adult. I know that love is a figment of human imagination rather than a fact of human relations. I'm not trapped in my innocence. And neither are you."

Gabe rose to his feet and followed silently. Joy went to the bathroom and turned on the shower that loomed above the old-fashioned bathtub. She looked over her shoulder, holding out her hand to him. He took her slender fingers and looked at them wonderingly, hardly able to believe that it was flesh rather than flames caressing his palm. He stepped into the bathtub and pulled the curtain in place, shutting out the world.

"But if you're pregnant—" he began, only to be cut off.

"It's not your problem, so don't worry about it," she said matter-of-factly, stepping into the warm spray.

In silence he took the soap from her hands and began creating a rich lather which he smoothed over her body. He felt subtly off-balance, as though he had been climbing a talus slope and suddenly sensed it quivering on the brink of landslide.

"You can't believe that," Gabe said slowly, caressing and cleansing Joy at the same time.

The feel of his hands sliding over her made Joy's breath catch and her eyes widen in surprise. A few moments ago completion had cascaded hotly through her; yet even as she denied the possibility of renewed desire, she could feel tension gathering in her breasts, in her body, heat coiling tightly, hungry for release. She saw Gabe's eyes watching the sudden, hard rise of her nipples, saw his slanting smile, saw the renewed heat of his blood in the male flesh stirring against her thigh.

"Listen to me," Joy say huskily, taking the soap from Gabe's hands and bathing him in return with rich lather. "When the sequel has been written, you'll leave. I accept that, Gabriel. That's the only truth, the only possibility that matters. No injured innocence, no responsibilities to anyone but yourself. It will be the same for me, I promise you. No past for us, no future. Just the hot, endless *now*."

"But—" began Gabe grimly, not liking Joy's summary of the past. Or the present and future, for that matter.

Before he could say anymore, Joy's fingers worked through the thick hair on his chest, teasing sensitive nipples, sending a shudder through his powerful body. Her small hands followed the black wedge of hair down to the point where it became a dark, soft line defining the center of his body. She followed the line until it flared out to define another aspect of his masculinity. Her fingers tangled in hair that was even longer, thicker, and his breath came out in a groan as she cupped him in her palm, savoring his very different flesh.

"I love your body, Gabe," she whispered as she caressed him. "So different from mine. So alive."

Her hands shifted upward slowly until she captured the blunt insistence of his desire. She felt a fierce pleasure as he became even harder beneath her sensual exploration.

"There are no ties, no traps," she breathed, stepping back, letting fresh water rinse completely over him, sending dissolving sheets of lather sliding down to the drain. "That's the past," she said, flicking the spent lather with her toe, "and there is no future." Her mouth brushed over his chest, searching through dark hair until she found the tiny, hard thrust of his nipple. "There is only now, Gabriel," she murmured, raking her teeth lightly over him, feeling the instant response in the flesh she held between her hands. "Let's make it last forever."

Her husky whisper was like her tongue—maddening, caressing every bit of him as her arms slid down his body until the hot water beat unimpeded against his back. He saw the flash of her smile against his dark hair, felt the sweet sting of her teeth testing the flexed muscles of his thigh. He knew he should stop her, knew they should talk; but when her soft, hungry mouth closed over him he could not think at all.

A shock wave of desire ripped through him. All the heat and power of his blood rushed into the flesh she was caressing so intimately. His body tensed until he could have been carved of stone. He endured the sweet agony for as long as he could before he called to her. She did not hear. She was lost to everything but the wild pleasure of loving him, and the taste and heat of him melting through her.

With a hoarse sound Gabe pulled Joy up his body and wrapped her tightly within his arms.

"Turn off the shower," he said, bending over, catching her erect nipple between his teeth as the water beat hotly over his head.

Blindly Joy reach around Gabe to find the faucets. When they eluded her, she gave up and returned her hands to the infinitely more rewarding territory of his body.

"To hell with it," muttered Gabe.

He pushed aside the shower curtain, pulled her out after him and yanked the curtain closed against the rushing water.

"The only thing I want to drown in is you," he said, lifting her into his arms.

Gabe put Joy on her bed and looked at her. Simply looked at her. Her body was smooth and creamy against the textured mauve of the bedspread. Desire flushed her skin, darkened her eyes, pulsed through her softness. He saw it, all of it, and it made fire burn within him.

"Do you remember the first time we made love?" he asked, running his fingertips from her lips to the aching peaks of her breasts.

"Yes," she said tightly, twisting against him, and neither one of them could have said whether she had answered his question or had encouraged a more satisfying touch than his teasing fingertips were giving her.

"So do I. Awake. Asleep. Dying. It doesn't matter. *I remember.* Do you know what that kind of remembering can do to a man?" he asked. His voice was soft, hot, like his tongue tracing her lips.

"N-no," she said raggedly, watching him with eyes that were almost black.

"I'll show you," he whispered. "So when I'm shaking with memories I'll know that you'll be shaking, too. You'll remember me. Always."

She saw the jade fire of his eyes, and hunger raced through her with each heartbeat. He came down on the bed beside her, not touching her, memorizing her with a hungry glance that went from her honey-colored hair to the trim nails of her feet. A moment later his shoulders blocked out the room as he bent over her, kissing her temples, tracing the spiral of her ear, thrusting languidly into the sensitive opening. Against the chill of the water drying on her skin, his textured heat was exquisite. She turned toward him, wanting him, needing to feel the hard thrust of his desire between her hands, in her body. He laughed softly as he evaded her by lifting her in his arms.

"No, sweet Joy," said Gabe, turning her deftly and placing her on her stomach, smiling down at her. "That's no way to make it last forever."

"Gabe—"

"Shhh," he murmured, running the ball of his thumb all the way down her spine in a loving movement that didn't end until he had curved down to find the incredible softness concealed within her body. He listened to the ragged intake of her breath and smiled again, a smile as slow and sensual as the caress tracing her hidden flesh. "I'm going to explore you, Joy," he said, bending down, kissing her shoulder, her spine, the delicate inward curve of her waist. "I'm going to know each softness, each golden curve, each beautiful peak and hidden valley."

As Gabe spoke, his hand moved slowly between her legs, spreading a sweet fire that made Joy want to roll onto her back and pull him into her arms, into her body. But when she tried, he just laughed deep in his throat and moved smoothly over her, covering her, pinning her in place with her arms stretched above her head and his fingers entwined with hers. The roughness of his hair caressed her back and the heat of him lay snugly between the shadow crease of her legs. She moved almost helplessly against him, wanting him, unable to touch him. Nor was he touching her. Not the way she wanted to be touched. Her breasts ached for his hands, his mouth; she cried out her need to be filled by him.

"It's like being caught in Small Favors again, isn't it?" he asked huskily, biting the nape of Joy's neck deliberately, delicately. "You can't touch me the way you want to, yet we're close," he said, moving his hips sinuously, "so *close*."

"No," she said raggedly. "This is worse than Small Favors. At least in the tunnel I could feel you against my breasts, my—"

Her words were lost in a gasp as he swiftly turned her over. He pinned her again in exactly the same way, settling over her. "Better?" he murmured, rubbing his body over hers, letting her feel his power, feeling her softness in return.

The long caress of his muscular body swept through her, making her tremble. She felt the heat coursing through her own flesh and wondered if he could feel it, too. She ached for him and he teased her with every look, every breath, the hot length of his desire moving intimately between their bodies. Her eyes closed as she moved helplessly beneath him, wanting him, his name coming as a moan from her flushed lips.

His laughter was expressed more as subtle movements of his body than as sound, and she moved again beneath him, trying to incite him to more than the exquisite torment of being so close and yet so far away from the consummation that called to her. She felt as though she were suspended endlessly in a hot, sensual grip that refused to give her the release she craved.

"This is much worse than Small Favors," she said, eyes closed, moving beneath him as though she were trying to force her way through a constricting passage within Lost River Cave's velvet darkness.

"Are you sure?" he murmured. "In Small Favors, I couldn't do this."

She felt his mouth take her breast in a fierce and tender suckling that made pleasure run through her like a hidden river that had neither beginning nor end, only the powerful, rushing present. She cried out Gabe's name and her need and felt something stronger than laughter shuddering through his body. He shifted slightly, rewarding her sensual struggle with enough freedom to move her legs until they were wrapped tightly around his hips.

"Better?" he asked again, stretching her arms above her head until her nipples were tight and quivering beneath his skillful tongue. The hard, sensual tugging of his mouth made her cry out in the same rhythms as his caress. She moved convulsively, using every bit of her strength, trying to capture the hot thrust of his desire within her body.

"Not yet, sweet Joy," he muttered. "You only think you want me."

"Gabe," she said brokenly, straining against him, "I'm going crazy. It's like my dreams, my nightmares, when I could do everything but feel you alive inside me."

His body trembled. "You had them, too?" he asked huskily.

"Yes! Awake, asleep—"

"Dying," he said against her lips. His tongue licked into her mouth in a rhythm that turned her bones to currents of desire.

"Ah, God," she sighed raggedly. "You're destroying me."

"No," he countered softly, sliding down her body, his mouth hot and damp and infinitely hungry. "I'm exploring you. There's a difference. All the difference in the world."

She felt him shift his weight, moving sensually over her skin, tugging at her with his mouth until tiny cries rippled out of her. He slowly explored the soft skin of her stomach and the sweet smoothness of her inner thighs; then she felt her heart stop, only to start again with a shudder as his explorations became unbearably intimate.

"A warm world opening for me. My God," he said raggedly, nuzzling against her incredible softness, tasting her, loving her as he had never loved another woman, "how did I ever leave you?"

Joy didn't answer. She couldn't. She could only twist sinuously against his hot, sweet caresses, forgetting the past and the future and even the present, succumbing wholly to Gabe's consuming sensuality. The golden pleasure gathered, coiling within her like a river caught within dissolving stone, demanding release. She called his name again, trying to tell him to come to her, but her body rushed ahead, knowing again the shivering, shimmering release that only this man had ever discovered within her.

"Gabe," she said raggedly, her fingers kneading through his hair to the hot scalp beneath. "I—"

And still he caressed her, stroked her, cherished her with exquisitely gentle teeth and tongue, each touch consuming her, creating her, discovering new levels of her passion.

"Oh, God, Gabe," she moaned. "Don't. I can't bear it."

"Yes, you can," he said, his voice husky and deep, words shivering against her violently sensitive flesh. "I promised it would last forever. It will."

He held her in loving torment until she was wild and crying his name with every broken breath. Only then did he come to her, moving inside her, calling to her, inciting her with dark words and darker caresses until her body tightened around him. She would have screamed his name and her own unbearable ecstasy if his mouth hadn't been as deeply joined with hers as his body was. The first waves of her seething, incandescent release washed over both of them, and his hoarse cry of discovery mingled with hers as they shared an ecstasy that kept every promise he had made.

It was unbearably good and it lasted forever. For both of them.

Chapter 11

Did you really find a new cave? Is it bigger than the old one? Can I see it?"

Kati's high young voice bubbled over with an eagerness that made Gabe smile. He had felt the same way when he was young and the whole world was one constantly unfolding miracle to be explored. He didn't know when that had changed for him, when he had become weary rather than excited, driven rather than lured. He did know the exact instant when he had once more felt a wild, incredible excitement at being alive—just a few hours ago, when he had first felt Joy soften and run like honey in his hands.

"I want to see the new cave, too!" said Laura Childer, dancing in place impatiently near the Jeep.

Susan Childer laughed and affectionately ruffled her daughter's dark hair. "The last time you talked Joyce into a cave expedition, you got twelve steps down below the en-

trance and decided to have a picnic up top with me instead."

"That was a long time ago," said Laura solemnly. "I'm
much older now."

"Mmm," said Susan, nodding sagely. "A whole five
months."

Joy spoke quickly, heading off the objections that she saw
clouding Laura's face. "No one has really been in the new
room, Laura. We just found it. And it looks like it will be
kind of a rough trip getting there."

"Does that mean I can't go?" asked Kati.

Joy hesitated. "Probably not, punkin. The only way into
the room so far is to rappel down a rope."

Frowning, Kati drew patterns in the dust with her toe.
"Worse than going into the old cave?"

"Uh-huh," said Joy. "Lots."

Kati sighed deeply. "Okay. But I still think I could do it.
I mean, I got born without any help," she said with a young
child's tangential logic, "so I've got to be good enough to
climb down a silly old rope."

Susan laughed again and ruffled Kati's flaming hair with
the same gesture of affection she had given her daughter.
"That's it, Kati. You tell 'em."

"Born without help?" said Gabe, puzzled.

Joy stiffened, but it was too late. Susan was already talking, telling one of her favorite stories.

"You mean you've been here almost two weeks and Kati
hasn't told you?" asked Susan in mock horror.

"Not a word," said Gabe, smiling with the easy charm of
a man who has made his living meeting new people and
drawing information from them.

"We'd better get—" began Joy.

It didn't work. Susan just kept talking.

"Kati is a real pioneer kid, just like in the old days," said Susan, putting her arm around Kati's shoulder and giving the girl a hug. "She was born in the desert a few miles from here. Literally."

Joy saw the color leave Gabe's face and stifled a groan. She was reluctant to have Gabe know the extent of her foolishness six years ago. She hadn't meant to have Kati on the side of the road. It had just turned out that way.

"What?" Gabe asked softly, his lips barely moving.

"Yeah." The older woman smiled wryly. "That was Fish's reaction. He came driving up here like a madman with Joyce and a squalling little scrap of life in the front seat. Poor man was white as salt—and him a field medic for the army! All his kids had been born in a hospital," continued Susan with a chuckle. "I still tease him about it. Just because there was blood here and there, he thought he was going to lose both of them. He didn't know that childbirth isn't Mother Nature's tidiest moment." Smiling, Susan shook her head at Fish's naïveté. "I knew better. All my kids were born right here, with my husband right by my side."

Kati smiled proudly up at Gabe. "Mommy and me are a team."

"Yeah," said Susan, slanting Joy a laughing glance. "Your mom does the work and you take the credit."

Gabe knew that he should smile politely or say something, anything, but he couldn't. He felt off-balance, as he had in the instants when his feet slipped on the water-smoothed pitch leading down into Gotcha. Only there was no safety rope belaying him now, nothing to catch him when he lost his balance and fell. And he was falling. The idea of

Joy giving birth to his child in the desert appalled him. He wanted to know what had happened, why she hadn't been in the hospital with doctors and nurses at hand if something went wrong.

But he couldn't ask Joy right now, no matter how much he wanted to know. Her embarrassment was as clear as the rose color staining her cheekbones. Questioning her would just make it worse. Besides, Gabe didn't trust himself not to reveal just how immediately the answers concerned him, and he had given Joy his word that he wouldn't tell Kati he was her father.

"Hold it," said Susan as Kati prepared to climb into the Jeep with Gabe and her mother. "I promised you and Laura some cookies. Run and get them, kids."

With small squeals of anticipation, the two girls pelted up the porch and into the weathered ranch house. As soon as the door slammed behind them, Susan turned toward Joy.

"I know you miss Kati when she isn't with you," said Susan quickly, "but Laura and I would very much like to have Kati stay with us."

"For the weekend?" asked Joy.

"For as long as you'd let her." Susan's mouth turned down at the corners. "Laura knows Kati will be leaving in a few weeks." The older woman smiled sadly. "So do I. We'd like to spend as much time with her as we can. And I know how hard it is for you trying to juggle Kati and all the underground work that has to be done before Lost River is closed. I thought that maybe you wouldn't mind if we sort of kidnapped her for a while after school is out."

The two girls burst from the house and leaped hand in hand down to the dusty yard.

"Think about it," said Susan quietly, then turned to greet both girls with open arms and a big smile. "Who brought one for me?" she asked.

Kati and Laura each handed over a cookie to Susan.

"What about Gabe and Joyce?" asked Susan.

Two more cookies changed hands. Gabe managed a smile at Kati as he took his, but it was one of the most difficult things he had had to do in his life. He kept thinking about Joy and the desert and all the things that could go wrong during childbirth.

I should have been with her.

Is she pregnant even now? If she is, where will she be when she gives birth?

Where will I be?

The thoughts came at Gabe like rocks careening down the face of a Peruvian cliff. And like the cliff, there was no cover for him, no place to hide, no way to deflect the battering tide.

Had she learned to protect herself? Had she simply cut the possibility of pregnancy from her life? Or did she know that now was a safe time for her, that she could be my lover for a few days and not conceive a child? Or had she wanted me so much that she had taken the risk without thinking?

That was the way it had been for me.

There were no answers to the pouring questions. On the way to the Childer ranch Gabe had tried to talk again with Joy about conception. He had promised to protect her in the future when they made love.

And she had told him that if he came to her wearing anything but his own skin she would refuse him.

Why?

Another question whose only answer was silence and futile speculation. The Joy of today was not the Joy of six years ago. She gave her body to him, yes. But the rest of her was like Lost River Cave, moments of glittering illumination against a backdrop of mystery as deep as time. It wasn't that Joy hid. It was that she didn't reveal.

Joy felt Gabe watching her as she drove the Jeep back to Cottonwood Wells. She fielded Kati's chatter with only half her mind. Joy knew that Gabe had been shocked to learn that Kati hadn't been born under the usual circumstances. Wryly, Joy conceded that she had been a little shocked herself in the beginning, when she had had time and energy and emotion left over for anything but the imperatives of giving birth. She also knew that Gabe would question her about it as soon as they were alone. She was grateful that he was waiting to satisfy his curiosity; six years ago he wouldn't have let anything get in the way of his questions. He had been rather ruthless, then. He still was now. He simply was more selective in applying that ruthlessness.

"Can Laura stay this weekend?" asked Kati eagerly. "You can pick us up after school and then you can take us to the bus on Monday. Then I can go home with her for the last week of school," continued Kati quickly, earnestly, reciting the latest in the two girls' continuing attempts to persuade both mothers that they should either have two daughters at a time, or none. "Then you won't have to get me to the bus stop all the time, and you'll have lots and lots of time to go caving, too. 'Specially since I can't go with you anyway," she finished triumphantly. "Don't you think that's a great idea, Gabe?" she asked innocently, turning to him with a bright smile.

"I think that you're asking the wrong person," Joy pointed out.

"But—" objected Kati.

"Your mother's right," said Gabe quietly. "It's not fair for you to try to get someone else to say yes for her."

Kati gave Gabe a very disappointed look out of big gray eyes. "You're no fun."

He smiled and shook his head slowly at her. "Won't work, punkin," he said, tapping the golden freckles on her nose with a gentle fingertip. "I was a kid once, too. I know all the ways to wheedle a yes out of parents."

Kati looked up at the man beside her in flat disbelief. "You were a kid?"

"Sure was."

"Really? Did you have a mother and father and everything?"

Gabe managed not to wince or look at Joy. "Yes. And a brother, too."

"Did you get to live with him all the time?"

"Whether we liked it or not," said Gabe, smiling crookedly, remembering the times when he and his brother had fought.

"Gee, were you ever lucky. I want a sister but Mommy says they don't grow on trees."

With difficulty Gabe kept a straight face. "That's true," he murmured.

"I used to think they did," admitted Kati. "Every morning I'd get up and run out and look at the big trees in front of the house." She sighed. "Just leaves. Lots and lots of leaves. Even on Christmas morning."

"Tell you what, punkin," said Joy, her voice tight, aching, hearing her own endless longing for a sister or a brother in her daughter's voice. "I'll call Susan and we'll work something out about Laura. Okay?"

"Okay! When? Could we have a cookout when Laura comes over? Will Fish bring his guitar and Gravy-bear sing?" She fairly bounced with excitement as she turned to Gabe. "Do you sing?"

"Not for a long time," admitted Gabe.

"Oh." Kati's face fell.

"For you, I'll sing."

"Oh, goody!" she said, her face lighting up with a smile that was very like her mother's. "It'll be so much fun! We'll have a fire and marshmallows and ketchup—"

"Ketchup?" asked Gabe, mildly horrified.

"Yeah. You know, for the hot dogs."

"Oh."

"And we'll stay up late and see the Glitter River and sing," continued Kati enthusiastically, listing her favorite parts of a cookout.

Gabe was almost afraid to ask, but in the end curiosity got the better of him. "Glitter River?"

"Yeah. That's the, uh, the—I forget the name. Mommy?"

"Milky Way, punkin."

"Milky Way," repeated Kati seriously. "It's not really milk, you know," she informed Gabe. "It's stars. Lots and lots of stars. Mommy showed me a book with lots of pictures. I want to go there when I grow up."

"To the stars?" asked Gabe.

"Uh-huh."

Gabe was shocked to feel the emotion tightening his throat, making it impossible to talk as he heard echoes of his own childhood in his daughter's eager voice. He, too, had wanted to go to the stars when he was Kati's age. He hadn't done it, but he had done the next best thing. He had seen as much of the earth as he could. It had been there for his taking, for his exploring, for his unending delight. He had drunk the wonder of earth's beauties until he had overflowed, then he had shared what he could in words; and for a time it had been enough.

But no matter how various, how extraordinary, how mysterious, the wonders of the world could no longer fill the emptiness he sensed growing inside himself. Yet the earth would always call to him, and he knew it. He could no more envision a life without exploration and discovery than he could envision being dead.

Glitter River.

Yes—and each possibility was a separate piece of shining beauty. How odd that it had taken a child to sum up his own feelings toward life and living.

And how chilling to realize that this child might slowly, unknowingly, become as empty as he had been, an emptiness he was only now beginning to measure as it was filled by Joy. He didn't want that emptiness for his daughter. He wanted life to be one magnificent glitter river, possibilities cascading endlessly into her outstretched hands.

For the first time Gabe sensed just a part of the agony that had made Joy pray that Kati would find life more gentle with her dreams than Joy had. Yet there was no guarantee that life would be kind to his child. The realization gave Gabe a feeling of helplessness that was horrifying, for he knew that he could not live Kati's life for her, could not choose for her from among the men who would come to taste her sweetness. He could only pray silently that she chose a better man than her father.

The prayer was no more comforting than Joy's had been.

Gabe finished the ride to Cottonwood Wells in a brooding silence that made Joy look at him almost apprehensively from time to time. She didn't know what Gabe's thoughts were. She did know that they were rubbing him raw as surely as Small Favors had, thoughts squeezing him, bruising him, forcing him to inch painfully forward into the unknown.

As the Jeep pulled up into the circle of cottages, Davy came out to greet everyone with a triumphant smile. "Fish's wife is on the way out with supplies. Said she'd play War with Kati while we go caving."

"I'll cook dinner tonight," said Gabe and Joy simultaneously. Then they looked at each other and laughed.

"Enlightened self-interest at work," said Gabe in a low voice.

Joy gave him a smile and a sideways look that made him catch his breath at the memories. In that instant he realized how little she smiled now compared to six years ago. The thought that he might have taken her laughter as well as her innocence was as painful to Gabe as the knowledge that he could not save his daughter from life's less pleasant surprises. He could only watch and pray and love.

"I'll clean up," said Davy quickly. "I hate cooking," he added to no one in particular.

"Really?" said Gabe, his dark brows lifting sardonically. "I thought it was just that everything you touched turned to—" he looked hastily at Kati "—er, *mulch*."

"Oh, but Kati loves my cooking, don't you?" Davy asked, lifting the little girl out of the Jeep and tossing her gently toward the sky.

"You cook just like a Gravy-bear," said Kati, laughing and tugging at Davy's blond hair.

"I think that child has a career as a diplomat," said Gabe.

"Stabbed!" said Davy, clutching his breast with one hand and supporting Kati in the crook of his other arm. "By my own sweet little girl, too."

"Where's the blood? Show me!" Kati giggled and pulled at the top of Davy's T-shirt until she could peer inside. "Yetch! Hair! Gravy-bear is hairy, Gravy-bear is hairy," she sing-songed as he carried her up the porch and into the house.

Gabe laughed softly, amazed by Kati's unending energy and acceptance of life. He looked over at Joy. "That's a fine little girl you've raised," he said. "She's so open. So alive."

Joy looked at Gabe with transparent gray eyes, unable to speak. She couldn't prevent the fine, sudden shimmer of tears as his words sank into her, dissolving away years of hidden fear, secret doubts. There had been so many days when she had wondered if she were doing the right thing by raising Kati alone, so many nights when she had been too tired or busy to give Kati all the time she deserved.

"Thank you," whispered Joy. "There are times when I feel I've done everything wrong as a parent."

Gabe looked into her eyes and saw the hesitations, the doubts, the relentless pressures of raising a child alone. He framed Joy's face with his hands and bent low, brushing his lips over her damp eyelashes.

"You've loved her," whispered Gabe. "No child can ask more than that."

Joy's tears felt hot on his lips. He sensed the tremor that went through her. She turned her face up to him and he took her mouth very gently, felt her breath sighing into his mouth as her hands opened against his chest.

"Dr. Anderson, I think we should try—" The front door slammed and Davy's voice stopped at the same instant.

Gabe nestled Joy against his body as he turned her face into his chest, concealing her tears. He looked at Davy's shocked face.

"We don't always fight," Gabe said quietly. "Sometimes we make up."

Davy looked from the hard-faced older man to the woman held so protectively against his chest. "Uh, yeah. Looks like this is one of those times." Davy ran his hand through his thick thatch of blond hair and sighed. "Guess I better get lost."

"No problem," said Gabe smoothly. "Just wanted you to know the way things are." With barely a pause he added, "I'll bet Maggie could use some help getting lunch ready."

"Maggie," said Davy.

"Yes. Maggie. If you're interested. If not, that's okay, too," said Gabe, shrugging. "She's nobody's fool. She'll find someone else."

Davy met Gabe's hard green glance for another moment, then smiled crookedly. "Funny. In the two years I've known her, she never mentioned your name."

Both men knew that Davy wasn't talking about Maggie. Gabe didn't answer. He simply continued to hold Joy against his chest, caressing her hair gently with his hand, shielding her from any eyes but his own.

Davy hesitated, then shrugged. "Looks like a good time to make sandwiches." He smiled suddenly. "If you see Dr. Anderson, would you ask her if we're going to take on Joy's Castle after lunch?"

"Yes," said Joy, her voice muffled against Gabe's chest. She shook her head and started laughing helplessly. "My God," she said, meeting Gabe's amused, gentle glance, "I feel like a teenager caught on the front porch swing!"

Davy smiled slightly. "You look like one, too. Didn't know you could blush. Or is that sunburn on the back of your neck?" he gibed.

Joy groaned and buried her face against Gabe's chest. She didn't lift her head again until the sound of Davy's laughter had faded behind the noise of Maggie's creaky cabin door opening and closing. Joy put her arms around Gabe and absorbed the sweetness of being held by him beneath the brilliant desert sun. She didn't care that Kati or Fish or Maggie might appear at any moment. She needed Gabe right now, needed his strength and his concern, his gentle, protective hug. It had been so long since anyone had held her, simply held her, giving to her rather than asking something of her.

Silently Gabe bent his head until he could rest his cheek against Joy's sun-streaked hair. He inhaled deeply, feeling as though he was breathing her into his very soul and she was a radiant light filling him. He couldn't remember the last time he had held a woman with no expectation of immediately making love to her. Then he realized that he had never held a woman like this, ever, absorbing her as though she were life itself.

"Mommy," said Kati, coming out onto the porch, "when are you going to call Susan?"

Reluctantly Gabe loosened his arms enough to allow Joy to turn and face their daughter.

"Soon, punkin," said Joy, leaning against Gabe, making no effort to stand beyond the circle of his arms.

Kati looked curiously from her mother to the tall man who held her. "Why were you hugging Gabe?"

"Because I like him," said Joy. She had never evaded Kati's questions in the past, no matter how difficult they had been to answer. She wouldn't evade them now.

"Don't you like Gravy-bear and Fish?" asked Kati.

"Of course I do. Very much."

"But you don't hug them."

"They aren't Gabe," said Joy simply.

Kati thought that over for a moment, her gray eyes as serious as her mother's. Then the little girl nodded, accepting both the explanation and the emotional logic beneath it. "When's lunch?"

Joy breathed a sigh of relief. "On to the really important things in life," she said so softly that only Gabe could hear.

"Like food?" he asked equally softly.

"Like food." She smiled at her daughter. "Maggie's fixing sandwiches right now."

"Oh boy! Suppose she's finished yet?"

"Suppose you could help her?" countered Joy.

Kati sighed. Fixing tacos was fun. Fixing sandwiches was work. On the other hand, she was very hungry. "I'll ask," said Kati, walking toward Maggie's cottage with about one third normal speed and enthusiasm.

Together Gabe and Joy walked through the cottage to the backyard, where a long clothesline was hung with freshly washed caving gear. As they took down the dry, sun-fragrant clothes, Gabe watched Joy as though he were seeing her for the first time.

"Tell me about Kati's birth," he said quietly.

Joy's hands hesitated over a piece of mesh underwear for just an instant before going on to lift the clothespins. "It was a classic case of too much too soon and then too little too late,'' she said.

Gabe stood with his arms out while Joy added a piece of clothing to the growing pile he carried.

''I was living with the Childers,'' she said.

''Were they friends of your parents?'' asked Gabe.

''No. Susan had advertised for live-in help, and after my parents died I had to have a place to live. The job was perfect. Room and board, enough time to study and enough pocket money to pay for gas.''

''Didn't your parents leave you anything?'' asked Gabe, startled. ''Insurance money or—anything?'' He had known Joy's parents weren't wealthy, but it hadn't occurred to him that she had been left without any money at all.

''They left memories,'' said Joy, unclipping another piece of clothing and handing it to him. ''Good memories.''

Gabe said nothing, for he had just realized that Joy had been penniless when she had rejected the check he had left for her. ''How did you manage to pay for everything?''

''The same way everyone else does,'' said Joy with a shrug. ''I worked two jobs. The second one was as a research assistant to several professors in the geology department.''

''Was the pregnancy—difficult?''

''The doctor called me his prize patient. Young, strong and flexible. Cave crawling keeps you in good shape. I was fine, physically.''

Gabe didn't ask about Joy's mental health. He didn't have to. He could imagine how difficult it had been for her to go through with her pregnancy in the face of her parents' death, his own total absence and the necessity of working two jobs while still going to school.

"What happened?" he asked finally. "Why was Kati born in the desert?"

Joy sighed and piled more dry clothes in Gabe's arms. "I'd had false labor pains for several days. I'd get halfway to town and the contractions would stop. Then I'd turn around and go back to the Childer ranch. I didn't want to go into the hospital any sooner than I had to."

"Money?" he asked.

She shrugged. "So the next time the contractions came, I just ignored them and kept working. All the men were out in the field. A tractor had broken down, or something, and Susan was already overdue with Laura." Joy pulled the last of the clothes off the line and folded them over her own arms. "Anyway, there was a lot to do around the ranch for everyone, and I just kept doing it. By the time I realized that my body wasn't fooling around anymore, it was too late. There wasn't enough time to get to town."

"What did you do?"

"The only thing I could. I pulled the Jeep over to the side of the road, dragged a bedroll out of the back, and—" She shrugged, trying not to remember how frightened she had been, and how alone.

"You must have been terrified," said Gabe, his voice raw as he imagined a scared nineteen-year-old giving birth alone in the desert.

"At first. Later on there wasn't any time for fear," she smiled wryly, hoping to lighten the moment. "Birth isn't exactly a voluntary process. Toward the end I was pretty much along for the ride."

Gabe almost couldn't force out the words. Yet he had to know. "Were you alone the whole time?"

Joy glanced up. The pain and regret in Gabe's eyes made her wish the subject had never come up. "No," she said quickly, touching his upper arm. "Fish came along. It was all right after that. He had had some emergency medical training, and he was very kind, very gentle with me. He knew how to help. Kati wasn't hurt at all. That's what really had terrified me—that something would go wrong and I wouldn't know what to do for her."

"When did Fish get there?" asked Gabe, each word distinct, harsh.

"I don't know. One moment I was alone and hurting and scared to death, and the next moment he was there, reassuring me. It was easier after that. Kati was born very quickly." The clenched strength of Gabe's muscles beneath Joy's fingers was almost frightening. He looked like a man who had never smiled and never would. "Gabriel don't. It wasn't your fault."

And even as Joy spoke she realized that it was true.

For a long time she had blamed him for leaving her to bear Kati alone. But it hadn't been his fault, not really. She had wanted his lovemaking, demanded it, and had not thought beyond the moment when he would move inside her. Yet she hardly had been stupid or uninformed as to the mechanics of conception and contraception. She simply had not cared. She had assumed childlishly that everything would turn out all right, that all she had to do was love this man and everything would work out in the end.

It had. But not the way she had expected. Was that Gabe's fault? Could she blame him any longer for her own willful naïveté and the fact that her parents had died so soon after he left her?

"Gabe, listen to me," she said urgently, hating to see the bleakness that shadowed his jade eyes. Once the sight of his suffering would have given her a vindictive pleasure. She didn't feel that way any longer. His pain was her own. It was also unnecessary, destructive. "I don't blame you anymore. I was smart enough to know better, but I didn't want to know anything except you. I wanted you. Period. I didn't have a thought beyond that." She smiled crookedly. "For a certifiably bright girl, I was very stupid."

"Don't," he said hoarsely. "Don't blame yourself. I'm the one who should have known better. I never should have taken a virgin."

"You didn't 'take' anything," retorted Joy. "I gave myself as freely and—and passionately as any woman ever has."

"Oh, God, *yes*," grated Gabe, closing his eyes, remembering. "There was never anyone like you, Joy. Never. You have haunted me to the ends of the earth."

The words went through her like a flood through Lost River Cave, sweeping up the shattered debris of the past and carrying it away, opening new passages where before only possibilities had been.

"That's only fair," she whispered. "You called to me in every one of the Voices."

"You hated me," he said flatly.

Joy started to deny it, but could not. "Yes. For a time. I hated myself, too. I hated life, Gabriel. But I'm growing up. Finally. Don't hate yourself. It's not worth it. Nothing is."

Gabe tilted back his head and let the sun's fierce light wash over him, unable to meet Joy's eyes. How could he not hate himself for what he had done to her? Was that what growing up was? Knowing yourself without evasion and yet not hating yourself? Was that one of the answers he had looked for when he had asked *Why?* and heard only silence seething within himself?

At last he took a deep breath and looked again into Joy's luminous eyes.

"You said that if I had come to Lost River Cave to find forgiveness, I'd come to the wrong place," said Gabe after a long silence. "Yet you're trying very hard to forgive me."

Joy's breath came in sharply as she realized that he was right. Seeing the Gabe of today had made her understand much better the Gabe of six years ago—and herself. She had participated in the passionate recklessness. And she had paid.

"Are you forgiving yourself, too?" he asked softly. "Do you still believe you were a fool to give yourself to love? To me?"

"I—I don't know," she admitted. "I didn't even know that I no longer blamed you."

"Joy," he whispered, bending over her, his arms full of sun-drenched clothes. "Kiss me. Please. I want to know what forgiveness tastes like. Then maybe, just maybe, I'll be able to forgive myself, too."

She stood on tiptoe, her arms as full of clothes as his, touching his lips with her own. When his tongue teased the curves of her smile she sighed and opened her mouth. For a long moment she leaned against him, knowing only the sweetness of his kiss.

"Well?" she murmured, nuzzling against his lips. "What does forgiveness taste like?" she asked, teasing and very serious at the same time.

"Sunlight. Peace. And peppermint."

Joy's laughter rippled through the afternoon. Gabe watched her transformation, the pleasure so clearly revealed in her smile, her eyes as radiant as his deepest dreams. This was one memory that had not been a lie. There was nothing on earth as beautiful to him as Joy laughing.

Chapter 12

The sound of steel ringing against steel echoed painfully within Small Favors as Gabe drove a piton deep into the limestone. He drove a second steel spike in, and then a third, carefully selecting his angles so as to ensure maximum holding power. The stone was dense. It took the pitons cleanly, with no visible fracturing. Gabe knew that two pitons would have been enough for safety. It was the knowledge that Joy would be the first one dangling from the rope that had made him drive in the third metal spike. Steel carabiners snapped securely into place, anchoring the rope Joy would use to rappel down into the unexplored room that bore her name.

Gabe wrapped the climbing rope around his body, braced his feet against the side of the tunnel and heaved, doing his best to break loose one of the pitons. Nothing gave. Nothing shifted. Nothing even hinted at coming loose. He heaved again and again until he was as certain as possible that the pitons and rope would hold. He wished that Joy had agreed to have a safety rope on her, too, but understood why she had refused. A safety rope was literally more trouble that it was worth on rappel, for the two ropes tangled at the smallest opportunity, leaving a climber knotted and dangling like a fly in a spider web, unable to go up, down or sideways.

Gabe tugged again at the rope, then went up to the lip of the overhang and began feeding the rope out over the edge a few feet at a time. The rope was one hundred feet long. If it didn't find bottom, he would substitute the two hundred foot rope that Davy had carried into the cave. There were about twenty feet of rope still remaining when Gabe felt the weight of the rope taken from his hands. Below him in the darkness the free end of the rope was resting on something. Bottom, hopefully, rather than a ledge jutting over another drop.

Gabe looked out into Joy's Castle. The green glow from the light stick that Joy had thrown earlier provided eerie illumination to a huge flowstone palette that was fringed with a beautifully fluted drapery. The bottom of the formation wasn't visible. Nor was the light stick itself. There was no way to tell whether the light was on the floor of the cave itself or caught within one of the many intricate formations.

Water danced and sang invisibly, ghostly conversations rising on the air currents caused by Lost River's undiscovered waterfall. Joy's Castle was an extraordinary place, as alluring as any Gabe had ever stood on the brink of exploring. And he was stalling rather than send Joy alone into its unknown territory.

So quit spinning on your thumb, Gabe advised himself sardonically. *She's exploring with the same eminently sane safety measures you would have used. She's doing it just the way you're going to do it when it's your turn. As she pointed out, what's sauce for the gander, etcetera.*

But the thought of losing Joy to an exploring accident made Gabe realize how hollow life would be without her, and how full it had become when he was close enough to feel her laughing within his arms.

When Gabe found himself seriously considering driving in a fourth and utterly unnecessary piton, he didn't know whether to laugh or swear. Instead, he eeled backward to the wide spot in the tunnel where Joy and the other cavers waited.

"Ready," he said. In a tone that brooked no argument he added, "I cut a very short section of rope and tied it to a third piton. Put the rope on and keep it on until you're out of the tunnel and in position to rappel. When you're on your stomach, the climbing rope is on the left and the safety rope is on your right. Got it?"

Davy and Fish exchanged a quick look and waited for Dr. Anderson to tear a strip off of Gabe Venture's overbearing hide. Not that they didn't think that the rope was a good idea. They did, for they knew that the most dangerous part of this kind of descent came in the scramble off the overhang. But Joy had never taken kindly to people who told her how to do things. Suggestions, yes. Orders, no.

Joy's head snapped up. She opened her mouth to tell Gabe that she had crawled a hell of a lot more caves than he had and had survived to tell the tale. Then she saw the tension drawing his face into hard lines and knew that he was worried about her safety, not her ability. He had explored enough wild country to know that luck was sometimes more important than skill.

"All right," she said, letting out the angry breath she had drawn. "Thank you, Gabe."

Davy swore softly. "Damn, Fish. I owe you five bucks."

"What for?" asked Maggie.

"Fish bet that Dr. Anderson would let Gabe belay her into the cave and drive the pitons to hold the rope. He was right both times," explained Davy.

"So Gabe's climbed a lot of rocks and knows more about pitons than we do," said Maggie, not understanding. "So what?"

Davy made a disgusted sound. "So Fish has crawled a lot of caves, too, but Dr. Anderson doesn't let him set anchor slings or cable ladders or—" Davy shrugged. "You get the picture."

Joy heard every word. As she did, she realized that each blunt word was true. She hadn't thought about it, but Fish was right. She never trusted her life to anyone if there was any way out of it at all. She belayed other people and climbed down alone when possible. When it wasn't possible, she let Fish belay her and then she searched until she found a route where she wouldn't need help. There was no conscious thought behind her actions. It was just the way she had been since Gabe had left and her parents died.

"Fish," Joy said quietly over her shoulder, pitching her voice so that Maggie and Davy couldn't hear, "it's not that I don't trust—"

"I know," said Fish softly, cutting Joy off. "Hell, if some bastard had left me helpless by the side of the road, I wouldn't trust a soul, neither, less'n there weren't no damn choice. Hard lessons stay learnt the longest."

Gabe heard every word. He crouched against the tunnel wall, feeling as cold as the stone itself, wishing he could crawl out of his own skin, disowning himself and a past that he had never meant to be. But the past had happened whether he liked it or not. The past couldn't be changed. It couldn't be forgotten.

And it couldn't be forgiven. Not by him.

Joy felt the rigidity of Gabe's body and knew that he was hating himself. *The bastard who had left her by the side of the road.* She also knew that it hadn't been that way. Gabe hadn't set out to seduce her and then abandon her to have his baby alone in the desert. He didn't have that kind of ir-responsibility in him, even then. He had never even ap-proached that kind of cruelty. If he had known how it was going to turn out, he would have prevented it somehow, even at the cost of his own freedom. She knew that as surely as she knew that she was alive.

But did he know?

She couldn't say anything to comfort Gabe without giv-ing away to Fish who Kati's father was. She could touch Gabe, though.

"I'm going to test our lights," she said tersely.

With no more warning than that, she unplugged the leads from her helmet and Gabe's, concealing their bodies within Lost River Cave's velvet night. She took Gabe's hand and peeled away the glove until her mouth could find his palm. He stiffened, trying to pull his hand away, refusing the comfort she was offering. She hung on, cradling his hand against her cheek and lips, murmuring softly, just one voice among the many whispering through the tunnel.

After a few instants Gabe no longer tried to retreat. In-stead he pulled Joy against him with a fierce, inarticulate sound. When his lips met hers she tasted the scalding heat of a man's tears.

"Gabe," she whispered brokenly. "Don't."

His only answer was a kiss that was both hard and gentle. Then he lifted her away from his body, turned his back to the people behind him and plugged in the leads to her helmet. She saw the tears glittering in the corners of his eyes and felt as though she were being torn apart.

"Get going," he whispered huskily. "If you need me, this time I'll be within reach. I promise you."

Blindly she touched her fingers to his lips.

He kissed her fingertips. "It's all right," he murmured. "Go explore your new world, Joy. I'll be right behind you."

For a moment longer she savored the warmth of his breath on her fingers, then she pulled on her glove and began to wriggle feetfirst into the last narrow stretch of Small Favors. After a short time she heard the scuffle and scrape of Gabe following her. It wasn't long before her boots connected with the thick metal eyelets of the pitons Gabe had driven into stone.

She turned on her side and inched down the tunnel between the pitons until her hands encountered the climbing rope. She attached it to the figure-eight descender which she had snapped onto her Swiss seat. The friction of the rope passing through the figure eight would act as a brake, slowing the speed of her descent.

Once the rope was properly attached, Joy quietly cursed and wriggled until the climbing rope was passed between her legs from the front, over her right hip, diagonally across her chest and then back over her left shoulder. Only when the rope was in position for rappelling did she attach the short safety rope to the Swiss seat with a locking carabiner.

It wasn't the easiest or neatest arrangement in the world, especially in the narrow tunnel. But the short rope did ensure that if she lost her balance while negotiating the tricky transfer from the overhang to a safe rappelling position, the fall would be frightening, bruising—and very brief. She inched backwards again, feeding the climbing rope through the figure eight with steady pulls. As soon as she was rappelling, her own weight would advance the rope through the descender. Until then it was a bit of a struggle.

Suddenly Joy's feet dangled over nothing at all. She kept going, using her arms to push herself backward. She tried to bend her legs back under her body, crouch at the mouth of the tunnel, and walk slowly backward over the lip in the normal manner of a climber initiating a rappel. There wasn't enough room. There was no help for it. She would simply have to take a few scrapes as the price of admission to her Castle.

Muttering words as dark as the unlit cave, Joy let herself bump over the edge of the overhang like a lumpy snake until she dangled from the climbing rope. Gabe had cut the safety rope short enough that there was little chance of a tangle unless she were out of control and spinning like an inexpertly thrown yo-yo. She wasn't. She let herself down until she was beneath the overhang and tapping gently against the cave wall. By then just enough slack remained in the safety rope for her to release the carabiner's locking mechanism.

Nicely calculated, Mr. Venture. Very nicely.

Joy positioned herself against the wall, feet spread as wide as her shoulders, climbing rope wrapped snugly in position for rappel. A look downward assured her that there were no immediate obstacles.

"Up rope," she called.

"Rope coming up," answered Gabe.

The safety rope went very slowly up the overhang until Gabe was sure that the attached carabiner was well beyond Joy's face. Then the rope disappeared at a brisk pace.

"Rappelling!" said Joy, kicking outward and releasing the tension on the rope with her right hand at the same time.

If Gabe had been belaying Joy, he would have answered in the normal manner. But he wasn't, so he didn't.

"Give 'em hell, sweetheart!"

After his husky encouragement there was an instant of silence, then Joy's pleased laughter floated up. The sound was surprising, exultant, vital, like the woman kicking out over unknown territory, confident in her own skills and those of the man who had anchored the rope to stone. She rappelled smoothly, controlling her descent with small pressures of her right hand. At the end of each outward and downward swing she met the wall feet first, absorbed the small jolt with her knees flexed, and then kicked out again, feeding rope as her controlled fall continued. Her headlight played over the fantastic subterranean landscape below as she checked for obstacles coming up to meet her. There were none. It was a clean fall right to the floor.

Soon she stood on the lip of what had once been a pool below a thundering waterfall. Now the basin was smooth, swirled with ancient water marks and contained a pool that had been there for unknowable years. As it glistened with her reflected helmet light, the water looked no deeper than her hand. Joy knew better. Long experience in judging the depth of Lost River Cave's incredibly clear waters told her that this pool was at least eight feet deep, perhaps more. The giveaway was the luminous shade of green that the water attained in some of the deepest curves and hollows of the pool. There was no color like it—except for Gabe's eyes when he became a part of her, wanting her with an intensity that made her shiver to remember.

Joy tilted her head back and felt like lifting her arms to embrace the cave itself. The overhang where Gabe waited was lost in a night that her light alone could not penetrate, but she knew he was there, waiting for her signal. Working quickly she pulled rope through her figure-eight descender. At first the rope was taut, eager, bouncing back from being stretched by her weight. When the rope was slack she unsnapped herself and stepped clear.

"Off rappel!" she called up, pitching her voice to carry through the murmurous sounds of water falling, sliding, dripping, water permeating Joy's Castle.

"Yo!"

Joy glanced around quickly, picking her way along the pool that was haunted by tints and tones and shades of green. When she was safely away from the area where Gabe would descend, she turned and yelled, "Clear!"

Moments later Gabe warned her that he was rappelling down. She stood transfixed, head tilted back, absorbing the sight of Gabe descending to her in a series of powerful, utterly controlled arcs. If any fear of being on a rope remained after the accident, he had conquered it. Joy deeply admired that. The nerve to climb *before* you had an accident was taken for granted. The plain courage it took to trust your life to a rope *after* a climbing accident was never taken for granted. As Fish had laconically pointed out, hard lessons stayed learned the longest. To take that kind of brutal lesson and use it to find out about life and yourself required not only physical courage, but courage of the mind and spirit as well.

Gabe had known that, and he had responded to the challenge with determination: *The mountain took a lot from me. I didn't want it to take my self-respect as well.*

Standing there in a vast darkness illuminated only by a single cone of light, Joy realized that Gabe had taken his accident and used its terrifying lessons to expand rather than contract the possibilities of his own life. Had she used the brutal lessons of her own past as well as he had? Had they expanded or contracted the boundaries of her life? Would she have had the sheer guts to dangle on a rope again as he was doing, knowing full well that any moment her life could peel away again strand by strand?

A grave two thousand feet deep.

Could she be like Gabe and learn to trust again? Could she love again, or was she still frozen within the moment of terror when her emotional world had given way beneath her feet and she fell endlessly, screaming deep inside herself because there was no one else to hear her?

The questions sank through Joy's barriers and seethed through her own inner darkness. She didn't know the answers—but she very much suspected that she had evaded learning anything subtle or profound from the brutal lessons of six years before. She had survived. Period. It had been enough at the time, all and more than anyone could have expected of her. But was mere survival still enough? Was a barren emotional existence all that she expected from herself for the rest of her life?

There was no answer as Joy watched Gabriel flying down toward her like his namesake archangel, darkness and light and power combined. He came to her where she stood in the midst of mystery, wrapped in a thousand nameless Voices whispering questions that had no answers but the taste of a man's tears on her lips.

Gabe called to her as soon as he had informed the people above that he was off the rope.

"Watch the pool," she called back, her voice husky. "It's deep enough to drown in."

"That little handful?" he asked, negotiating the last stretch of rock between himself and Joy.

"I'm little," she pointed out.

"Yes," he said, bending down, kissing her. "And you're deep enough to drown in, too." Then he added softly, "But what a sweet drowning."

Joy hugged him suddenly, fiercely. "Gabriel," she whispered, "have I told you that I'm glad you're here?"

He closed his eyes, letting her words sink into him, unable even to speak as he held her.

"On rappel!" came Maggie's voice from the darkness above.

"Yo!" answered Gabe. His voice was almost rough as it rose above the compelling murmurs of water flowing, water dissolving away the old, creating the new, changing everything.

Gabe looked at Joy's eyes. He saw both the clarity and the shadows, and he accepted both. She was a woman now, light and darkness in a fascinating mixture, unique. He wanted her even more for her shadowed depths than he had for her innocent clarity. She could share so much more of life now, understand so much more, hold so much more.

Deep enough to drown in.

Did she realize it? Did she know that he was drowning? Would she even care if she did know?

Maggie hit the floor with a thump, staggered slightly, and began feeding rope through her descender until there was slack. She unclipped, called up to Fish and came over to where Joy and Gabe waited.

"What a gorgeous green," she said, looking into the depths of the pool. "Just like Gabe's eyes."

Gabe almost laughed aloud. The comment was like everything else about Maggie—matter-of-fact rather than flirtatious. He rapped his knuckles lightly against Maggie' helmet.

"Keep it up," he said lightly, "and I'll have to buy a new helmet when my head outgrows the old."

"You should anyway," said Maggie. "I get chills just looking at the dents. Was Davy right? Did you really wear that through a landslide?"

"Yeah. One of life's little surprises."

Maggie grimaced. "I don't know how you can be so casual about it."

"I survived," he said, shrugging. "That's all anyone can ask."

"Is it?" asked Joy suddenly, looking up at him. "Is that all you ask of yourself and life?"

Gabe's green eyes searched Joy's face as he sensed the intensity behind her question. "No. I'm asking a hell of a lot more now. I don't deserve it—but I'm asking for it just the same."

She wanted to ask what Gabe meant, but couldn't because Maggie was there. So Joy simply returned Gabe's unflinching glance and the pressure of his hand holding hers

Fish's light seesawed gracefully through the darkness as he rappelled down the wall. Once all the equipment had been lowered, Davy wasted no time in following. After the picked up their equipment, everyone split into two groups. Gabe and Joy took the west wall. Maggie and Fish and Davy took the east. Normally they would have stayed in a single group, but there was nothing normal about this situation. They had to explore as much as possible of the room, as quickly as possible.

"Remember," said Joy. "This is a fast reconnoiter only. Davy, don't be a perfectionist with your map. Don't even be good. Just mark down the rough positions of possible passages, pits and chimneys. Don't explore them. We'll do the same. Stay in sight of us when you can, and be damn sure you're within yelling distance at all times. Questions?"

There were none. Joy twisted a light stick, left it a few feet from the climbing rope, and the exploration began. Using Gabe's compass, they stayed as close as they could to the right-hand perimeter of the Castle. Joy expected the sound of the hidden waterfall to become louder as they went farther into the room. Instead the muted thundering sound faded imperceptibly, telling her that, like the Voices, Joy's Castle didn't hold the enigmatic river that had shaped the cave.

Yet there was water in abundance. Sounds both mysterious and musical filled the air, as though somewhere just beyond the range of light the cave dreamed, and in dreaming, sang.

"Waterfall?" asked Gabe, turning his head slowly from side to side, trying to pinpoint the rushing, singing sounds.

"Maybe a small one," said Joy. "Not the source of the Voices, though. The Voices come from a good-sized fall that is either distant or largely muffled by stone."

Water gleamed in runnels among tiny stone channels, pooled transparently in hollows and glittered swiftly as rivulets met and braided. Sometimes the hand-sized streams ran musically among stalagmites and columns. Sometimes the braids came unraveled and vanished among cracks in the floor, sinking down and down through a network of channels far too small for men to explore.

Yet still there was water everywhere, gleaming from stone surfaces, shining from the hems of draperies both tall and elegant. Formations grew out from the wall; limestone precipitated into something that resembled the palettes used by artists. From the edges of the palettes hung fine, banded draperies, shapes so graceful and fluid it seemed impossible that they were made of unbending stone.

Small pools were everywhere, winking back from darkness when brushed by light, shivering as though alive when touched by a falling drop of water. And through it all came the rising murmur of water, the lifeblood of Lost River Cave flowing through hidden arteries and veins, rushing through darkness, singing over stone.

"Gabe," said Joy, her fingers closing over his wrist. "Look."

The white cone of her light showed what appeared to be very round eggs lying within a stone nest as big as a dinner plate. Gabe's sound of surprise and wonder joined the other murmurings of the Castle.

"What on earth?" he asked softly.

"Oolites," said Joy, kneeling next to the nest, careful to disturb nothing. She took readings on several landmarks, fixing the position of the rare formation as best she could for her rough map.

"That's a textbook word," said Gabe, kneeling next to her as she wrote quickly. "What do cavers call them?"

"Cave pearls."

"Scratch a caver and find a romantic every time," he said.

Joy looked up at him, smiled, and said, "Now I suppose you want me to tell you all the theories about how they're formed."

"Romantics?" he asked dryly.

"Oolites," she corrected.

"Do I have a choice?"

"Nope. You see, none of the theories satisfy me, so I'm not going to tell you a single one of them."

"Oh? How do you explain cave pearls, then?"

"They're fantastic, utterly miraculous seeds," she said, her voice both serious and subtly teasing. "Like the ones that Jack of Beanstalk fame grew. Only my magic seeds grow down, not up. They're tomorrow's caves in embryo, waiting to be born. Someday the shells will split and new caves will develop out of the old, branching and spreading, alive with water, beauty growing through darkness, waiting only for the first touch of light to be revealed." Joy leaned closer and whispered against Gabe's mouth, "But if you tell my colleagues what cave pearls really are, I'll be out of a job."

Gabe kissed her swiftly. "My lips are sealed."

"I noticed," she retorted.

He kissed her again. Slowly. Thoroughly. Finally he lifted his mouth. "Better?" he murmured, teasing her with his tongue.

"Much." She caught his lower lip delicately in her teeth, then reluctantly released him. "But not enough."

"I know what you mean," groaned Gabe as he stood and pulled her to her feet. "If we don't get moving, I'm going to do the kind of exploring that doesn't require ropes, safety lines and layers of clothing. Especially the clothes!''

Joy looked away from Gabe's face, for it was already taut, dark with desire. Just looking at him made her ache. With a wrench she turned her thoughts back to exploring the cave rather than the man. It wasn't easy. She knew that the time she had for both man and cave was very short. Not enough time. Not nearly enough. A lifetime wouldn't be enough to discover all of Lost River—or Gabe. Why had she been given only a few weeks?

Greedy little girl. You want it all, don't you?

Joy didn't answer herself. She didn't have to. She wanted Gabe with an intensity that she hadn't ever expected to feel for any man again. The realization frightened her, making her heart race and her mouth dry and her palms damp. She wondered if he had felt like this when he went back to the mountain that had nearly killed him. Terrified. She turned to ask him, and as she turned her light swept along the wall of the room.

The wall returned her light in glorious bursts and ripples. The surface was alive with water, a fantasy of banded flowstone veiled in liquid silver and gold. Water seeped from cracks and tiny channels high in the limestone wall. Water fell in fluid braids and golden veils, clothing the stone in grace.

The massive flowstone formation suggested a seated woman with her skirts swirling around her and her head thrown back to a timeless sky. Her long, unbound hair was transparent silver strands of water, and her dreams were heard in the thousand pure voices of water singing. At her feet lay curve after curve of multileveled rimstone pools, a fantastic lotus of silver and gold and jade unfolding to reveal the woman seated amid a beauty that could only be equaled by the singing of her dreams. Water slipped from pool to pool, each movement a separate voice, a separate song, a separate dream dancing through darkness and sudden illumination.

Slowly Joy realized that another light was moving in tandem with hers over the face of the Dreamer, doubling the area of illumination. Gabe's arms were around her, holding her, sharing the moment of discovery, and his name was one of the Dreamer's songs. When she heard him call to her, she turned to him, answering him.

Wrapped again in velvet darkness, the Dreamer whispered around them, adding two more names of love to its endless song.

Chapter 13

"Mommy, is Gabe on the phone again?"

Joy made an absent sound without looking up from the piled paperwork on her makeshift desk in the living room.

"Mommy?" asked Kati insistently, although she could see very well from where she stood that Gabe was in the kitchen talking on the phone.

Reluctantly Joy forced herself to confront her daughter. "Yes. Gabe is on the phone."

"Why?" retorted the child.

"Why do you think?" asked Joy briskly, for she and Kati had had this conversation several times in the last week.

"He's going away." Kati made it sound like an accusation.

Joy's mouth turned down despite her effort not to show emotion. "We're all going away from Cottonwood Wells, remember?" she asked quietly.

"Together?" asked Kati, hope leaping in her transparent eyes.

Pain twisted through Joy. She looked back down at the papers stacked in front of her, forms and more forms, epitaph for a dead government grant. "Just you and me, punkin."

"Can't they all come with us?"

Joy tried not to show her impatience and pain at Kati's insistence that everyone could just find another cave to explore and go on living together forever. "What do you think, Kati?" she asked evenly.

Kati's mouth flattened into a stubborn line that was very like Gabe's. She knew the answer and she didn't like it. "I don't want to leave."

"No one *wants* the cave to close," pointed out Joy. "That doesn't change anything, though. The cave will close. Maggie and Fish and Davy all have work to do in New Mexico. Our work here is done. We have to find another place to live."

"Don't want to," repeated Kati.

"I know," said Joy calmly.

"What about Gabe?" persisted Kati. "He likes me. Can't he stay with us? He'd be a won-der-ful daddy."

Joy winced and ran her hand distractedly through her hair, trying not to think of Gabe, of him leaving, of the pain his leaving would cause.

And the worst of it was the knowledge that she definitely was not pregnant. Her period had just ended. Soon the cave would close. She and Gabe would go in different directions. There would be no hope of a sibling to ease Kati's only-child status. There would be only memories. Memories and dreams. A lifetime of them, defining the lonely present.

"Isn't that a good idea, Mommy? Having Gabe for my daddy?" said Kati, her young voice more than a little belligerent, challenging.

"Mommy's busy right now, punkin," Joy said grimly, knowing that Kati was spoiling for a fight and trying to deflect her. Right now Joy's temper was more than a little uncertain. "Laura and Susan are in Maggie's cabin. Weren't you going to help them fix cookies for the barbecue tonight?"

"Don't want to!" Kati's voice and eyes said she didn't want to do anything now except fight, blow up, vent the pressures that had come with the growing, unwanted knowledge that the cave would close and they would move and nothing would ever be the same again. "Don't want to!" she repeated, almost yelling.

"That's enough, Kati," said Joy in a clipped voice. "Gabe can't hear the man on the phone if you're shouting."

"Don't care!" retorted Kati, her voice rising. Her face was flushed and her eyes were narrow. "He's leaving and I don't care!"

As Gabe hung up he heard the anger and the underlying pain in Kati's voice. He crossed the kitchen quickly, silently, not stopping until he saw Joy's face. The pale exhaustion of her features told him more than he wanted to know.

Gabe had said nothing to her about his editor's frequent and increasingly irritated calls, beyond the fact that the man wanted to know how the Lost River Cave article was progressing. But Gerald Towne had wanted to know more than that. He wanted to know why Gabe hadn't left Cottonwood Wells ten days ago, when the Russians had come through with their incredible, totally unexpected offer.

Chrissake, Gabe, the damned cave's been there forever. I have enough pull to get it opened again for whatever odds and ends need wrapping up for your article. But the Russians could change their minds in the next hour. You've got to grab that story, Gabe. It's the chance of a lifetime!

"I think it's time for you to pack your clean clothes," said Joy. "Susan will want to leave right after dinner, and—"

"Don't want to! Don't—"

"Kati," interrupted Gabe firmly, "your mother has work to do. I'll help you pack." He eyed the mutinous young face with sudden understanding. "Hey, punkin," he said in a gentle voice, "even if you bug your mom until she can't get any work done, the cave will still close right on time. There's nothing you can do about it except help make it easier for your mom—and for yourself—by being as cheerful as you can."

It was the truth, but that only made it harder to take. Kati had finally found the excuse she was looking for.

"I hate you!" screamed Kati suddenly. "I'm glad you're leaving! I'm glad you aren't my daddy!"

She turned and bolted to her bedroom before either adult could stop her.

Joy stood up swiftly, heading for Kati's room. Gabe intercepted her.

"I don't want her punished for being honest," he said, his face pale, grim.

"That wasn't honesty," retorted Joy, her eyes dark with anger. "That was plain, old-fashioned revenge."

"For what?"

"What do you think?" asked Joy angrily, her own temper slipping from control. "Because she loves you and you're leaving, and she wants you to be her daddy very much!" Joy closed her eyes for an instant, realizing what her own temper had led her to reveal. "I'm sorry Gabe. I didn't mean that the way it sounded."

"How do you think it sounded?" he asked, his voice husky.

"Like the door of a cage shutting," she said succinctly, turning away. She sat down at the table again. "I'll give her ten minutes to get a handle on her redheaded temper, and then I'm going in after her."

By then I might even have a handle on my own temper, Joy added to herself sardonically. *Right now I'd like to wring my daughter's little neck for hurting Gabe like that. He has been more of a father to her in the last few weeks than some kids get in years of living with a dad. He has played War and Go Fish and Old Maid with her, talked to her about mountaintops and coral reefs, walked with her while she showed him lizards and coyote tracks and cactus, washed her clothes, fed her peanut butter sandwiches and tucked her into bed at night with a story and a kiss. He's given her so many beautiful memories—and what does she do? She throws it in his face.*

Because she wants it all. Like her mother. Greedy little girl.

Gabe watched as Joy again bent over the endless, frustrating government forms. He knew that each hour, each minute, each second that Joy spent on paperwork meant less time between now and the moment that Lost River Cave would be closed to her. He had shared the magic of its exploration with her, the almost overwhelming instants of beauty and discovery. Yet instead of being out exploring right now, she was stuck here filling out forms in quintuplicate, hearing seconds tick away in her head. No wonder she was ready to scream.

Gabe wanted to go to Joy, to ease the knots in her shoulder muscles that came from tension, to feel her warmth flowing up through his hands and to hear her groan of thanks as muscles relaxed beneath his touch. He wanted to help her, to take some of the load that she was carrying, to—what? What did he want? What the hell was he thinking of?

He sank onto the couch and realized that he was ready to scream himself. Like Kati. Like Joy. But his reasons were different. It wasn't the impending closure of Lost River Cave that was grinding on his nerves. It was the fact that the only time he heard Joy say *I love you* was in his memories and dreams. The words that she had given to him so freely six years ago didn't exist on her lips now. And without those words he could not believe that she had forgiven him.

He wanted those words. He wanted them as deeply as he wanted her. He wanted to know that she cared for more than the physical ecstasy he could give her. He wanted—what?

Yeah, fool, what in hell do you want? You're looking at six years ago all over again. Like the Orinoco River expedition, the Russian offer is literally a once-in-a-lifetime gig. Not only have you never been to the Arctic, but you'll be the first man in two generations to have the freedom of the northern ice. All of it. No boundaries, no political flack, nothing but a glittering undiscovered landscape stretching across the top of the world. Are you going to turn that down, settle down in a town somewhere, sink down beneath layers of respectability and resentment and regrets?

Six years ago all over again.

With a few differences. She's not pregnant, she isn't a nineteen-year-old virgin and she doesn't love you. You're free to go. The Lost River Cave story was wrapped up two weeks ago, in the bag, everything ready to go. Except you. You've been stalling for the last two weeks. You're still stalling. Why?

One more cruel, unanswerable question.

Gabe heard the bedroom door opening and light foot-steps coming across the bare wood floor. He expected the footsteps to stop at Joy's chair, but they didn't. They came right across the room to where he sat with his head resting against the back of the sagging couch and his eyes closed. He opened them. Kati's wan little face was watching him. He held out his arms and she ran into them, holding onto him as he lifted her into his lap. She cried against his shoulder as though she had a lifetime of tears and only a few seconds to spend them in.

With a gentle hand Gabe stroked the little girl's fiery hair and shaking body while he murmured assurances between her incoherent apologies. After a time the storm ended, leaving Kati spent and silent but for an occasional ragged breath. When even that had passed, Kati lay quietly, watching his face. Then she wrapped her arms around his neck, kissed his cheek, and said, "I love you better than anyone but Mommy."

Before Gabe could respond, Kati was off his lap and dancing away across the living room. The front screen door slammed behind her.

"Susan!" called Kati's voice across the yard, bubbling with life again. "Is it time to make cookies yet?"

Gabe looked up and saw the tears glittering in Joy's eyes in the instant before she returned to her paperwork. He wanted to go to her, to comfort her and himself. But there was neither comfort nor the possibility of it unless they could reach out and wrench time off its track, bend it around, make of it a closed loop that went nowhere, nothing changing, Joy in his arms and he in hers. No Orinoco six years ago. No Arctic six days from now.

Fool. Time doesn't go backward or in circles. One way only. Forward. You have to go with it.

Don't want to! mocked part of Gabe's mind, echoing Kati's passionate declaration.

Then stay.

With a woman who doesn't love me and no job at all?

How do you know she doesn't love you?

I betrayed her. How could she love a man who betrayed her?

She forgave you.

Did she? Did she really? Then why doesn't she tell me that she loves me? Because she doesn't, that's why!

Fool. Why do you think she's sleeping with you?

Passion. With her I'm one hell of a lover.

Yeah. And without her you're one hell of a fool.

Gabe's internal argument continued in silence and darkness, raging like the hidden Lost River itself, pummeling and grinding against existing channels and tunnels and troughs, trying to find new solutions to old questions of how to get there from here. He had until tomorrow morning to decide. Then Towne would demand an answer. *Don't want to* wouldn't get it done.

Rather grimly Gabe wondered what he was going to tell Towne—and himself.

It was one more unanswered question shoved deep beneath Gabe's consciousness, because he didn't want to brood through the barbecue Kati had looked forward to as though it were Christmas. Instead he held his daughter on his lap and his woman curled against his shoulder and they sang all the old camp songs. He ignored the unanswered, unanswerable questions because he refused to spoil what might be his last chance to look up with Kati at the Glitter River and try to count the timeless, pouring possibilities of life.

When the last note of the last song was sung, he carried his sleeping daughter to Susan's car. The station wagon had been made up as a bed. He put Kati gently in the back next to her sleepy chum, kissed Kati's soft hair and tucked the blanket in around both girls. When he looked up he saw Fish watching him with speculation in his shrewd eyes. Abruptly Gabe turned away and went to Joy's darkened cottage to wait for her.

Through the window he saw Susan's car move out into the desert, leaving the cottages behind. Beneath the full moon Joy crossed the dusty yard toward the cottage. Her hair shifted and shimmered with subdued light. She looked unreal, ethereal, as impossible as the secret Dreamer singing among transparent pools. The sight of Joy coming to him through the moon-silvered darkness made Gabe ache with emotions he had no name for. He knew the hard rise of passion, though. He had always known that with Joy.

He pulled her into his arms as the screen door snapped shut behind her. His voice was husky when he spoke, and his caresses had a lifetime of hunger burning in them. He wanted to seduce more from her than her passion tonight. He wanted a question answered. He wanted the words that he heard in his dreams and memories.

I love you.

"I miss Kati when she's gone," he said, kissing Joy hotly, sweetly, "but I sure as hell don't miss sleeping alone. I like falling asleep with you curled in my arms and waking up to feel your breath warm on my skin. I like looking at you, talking to you, exploring with you. Ah, God," he said huskily, lowering his mouth to her neck, "how I love exploring you. You're different each time. Like the Voices and the Dreamer seething in my blood, in my mind."

Joy sensed the passion beating in Gabe's veins, an urgency that made his hands tremble as he began to undress her. Instinctively she knew there was something more than simple desire driving him, something deeper, wilder. It was time rushing toward them, the future coming down on them, bringing the end of passion and the beginning of unanswerable questions and haunted dreams.

The realization was like falling, twisting, turning, rope burning flesh to the bone beneath. It was all Joy could do not to cry out her protest aloud. Then within the storm of her emotions condensed a single, absolute certainty. If memories were all she would have of Gabe for the rest of her life, then she would see that the memories were as perfect as the Dreamer veiled in water, singing within stone.

With a sigh that was Gabriel's name, Joy threaded her fingers into his thick, soft hair and held his mouth against the pulse racing at the base of her throat. His lips moved down, retracing the path of his fingers as he brushed aside her clothes, baring her to the silver moonlight. The tip of her breast was another shade of velvet darkness crowning the soft luminous flesh. When his tongue touched her, she tightened into a shining peak that tempted his tongue again and again.

"You're so beautiful," he whispered, and his breath ca
ressed the taut, hungry nipples he had called from her soft
ness.

"No," said Joy, watching the dark planes of his face and
the glistening tip of his tongue caressing her, "it's you who
are beautiful, Gabriel." Her finger traced the dark eye
brows, the lean cheeks, the sensual lips, the hot and teasing
tongue that was making her shiver with anticipation. "You
touch me so perfectly." A low sound came from her as his
teeth closed with exquisite care, tugging at her breast unti
liquid heat uncurled within her body. She gasped as his hand
slipped inside her unfastened jeans, discovering her hot
layered softness. "I want you inside me," she said ur
gently. "Oh, Gabe, don't tease me anymore. I want—"

Joy's thoughts scattered in a burst of sensation as Gab
caressed her intimately, deeply, melting even her bones
Dizzy, her breath ragged, she clung to his touch, telling him
without words how much she wanted him to be a part of her
She had done the same thing six years ago, instinctively, and
he had responded in the same way, a groan of discovery and
need. Her hips moved sinuously, promising both a wel
come and a release for the hunger that stretched rigidly be
neath his jeans. Her hand found that hunger, traced it
rubbed over it with a hot, searching intent that equaled hi
exploration of her softness.

Gabe saw the passion tightening Joy's face, making of he
eyes a midnight darkness, flushing her lips and her breast
with heat. With a harsh sound he took her mouth, holdin
her straining hips against him with one hand and with th
other caressing her until he felt her heat flow over him
joining them in a promise of the deeper union to come.

Abruptly Gabe stepped away from Joy. "If I touch you now, I'll take you now," he said hoarsely. "It's always been like that. You fill me to overflowing and yet I can't get enough of you."

Joy trembled and swayed toward him. "Yes. It's the same for me. Take me, Gabe," she whispered against his lips. "Let me take you. Fill me to overflowing and then hold me, *hold me*. Give me enough memories for a lifetime."

She felt the shudder that swept through Gabe's powerful body even as his arms closed around her, lifting her. He carried her to the bedroom and lowered her into the silver light pooled on the bed. With slow, caressing motions they undressed each other. When they both wore nothing more than moonlight, he simply looked at her. She started to speak but the sight of his taut, almost tormented face froze the words in her throat. He had looked at her like that six years ago, just before he took her for the first time.

Was this to be the last time? Was that why he looked like a man being torn apart?

"Gabriel, what's—"

The question died as he accepted the invitation of her body and slid deeply inside her. The sensation of fullness was so exquisite that Joy shivered and made tiny sounds at the back of her throat. It was the same for Gabe, tightly sheathed in her resilient softness, able only to make a deep sound of pleasure. He wanted to burst with the hot perfection of their joining, but he knew that even greater levels of ecstasy waited to be explored. He moved slowly, powerfully, and she was with him, moving as he did. He saw the first level of pleasure break over her, felt the ripples hot and sweet around him, and arched against her, increasing the intensity of her response.

When she no longer cried out and clung to him fiercely, he moved again, deeply, calling to her with words as the potent sensual pressure of his unreleased passion filled her. Her eyes were half opened, dazed with the aftershocks of ecstasy still coursing through her. At each sliding caress of his body within hers, desire grew again, curling hotly through her, tightening her around him. He took her mouth as completely as he had taken the rest of her softness, inciting her with teeth and tongue and words that made her arch wildly against him. Then her hand slid down the gleaming muscles of his back and buttocks, seeking the tight male flesh, caressing him until he could reach no higher level of pleasure.

"No," he said hoarsely, biting her lips, burying himself deeply in her straining softness. "Don't let me leave you behind. Come with me, sweetheart."

The words and caresses burst within her even as he did— and she was with him, ecstasy racing wildly through their joined bodies until nothing existed, neither memories nor dreams nor even time itself.

Moonlight lay softly over them, making them shimmer like the Dreamer bathed in silver water. Gabe kissed Joy's forehead and cheeks, her lips and the curve of her throat, her sweet-smelling hair and the quivering lashes veiling her eyes; and he said the only truth he knew, the only answer he had to his many questions.

"I'll come back to you as soon as I can."

The words poured over Joy like cold, black water, chilling her to the bone. She had heard words like them before—six years ago, when she had pleaded with him to stay for just another day, an hour, a minute. For a wild instant she thought that she was pleading still, that time had indeed turned around on itself, making a full circle of anguish and regret.

No. Not this time. This time he won't destroy me. This time I don't love him.

Do I?

Fear froze her, driving every bit of heat out of her body. She looked wildly for a place to hide, a place to pull darkness around her, a place where she would never again know the threat of light. It was the past repeating itself, time eating itself, eating her. Six years ago all over again.

Only this time she wasn't pregnant. And she wanted to be. She wanted to be and it wasn't going to happen.

It wasn't quite the past after all. It was worse.

"Joy," said Gabe, turning her face toward him with a gentle fingertip. "Did you hear me?" His breath came in sharply as he saw her face. There was nothing of joy there, neither light nor laughter nor the hope of either. Words tumbled out of him quickly as he tried to make her understand. "Sweetheart, it won't be for long. I swear it! It's just this one assignment. I've been wanting to go to the Arctic since I was a kid. I'm the only western writer the Russians will allow into their part of the Arctic. There will never be another chance like it. Towne has a publisher who wants me to do a book on it and—"

Joy heard nothing beyond the fact of his leaving and her emptiness.

"I'm not pregnant!" The words were blurred, almost strangled by her sobs as anger and despair overwhelmed her. She gave herself to tears as passionately as she had given herself to him.

"You're pregnant?" asked Gabe, misunderstanding. For an instant he was frozen, watching Joy shudder with her wild grief—and then elation shook him and he pulled her fiercely against his body. "Pregnant!" he said, laughing, hardly able to understand his own shattering pleasure in her pregnancy.

She hadn't protected herself after all. She gave herself to me as completely this time as she did six years ago. She must love me, even though she won't say the words.

He buried his head in the curve of her neck. "It's all right, sweetheart," he said fiercely. "I'll stay with you, hold you, care for you. Our baby will be born into my hands, not some stranger's. I won't leave you alone again."

A few of Gabe's words penetrated Joy's sobs, enough so that she knew he had misunderstood. She lifted her head and said as clearly as she could, "No, you d-don't understand. I'm *not* pregnant and I w-want to be! I don't want K-Kati to be a lonely only child all her life. Having your baby was the perfect solution, just the kind of relationship you're suited to," Joy continued, words rushing out, pushed by grief and despair. "Anonymous fatherhood, no strings, total freedom to go wherever you want whenever the chance came. But it came to soon. You're leaving and I'm not pregnant and there's no chance for another baby!"

Joy's tumbling, broken words punctured Gabe's elation.

"That's why you slept with me?" he asked harshly, feeling her words going into his soul like a steel piton into stone, anchoring him forever to pain and betrayal. "Just to get another baby? You didn't forgive me after all, did you— much less love me!" His hands balled into hard fists. "Christ! And to think I would have given up everything to stay with you!"

Joy didn't answer because she was able to hear only the sound of her own sobs; but even through her tears she saw betrayal set its bleak stamp upon Gabe's features. He rolled out of bed with a swift, powerful movement and began dressing in a silence that seethed with fury. Like his mind. Seething.

She used me like a goddamned stud.

And just what did you have in mind for her? Till death do you part? Or until the next article, whichever comes sooner? Fool.

Go to hell, Gabe snarled silently to the sardonic voice within himself, *and take your sneering questions with you!*

Gabe turned at the bedroom door and raked Joy's naked body with an icy glance. "If you've made a mistake and you're pregnant, give my brother a call. You two can talk about old times."

A few seconds later the front door slammed, followed by the sound of Gabe's rented Toyota scattering sand and gravel in a wild rooster tail as he accelerated out of Cottonwood Wells. The engine sounds rose in a series of screams while he slammed through the gears as though his life depended on outracing the voice within his head.

But he couldn't go fast enough, for wherever the road turned he was already there, waiting for himself.

Fool.

Long after the sound of Gabe's anger faded, Joy lay without moving in the middle of the bed, feeling as though she were sinking endlessly, helplessly, layers of loss and regret closing around her until she could not breathe. She hadn't felt like this in years—used up, spent, incapable even of crying. Yet at the same time her body seethed to be free, to move, to do something besides lie here waiting for the sound of a car coming back over the desert toward her,

Gabe's beloved arms closing around her, his voice telling her that he would never leave her again.

But he would. He had.

As she had done years before, Joy dragged herself out of bed and stood beneath the stinging needles of a cold shower. Mechanically she dressed, pulling on layer after layer of caving gear, turning to the only comfort she knew—Lost River Cave's unearthly beauty. Silently she closed the back door of the cottage behind her.

"Going caving?" asked Fish, his voice casual, his eyes penetrating.

Joy was too intent on her own needs even to be startled by Fish's unexpected appearance. "Yes," she said. It was a stranger's voice—remote, lifeless. She didn't care. The stranger was also herself.

"Was that Gabe tearing out of camp?"

"Yes."

With a swift movement Fish plucked the Jeep keys from Joy's hand. His shrill whistle split the night. "Yo! Davy! Shag your butt out here! We're going caving!"

"But Maggie and I were just—" began Davy.

"Shag it!" snarled Fish over Davy's protest.

Joy's protest was also futile. Within minutes Davy and Fish were in their gear and headed for the cave with her. Davy took one look at Fish's grim face and Joy's unnatural pallor and decided that he would ask questions later. In silence the three of them pulled up to the entrance of Lost River Cave.

"I'm belaying you tonight, Dr. Anderson," said Fish quietly, settling into the anchor sling.

Joy didn't argue. She simply snapped herself to the rope and let herself down into the cave's seamless, welcoming embrace with all the speed she could command. When the rope went slack, Davy reached for it. Fish stopped him.

"Nope," said Fish, releasing himself from anchor position. "You stand by up here to belay Gabe."

"Huh? When is he getting here?" asked Davy, confused.

"Maybe never," admitted Fish, "but it'd be a damn shame to lose him to an accident if he finally got the brains to count to two and came back to her."

"What the hell is going on?" said Davy plaintively, automatically settling in to belay Fish into the cave. "Why should I wait around for Gabe? And why does Dr. Anderson look like death warmed over?"

"Gabe left her again," said Fish bluntly.

"Again?"

"Gabe is Kati's father."

Fish dropped swiftly into the cave, knowing he would have to hurry to catch up with Joy. She retreated in front of him in a ghostly aura of light, pausing only to be belayed down the steep slide leading to Gotcha. Neither of them said a word as they went deeper and deeper into the cave and the Voices condensed around them.

Joy managed to shut out the silky murmurings all the way through the Maze, hearing only her own heartbeat until she emerged from Small Favors and rappelled into the fantastic castle that bore her name. She walked quickly through the glistening formations, giving them barely a glance. She had room in herself for only one thing—the knowledge that Gabe was gone.

Fish followed at a discreet distance. He saw Joy stand motionlessly in front of the stone she called the Dreamer and realized that she had found whatever she had sought within the cave's darkness. He was no longer needed. Silently he retreated to the rope dangling from the mouth of Small Favors.

With a tiny part of her mind Joy knew that Fish had gone, leaving her alone. She let go of the aching control she had held over her mind and body. In that instant the Voices rippled through the barriers of her fear and anger and grief, speaking directly to her core, whispering words that shook her to her soul.

I love him.

I've always loved him. I always will. He is within me as deeply as water is within Lost River Cave, water dreaming through stone in darkness and mystery. Whether I'm here or not, whether I see it or not, the cave goes on living, changing, becoming more beautiful with every glistening drop, every extraordinary instant of time.

Like love. Growing whether I will it or not, spreading through me, destroying and creating me in the same sweet and terrifying moments.

Slowly Joy sank to the floor, her posture echoing the Dreamer as she let the thousand Voices sing through her. After a long time she removed her helmet and gloves and shut off her light, watching with more than her eyes, giving herself to the dreams that lived in every movement of water sliding over stone, creating beauty where once there had been only emptiness.

Somehow I'll find you again, Gabriel. If it takes another six years, so be it. My love will be there the whole time, growing like the Dreamer within stone, singing to us with a thousand voices. But even if you leave me again and again, our love will still be growing, singing in darkness, waiting to be discovered.

Yes. Our love. Because you love me, too, Gabriel.

*Your love was written in the fury and despair on your face
when you left me tonight. You felt betrayed, as I once did.
To feel betrayed like that, my bittersweet lover, first you
must give yourself to love.*

And lose.

Eyes closed, her mind deep within the Dreamer, Joy heard
nothing around her but the hushed songs. The sound of
footsteps winding through the room toward her were consumed by the sweetly rushing whispers of water. The cone
of light that swept over her was intangible, unnoticed,
quickly extinguished.

After one glance Gabe didn't need the light. He knew he
would never forget the sight of Joy seated in front of the
Dreamer, her face washed in tears, glistening even as the
Dreamer did. Slowly he pulled off his helmet and sank down
next to her. With motions that were both gentle and determined, Gabe removed his gloves and took her hands in his.

"I'm not going to be a fool twice," said Gabe quietly, his
husky voice sliding among the Dreamer's songs, sinking
deeply into Joy. "Without you I might as well be in a cage,
because wherever I am I'll be looking for you through the
bars of my loneliness." He cradled her hand against his
cheek, kissed her palm swiftly. "I'll give you that baby you
want, Joy, but first you'll have to marry me, live with me,
let me care for you and Kati as I should have cared for you
all those long years ago."

Joy's hand stirred beneath Gabe's palm, warmed by his
flesh. She laced her fingers through his slowly, completely,
and he began to breathe again.

"What about the Arctic?" she asked softly.

She felt the shrug of his shoulder against hers.

"There will be other articles," he said, "other books. There is only one Joy, one Kati."

"But—"

"Sometimes being an adult boils down to facing and making choices," he continued gently, relentlessly. "I didn't understand that six years ago. I do now. I choose you, Joy. You and Kati. You see," he added huskily, rubbing his lips blindly along her palm, "I love you. It took me too long to discover that loving you was the answer to so many questions, but I know now. I love you, Joy, even though you don't love me in return. But I want your love. *God how I want it!*"

Joy's throat closed as she felt the heat of his tears flowing between her fingers. She turned toward him blindly, going into his arms and holding him with aching strength, and once again he heard the words that had haunted his memories and dreams, the hidden answer to so many questions.

"I love you, Gabriel," she murmured, kissing him, not knowing whose tears were on her lips. "I'll go with you wherever you want, stay behind whenever I must. But—" She hesitated, then said in a rush, "Kati and I would love to see the Arctic with you. She's as hungry for a piece of the Glitter River as her parents are. If not this time, then maybe the next, or the next. You're so good at what you do. I don't want you to give it up. Just come home to us. To love. We both love you so much."

"Do you mean that?" he asked, holding her as though he were afraid she would run between his fingers into Lost River Cave's limestone floor and vanish forever. "Would you and Kati really travel with me?"

"Anywhere," Joy said simply.

Gabe buried his head in the curve of her neck and felt possibilities pouring through him. "We can have it all, can't we?" he said, his voice husky. "Love and children and the whole world to explore."

"We can try," she said, sliding her fingers through his thick warm hair. "But it won't be easy," she admitted.

"Have we ever done things the easy way?" he asked ruefully.

"No," she said, laughing softly. "We never have."

Her laughter and Gabe's newly discovered words of love mingled with the sounds of Joy's Castle, becoming part of the Dreamer's thousand songs . . . love murmuring through stone, creating a world that would always be new, always changing, as unexpected and enduring as Lost River Cave itself.

READERS' COMMENTS ON SILHOUETTE INTIMATE MOMENTS:

"About a month ago a friend loaned me my first Silhouette. I was thoroughly surprised as well as totally addicted. Last week I read a Silhouette Intimate Moments and I was even more pleased. They are the best romance series novels I have ever read. They give much more depth to the plot, characters, and the story is fundamentally realistic. They incorporate tasteful sex scenes, which is a must, especially in the 1980's. I only hope you can publish them fast enough."

S.B.*, Lees Summit, MO

"After noticing the attractive covers on the new line of Silhouette Intimate Moments, I decided to read the inside and discovered that this new line was more in the line of books that I like to read. I do want to say I enjoyed the books because they are so realistic and a lot more truthful than so many romance books today."

J.C., Onekama, MI

"I would like to compliment you on your books. I will continue to purchase all of the Silhouette Intimate Moments. They are your best line of books that I have had the pleasure of reading."

S.M., Billings, MT

*names available on request

If you're ready for a more sensual, more provocative reading experience...

We'll send you
4 Silhouette Desire novels
FREE
and without obligation

Then, we'll send you six more Silhouette Desire® novels to preview every month for 15 days with absolutely no obligation!

When you decide to keep them, you pay just $1.95 each ($2.25 each in Canada) *with never any additional charges!*

And that's not all. You get FREE home delivery of all books as soon as they are published and a FREE subscription to the Silhouette Books Newsletter as long as you remain a member. Each issue is filled with news on upcoming titles, interviews with your favorite authors, even their favorite recipes.

Silhouette Desire novels are not for everyone. They are written especially for the woman who wants a more satisfying, more deeply involving reading experience. Silhouette Desire novels take you *beyond* the others.

If you're ready for that kind of experience, fill out and return the coupon today!

Silhouette ❦ Desire®

Silhouette Books, 120 Brighton Rd., P.O. Box 5084, Clifton, NJ 07015-5084

Clip and mail to: Silhouette Books,
120 Brighton Road, P.O. Box 5084, Clifton, NJ 07015-5084 *

YES. Please send me 4 FREE Silhouette Desire novels. Unless you hear from me after I receive them, send me 6 new Silhouette Desire novels to preview each month as soon as they are published. I understand you will bill me just $1.95 each, a total of $11.70 (in Canada, $2.25 each, a total of $13.50)—with no additional shipping, handling, or other charges of any kind. There is no minimum number of books that I must buy, and I can cancel at any time. The first 4 books are mine to keep.   **BD18R6**

Name _____ (please print) _____

Address _____ Apt. #

City _____ State/Prov. _____ Zip/Postal Code

* In Canada, mail to: Silhouette Canadian Book Club, 320 Steelcase Rd., E., Markham, Ontario, L3R 2M1, Canada
Terms and prices subject to change.
SILHOUETTE DESIRE is a service mark and registered trademark.   D-SUB-1

Silhouette Intimate Moments

COMING
NEXT MONTH

MIDNIGHT RAINBOW
Linda Howard
Traipsing through the jungle one step ahead of terrorists was a strange situation for a confirmed cynic and an eternal optimist to fall in love, but Grant and Jane fought the odds and won each other.

PRICE ABOVE RUBIES
Mary Lynn Baxter
McKenzie Moore had learned to live a comfortable albeit unhappy life without Jeb Langley. But he was back now, and his presence shattered McKenzie's hard won calm as he strove to reclaim her heart.

THE ART OF DECEPTION
Nora Roberts
Adam was cool, calm and very discreet, an excellent spy. But he had never encountered anyone as beautiful or as eccentric as Kirby, and he soon found himself losing his cool—and his heart.

THE DI MEDICI BRIDE
Heather Graham Pozzessere
For Chris, the beauty of Venice began to fade when circumstances conspired and she found herself a permanent resident of the city, a target for murder—and married to a man she hardly knew.

AVAILABLE NOW: